Like It or Not

by

Eva Fox Mate

Hughes Brothers

Like It or Not

COPYRIGHT © 2025 by Eva Fox Mate

Cover Art by *Tina Lynn Stout*

The Wild Rose Press, Inc.
PO Box 708
Adams Basin, NY 14410-0708
Visit us at www.thewildrosepress.com

Publishing History
First Edition, 2025
Trade Paperback ISBN 978-1-5092-6215-1
Digital ISBN 978-1-5092-6216-8

Hughes Brothers
Published in the United States of America

Dedication

To my mother, Ann, and sister, Catie, with love.

Prologue

"Look, I just need a little more time. The current owner went out of town suddenly, and that messed up the timetable." It was a bold-faced lie, and Liam O'Brien knew it. And he knew Jonathan Bannion, the buyer on the other end of the phone, knew it, too. Liam was swimming in dangerous waters with very big sharks. But if he sewed up this deal, he'd be free. Set for life.

"I'm a generous man, Mr. O'Brien." The voice at the other end of the line was relaxed, almost jovial. "I'll tell you what I'll do. I'll throw in another million if you get it to me within the week. That gives you six days. However…" A hard note of warning entered the voice. "That's stretching my generosity to its limits. If you don't deliver by then, I'll subtract a million and keep on subtracting, every day, until I have it in my hands. Is that clear?"

Liam swallowed around the lump in his throat. He was taking on water and starting to go under. Bannion wasn't a man to trifle with. How had he gotten himself into this mess?

Greed. Pure and simple. Money was the bane of the O'Briens, be it too little or too much.

"Clear as crystal. I'll deliver. You can count on it." Liam winced. Could he sound more pathetic?

"I'm glad to hear it." The hardness was gone. They were friends again.

1

"I'll be in touch." Too late, Liam tried to reassert dominance over the conversation.

Bannion laughed. "You'd better be," he said, and ended the call.

Liam looked down at his phone's home screen. The wallpaper was a picture he'd taken of an old photo, discolored with age. His teenaged self grinned up at him, happy and proud in his high school football uniform. Beside him stood a ten-year-old girl, her long hair in messy pigtails he'd braided himself. Both of her knobby knees sported scabs. The hero worship in her eyes as she smiled up at him gnawed at his present-day self. Squashing the emotion, he pulled up a number and hit the dial button with his thumb.

"Liam." Priscilla spoke his name like a curse. "What do you want? I've told you a thousand times, this is your problem. I'm out of it."

"No. You're not out of it until I say you're out. I need that Bible, and I need it now." He regretted the menace in his voice, but she had to understand he meant business.

"You're out of your mind. They just found the Gutenberg a week ago, and it went straight to the university for authentication. I didn't see it, sniff it, or touch it. And I don't want to. Ever. I've left that life behind."

The defiance in her voice made him smile. Good old Priss. She didn't back down, not even for him. And she was loyal. Loyal to that new husband of hers and his bright, shiny, squeaky-clean family.

"Un-uh. It's not that easy." He pulled in a deep breath, sorry to sink so low. "You know, I really like that hubby of yours. Not that you've introduced us or anything. In fact, given the rock-solid fake identity I built for you, I'm guessing Mason doesn't know anything about us O'Briens. Wouldn't it be a shame if he found out what the family business is? Remember," he hardened his tone. "I created you. I can destroy you, too."

"You wouldn't dare!"

Bingo. Her husband was her Achilles heel. "Why not? I'm not the one with so much to lose. I mean, Lover Boy would have a lot of explaining to do if your real name ever came out."

Her sharp intake of breath told him he'd scored another hit.

"No!" The word was almost a sob. "Lee, you're scaring me. It isn't like you to be this cruel."

Closing his eyes, he shrugged off the prick of guilt. *Life or death, man. Life or death.*

"Let me spell it out one more time." He gritted his teeth. "You are Mrs. Mason Hughes. It wasn't part of the original plan, but it's even better. You get me the Gutenberg and everyone lives happily ever after."

He waited, allowing that to sink in.

"No," she repeated, after several beats. "I won't agree to it. I did everything you asked and now I'm out of it. Leave me and my husband alone."

Liam stared out at his view of the Charles River, still frozen solid despite the recent break in the weather. Good old cold and gray Boston. He couldn't wait to get out of this shit hole. Maybe he'd buy a nice little beach cottage, somewhere without extradition.

But for that, he needed cash. Lots of it, to do it in style and with adequate protection. So, he'd keep on squeezing.

"I wish I could, kid. I really do. But you don't

understand the, um, *situation* I'm in. It's become imperative that I get the hell out of Dodge. That doesn't happen unless this deal happens. If I have to use you and your precious husband as leverage, I will."

"No." She sounded frantic now. "So help me, I'll leave him. Then your leverage is gone."

He laughed again. "Tell me another one. You're head over heels about him."

"That doesn't matter." Her voice was stronger, more determined now. "I'll do whatever it takes to keep you from hurting Mason or his family."

He fisted his free hand. Why did she have to make this complicated? "You'll stay right where you are. Do you hear me, Priss? Priss!"

God damn it. She'd hung up on him. That made two: First Bannion, then Priss. No one hung up on Liam "The Lion" O'Brien. *No one.*

Especially not his little sister.

Chapter One

Life could really bite you in the ass.

Three weeks ago, Priss Hughes had everything she'd ever dreamed of: A loving husband, a supportive family, a fun job. Now, she was hiding out in a shitty apartment with no job, no family and, worst of all, no husband.

"I will not cry. I will *not* cry." Blinking, she surveyed the apartment's postage stamp-sized kitchen, her hand hovering over a box of tissues.

Who was she kidding? Of course she was going to cry. The real question was whether she'd manage to do anything else. Snatching the half empty box off the counter, she sniffled her way to the tired sofa, sitting flush under the room's only window. Dropping the tissue box onto the scarred coffee table, she raised the neon pink window shade a few inches. *What a view*. Two dumpsters and a graffiti-covered brick wall. Not to mention the occasional drug deal. But she couldn't afford to be picky. If her sister-in-law, Callie, hadn't offered up her old apartment, Priss would be sleeping in her car.

She shouldn't be surprised. She was an O'Brien after all, and O'Briens were blessed with the worst kind of luck. Despite the generations her family had spent in Ireland, Priss would bet there wasn't one single member of the clan who'd found a four-leafed clover. But plenty of them had kissed the Blarney Stone.

Which was why her good fortune in tumbling head over heels for Mason Hughes almost a year ago had been so incredible. Not because he was one of *the* Hugheses, a family with plenty of smarts, good looks, and money to go around. That wasn't a bummer, but the amazing thing was Mason's…niceness. He was a thoroughly decent person with a thoroughly decent background. No lies, no hidden agendas.

No Mob, with a capital "M."

Her lips twisted as she blew her nose. A secret mob princess falling for a member of one of the most respected families in American history? If that wasn't irony, she didn't know what was. Mason's grandfather was a freakin' former US president, for crap's sake, and his father was the sitting Chief Justice on SCOTUS, the nation's highest court.

Was it any wonder she'd claimed to have been orphaned at a young age?

She shoved the heavy mass of her uncombed, unwashed hair over her shoulders, coming away with a few brown strands. Great. She was so stressed she was shedding. Good thing she'd brought the tissues over. Potential baldness brought on a fresh onslaught of tears.

She was contemplating a full-fledged crying jag when a heavy knock sounded at the door. It was either Callie or the sweet but nosy landlord again. No one else knew she was here.

After another quick blow of her nose, she launched herself off the crappy couch and crossed the room. It took a second to unlock the industrial-sized deadbolt, and a moment or two longer to coax open the warped door. Two men stood in the hallway, their dark suits and mirrored sunglasses telegraphing their identities faster than the ID badges they flashed.

Shit. No self-respecting mob daughter in the country would mistake the duo for anything but FBI.

"How did you find me?" The question tumbled out before she'd fully vetted it. All the years away from the family had made her rusty. No self-respecting mob daughter would be surprised by anything the Bureau did either.

The taller, younger one tilted his head toward his partner. "This is Agent Peters, I'm Agent Young. May we come in, please?"

Priss hesitated, torn between the hard-wired O'Brien instinct to shut the door and flee via the fire escape, and the much more rational desire to hear what the agents had to say. She'd spent her entire life staying off their radar. The rest of her family, not so much. Their visit today confirmed what she'd been suspecting for months: Her brother was in over his head.

She waved the duo into the low-ceilinged room. Three people in the tiny apartment was two too many, but Priss ignored the claustrophobia rising in her throat and dropped back down on the couch. The Feds could stand or sit as they chose. She was still enough of an O'Brien not to worry over their comfort.

Young snatched the solo kitchen chair away from the tiny café table and straddled it backward, letting his forearms dangle over its back like useless T-Rex arms. Peters, the more seasoned and less debonair of the two, gave the apartment a once-over before perching on the sofa's oversized arm, his long legs stretched out in front of him, crossed at the ankles. The colorful alien motif on his socks reminded Priss of her brother-in-law, Adam, whose cartoon ties broke up his usual buttoned-up look. However, the sense of impending doom the Fed triggered was a far cry from her affection for her BIL.

"You look like your brother, Ms. Hughes." Young flashed a smile full of gleaming white teeth, but the friendliness didn't reach his eyes.

Priss folded her arms across her stomach, battening down the troop of butterflies dancing within. Should she lead with righteous indignation or cautious resignation? She chose the latter, since they obviously knew the identity Liam had created for her was as phony as a three-dollar bill.

"I'll take that as a compliment. Since you've done your research, I'm sure you're aware I left home when I was sixteen and legally changed my name at eighteen. I have nothing to do with the, ah…family business." Pressing her lips into a straight line, she sank further into the lumpy couch cushions and waited.

Always keep them dangling, her father had said, and Seamus O'Brien had been a consummate dangler when it came to law enforcement. Priss didn't have anything near his experience or skill, but even she knew it was better to say too little than too much.

Young nodded and gave her a sympathetic look he no doubt practiced every morning in his bathroom mirror. "Of course, of course. We understand. But we also know you've remained in steady contact with your brother, Liam "The Lion" O'Brien, through the years."

Priss forced her muscles to remain relaxed, aiming for interested but not *too* interested. "Is there a law against that?"

Again, Young flashed the results of some good orthodontia, the epitome of Mr. Cool. "Of course not.

Although we have wondered if the O'Briens are aware of your connection to the Hughes." The arrogance factor in his smile went up a couple notches. "And vice versa."

She doodled along the frayed arm of the sofa with her fingertip before raising her head in a direct challenge to Young's faux look of understanding. "If you're here to try and manipulate my connection to the Hughes family, you're too late. My husband and I have recently…" She gulped down a painful swallow. "Gone our separate ways."

Young raised an eyebrow and lowered his chin a fraction, though whether in admiration or disappointment, Priss couldn't tell, since the tough demeanor she'd adopted took the bulk of her concentration.

"I can assure you we have no intention to try and manipulate you or your in-laws." Young shook his head, as if the very words were distasteful.

"Huh!" Priss clenched, then unclenched her fists. *I will not lose my temper.* "I may not be my father's daughter in many respects, but I do know bullshit when I hear it."

A muscle in Young's jaw jumped, and she gave herself the point. Ready to quit this conversation while she was ahead, she began to once more wiggle her way out of the jaws of the sagging couch. She hadn't moved so much as an inch when, with a quelling look at his partner, Agent Peters hijacked the conversation.

"Ms. Hughes, while your father was alive, your brother was a guppy in a very large pond." Peters' voice was gruff, as if he'd smoked a few thousand cigarettes in his day.

"More like an ocean," Young added, chuckling at

his own joke.

Peters didn't break stride. "Lately, however, The Lion's been experiencing some growing pains, showing interest in some of the more, shall we say, *questionable* sides of the business."

The older agent looked straight at her when he spoke and didn't waste time with smiles. His broad, lined face, with its derisive expression, didn't waver. Priss suspected he was aiming for "bad cop" to Young's good one, but he came off as "complete asshole cop" instead.

"We'd very much like to know what *you* know about any new ventures your brother might be pursuing."

Ah ha. Peters had cut to the chase at last.

Priss freed a piece of fluff clinging to the fleece lounge pants she'd worn for three straight days and watched it drift to the floor. *Oh, Liam. If you were here, I'd smack you. Hard.* Her brother had always had a magnetic response to the seamier side of their father's—now Uncle Sean's—business. He was both attracted to and repelled by the secretive, backroom deals and other, more unsavory tactics. But Lee had shown her the only love she'd experienced as a child, and this agent's pompous way of speaking rubbed her the wrong way. Besides, O'Briens were a lot of things, but they weren't narcs.

"I'm not sure what I can do for you, Agent. Lee and I never discuss business." That wasn't a lie. In the past months, Liam had done all the talking. She'd just submerged herself in the Lalaland of the newlywed and hoped her brother would wise up.

He hadn't.

"Has your brother ever mentioned a man named Jonathan Bannion?"

Priss studied Peters. At first, she'd assumed Young, with his tailored suit and 900-kilowatt smile was in charge, but that wasn't so. Despite his somewhat rumpled exterior—unusual for a Fed—Peters ruled the roost. Not that it mattered much. She didn't trust either one of them.

"Nope. I've never heard that name." That was also true, but she made an educated guess. Bannion had to be the mysterious "buyer" Liam kept talking about.

Peters made a notation in his phone, using the thumb of one hand and forefinger of the other. "Do you know why this man Bannion, a known dealer in stolen antiquities, would be keeping tabs on your husband?"

She stiffened as the butterflies in her stomach reawakened. "No, I don't."

Except that she did.

Damn it to hell, Lee. You and your stupid wheeling and dealing. How dare you hang Mason out to dry!

She needed to warn her sweet, charming, clueless-as-to-the-ways-of-the-Mob husband, ASAP.

There was only one problem with that plan. She'd cooked her goose but good, and Mason now wanted nothing to do with her.

Both agents spent a few seconds tapping on their phones, Young with much more dexterity than Peters, before rising to their feet, as if by some secret signal.

"Ms. Hughes, I can't emphasize this enough. Mr. Bannion is bad news. If he has eyes on you or your husband, it's serious. Your husband's grandfather and parents have security details. However, Dr. Hughes and his brothers don't qualify for that kind of protection." Peters once again glanced around the room, his gaze lingering on the solitary, unbarred window. "You're living here?"

Priss broke free from the suction of the couch without losing too much dignity. "Not for long." The question reminded her of the first one she'd asked, when the agents first arrived at the apartment. "How did you find me?"

Peters stared back at her without blinking, but Young's gaze dropped to his shoes.

Priss narrowed her eyes. "Are you kidding me? You're tracing my phone?" Her hair spilled forward as she shook her head, and she shoved it behind her ears once more. It was a little different from wiretapping, which was illegal without a judge's sign-off, but it still left her feeling violated. Legal rights—or the suppression thereof—had been popular dinnertime conversation in the O'Brien household. "That's an invasion of my privacy," she said, even though her words appeared to have zero impact on either of the two men.

Young cleared his throat. "Your father was Seamus O'Br—"

"My father is *dead*, shot and killed by the Federal Bureau of Investigation." Tears threatened again as she stormed across to the door, opened it wide. "That's your cue to leave, gentlemen."

Both agents stepped forward but paused at the threshold. Young offered her his card. She snatched it from his fingers and crumpled it into a ball.

The younger agent didn't bat an eyelash. "Whether you like us or not, Ms. Hughes, doesn't matter. We believe you—and through you, your husband—are in danger. We came here today to discuss the possibility of your testifying as a federal witness. We'd give you protection, a new identity." He glanced around the room again. "A nicer place to live."

Her jaw dropped. Good God. These guys had balls; she'd give them that. They'd killed her father, but they thought she'd cooperate. "I'll give you three guesses as to my answer, and the first two don't count."

"We would keep you safe." Peters added his two cents' worth. "With you out of the picture, your brother ceases to have any leverage with the Hughes family. Takes the heat off your husband."

Damn it. That made some sense. Ensuring Mason's safety was Job Number One. But working with the Feds after everything that had happened... Even vigorous brushing wouldn't get that taste out of her mouth.

She uncreased the business card, flattening it between her palms. "I'll think about it." At the words, her gut clenched. Without a doubt, her father was rolling in his grave right now.

Peters gave her a quick nod and he and his partner stepped into the hallway. Young, his complexion gray in the harsh fluorescent light, gave her a lingering look over his shoulder. "It's a good offer, Ms. Hughes. And it won't be on the table forever."

Priss shut the door and shot the bolt home.

****

"Sonofabitch! Mace, you turd. What's with the elbow?"

Mason shrugged off his eldest brother's comment and took to the air for a picture-perfect slam dunk, one of the perks of being six foot six. So what if Jeep was mad? So was he. All the time, these days.

"Still no word from Priss, I take it." Lunging sideways, Mason's other brother, Adam, swatted the ball back into the court before it bounced into the boxwood hedge. Nearly as tall as Mason, Adam's wingspan was equally impressive.

"I don't want to talk about it." Mason spat the words out, knowing full well his brothers would ignore his request.

"Too fucking bad," Jeep said, with his usual eloquence. "You need to get a grip, Little Bro. Before that head of yours explodes." Despite his shorter height—he was a mere six-three—he caught Adam's pass with ease and rose on tiptoe for a three-pointer that was nothing but net.

"I'm fine." Mason was living at the hospital, eating little and sleeping less, but other than that, he was just peachy.

"Callie assures me Priss is safe, just needs a little space." Adam raced after the rebound again.

Mason gritted his teeth. That was the fifty-sixth time he'd heard that phrase in the past twenty-four hours. Everyone said it, as if it made things feel less shitty. It didn't. Not where he stood. His wife had left him. Period.

And, God help him, he had no idea why.

From day one, they'd been kindred spirits. Soulmates. Totally in sync. Then, all of a sudden, *wham*. She'd left. What the hell had happened?

He zigged, then zagged, catching Adam's pass. "It's that damn book's fault. If I hadn't spent so much time with you losers, looking for the frickin' Gutenberg…"

Jeep appeared before him like a human brick wall. "Ooof." Mason clipped his brother's broad shoulder, which jarred him enough to drop the ball. "Geez, man." Grabbing his arm, he watched the ball roll into the boxwoods. "Who are you, Iron Man? Go easy on us mere mortals."

Jeep grinned and patted his six pack. "Once a SEAL, always a SEAL." He jabbed a finger into Mason's chest. "You showed us the note, bro. I hate to say it, but that book—if you can call something that weighs thirty-five pounds a 'book,'—had nothing to do with the breakdown of your marriage."

"That was a fairly standard size for a book at that time," Adam, always the professor, offered from the hedge. After a moment of searching, he stood up with the ball. "The vellum, or paper, was folded in the folio manner and—"

Deep snoring noises came from Jeep. "Thanks, Poindexter, but we're here to shoot hoops, not attend one of your lectures on ancient manuscripts."

Adam flipped Jeep the bird. "Philistine."

Jeep shrugged. "I'm just saying. I'm glad we found the damn thing. Shocked, and glad. Now that it's in the hands of the university, we can relax and get back to what really matters." He gave Mason a hard stare. "Like what a complete mess you are."

Mason glanced down with a frown. While he wasn't as muscle-bound as Jeep, he kept himself in decent shape, so it must be his T-shirt his brother was talking about. He'd lived in it or his scrubs for the past several weeks. It sported a large ketchup stain, another that might be soy sauce, and was ranker than a skunk. Still, he stuck his chest out, hands on his hips. "I thought we were here to play basketball, but if you'd rather spend the time discussing my laundry…"

Adam, the peacemaker of the family, inserted himself between them. "We came to play." He gave Jeep a clear warning look before unleashing a concerned gaze on Mason. "But we're worried about you. You're always at the hospital—"

"I'm a doctor. Where else would I be?"

Jeep threw up his hands and took a step backwards. "Told you we'd get nowhere with the kid. If he wants to work himself into the ground, so be it."

Mason caught the worry in Adam's blue eyes, knew his brothers' concern came from love. He relaxed a fraction. "Okay, so I'm a little out of balance. My wife just left me. I'm entitled."

Jeep leaned forward and set a heavy hand on Mason's shoulder. "You are. We just don't want to see you crash and burn." The warmth in his usually clipped tone spoke volumes.

Sighing, Mason stared down at a long, black scuff mark on his left shoe. "I don't know what else to do."

"You know what Mum always says. 'When you're in need of some introspection…'" Adam's falsetto was a perfect imitation of their mother's proper British accent.

Mason raised his head and managed half a smile. "Go to the cabin?"

"Go to the cabin," his brothers said in unison.

It wasn't a half bad idea. Heaven knew he had the time off coming. "I'll think about it. But first, I need to see Gates. Priss asked me to start divorce proceedings."

Both Adam and Jeep looked poleaxed.

"Dude, she's only been gone six weeks. Don't you think that's a little rash?"

Once again, Mason bristled at Jeep's words. "No…maybe." He shrugged and blew out a long breath. "I don't know. We got married in a crazy, Vegas-fueled daze. Given that, it's surprising it lasted this long."

Wow. That performance deserved an Academy Award.

Or not. His brothers' stares told Mason they weren't buying what he was selling. "C'mon. I'm not saying anything you guys haven't thought a thousand times."

Adam nodded. "That was true, in the beginning. But now, after seeing you two together…"

"You're fucking perfect for each other." Once again, Jeep skipped the bullshit and got right to the point.

"Plus, you're a forgiving soul," Adam added. "Much to your credit. I've learned quite a bit about forgiveness lately, and I have to say, it brings some awesome rewards."

Mason understood that Adam was referring to his own marriage, which had begun with more than a little deception and secrecy. However, his relationship with Priss was different from his brother's and sister-in-law's. What had begun with a mad impulse was ending the same damn way. That was poetic justice for you.

"You know what your problem is?" The determined glint in Jeep's eyes flashed like a neon sign.

"No," Mason said, with a huge exhale. "But it looks like you're gonna tell me." Sometimes being the youngest sucked. Neither of his brothers realized they weren't his boss.

"Damn straight I am. You've never had to fight for anything in your life."

Clenching his fists, Mason took a jerky step toward Jeep. "Are you kidding me? We can go right now if you want."

For the second time in as many minutes, Adam maneuvered between them and set a hand on Mason's chest. "Hang on, Rocky. He doesn't mean that kind of fight."

Mason kept his eyes on Jeep. "Oh, yeah? What the

hell does he mean, then?"

"He means…" Adam paused, as if searching for the right words. "I think a better way to say it is that you've led a charmed life."

Stepping back, Mason glanced around at their surroundings, including the sprawling, multi-million-dollar ranch house in which they'd all been raised, and shrugged. "That's true of all of us. But you don't choose your family. Besides, it's not like Mum and Dad handed us everything. We worked. *I* worked. Worked my ass off."

Adam gave him a lopsided smile. "I said *charmed*, not easy. You have worked hard. In fact, you've achieved every goal you've ever set for yourself."

Mason muttered one of Jeep's favorite words. "Isn't that the whole idea?"

"Yes, but—"

"You've never been thwarted," Jeep barked. "Never had your path blocked before. As a result, you don't know what to do when you hit a roadblock."

Mason's gaze flickered between his two brothers. He couldn't believe this. They were dead serious. "You two don't know what the hell you're talking about."

It was Jeep's turn to curse and, JAG lawyer that he was, he made the Navy proud. "I give up." He turned to Adam. "He'll do just what he always does on the rare occasion when something goes sideways. Buy a giant rug and sweep everything under it. Let's get back to the game." With a perfect military pivot, he stalked off to retrieve the basketball.

Adam stayed put, his eyes boring into Mason's. "Do you love Priss?"

Sucking in air, Mason rubbed at his chest. The ache

that had formed the day he'd found her note intensified every day they were separated. "I want to say 'no,' but, yeah. More than I ever thought possible." He lifted a hand as Adam started to speak. "Which means I want what she wants, and she wants a divorce. She's made that very clear."

Adam ran a hand through his dark, sweaty hair. "That's what we've been trying to tell you. Maybe Priss is mistaken. Maybe she doesn't know what she wants. If you love her even half as much as I think you do, now isn't the time to cave. Now's the time to fight, man! Convince her you belong together. Make her stay."

Mason frowned. "Were we raised by the same bra-burning, glass-ceiling-busting feminist? Because that sounds a little Neanderthal to me. I don't own Priss. She's her own woman. Plus, we agreed—back in that ridiculous Elvis chapel in Vegas—that if it didn't work out, there'd be no guilt. Each of us was free to walk away."

And he didn't want her staying if she was as miserable as she claimed to be.

Adam gave him a not-too-subtle shove. "Come on, don't be so obtuse, man! I'm not suggesting you carry her off to a cave somewhere. I'm just suggesting that what you guys have is worth fighting for, that's all. For both your sakes."

Mason drew in another deep breath. It was simple for Adam to say that, but he hadn't read Priss's note. She'd sounded like a woman who wasn't coming back.

Jake jogged up with the ball under his arm. "Any luck?" he asked Adam.

Adam lifted his shoulders. "Mace. We love you, man, and we'll always have your back. But now isn't the time to make any drastic decisions. Why don't you spend a week or so at the cabin and think about things? Chop some wood, take a hike, inhale all that clean mountain air. Then, and only then, do you decide what to do, moving forward."

Turning away, Mason let his gaze wander across the rolling Virginia hills, purple in the afternoon shadows. Closing his eyes, he soaked up the gentle lapping sounds of the Potomac River as it flowed toward the sea. This combination of sights and sounds usually brought peace. But his brothers were correct, up to a point. Nothing was working for him right now, not even the familiar lull of his childhood home.

He swiveled back to his brothers. "Okay. I'll give the cabin a try. I'm not promising I'll change my mind about anything, but I'll consider my options."

Adam smiled. "That's all we're asking."

The deep intonations of Big Ben echoed around the court. Mason's ring tone was a nod to their mother's homeland.

"Crap. I gotta get this. I'm on call." Three strides brought Mason to the bench along the side of the court, where he'd dumped his backpack prior to the game.

"Of course you are." Jeep sent up another three-pointer.

Mason pulled his blaring phone out of the unzipped front pocket. The photo on the screen was the last one he expected to see. A jolt of pure panic coursed through him. "What do I do?"

"What do you think you do, dumbass? You answer it," Jeep said, sauntering over.

Mason's gut clenched as he stared down at Priss's image. Long, luscious hair, impish violet eyes, smiling full lips. He missed her so much it scared the shit out of him.

Groaning, he silenced the call and slid the unanswered phone back into his bag. "I can't talk to her right now." He was too…raw.

In a fluid move, Jeep reached around him and withdrew the phone before Mason could react.

"Hey, Priss. It's Jeep."

Mason made a mad scramble for the phone, but his brother stiff-armed him.

"Um-hmm." Jeep nodded. "You doin' okay? Need any help?"

Half holding his breath, Mason scoured Jeep's face for a reaction. As usual, there wasn't one. What was Priss saying?

Jeep nodded again. "Okay…Yeah, he'll be there. You take care." He ended the call and handed the phone back. "Your wife wants to see you, pronto. You're meeting her in an hour, at some dive diner near Callie's old apartment. Macee's, with two 'e's."

Wide-eyed, Mason turned to Adam. "Is *that* where's she's been staying? Callie's old place? That stings, bro." And it heightened his concern. The apartment was in a sketchy part of town, to say the least.

Adam raised his hands in defense. "The universal sisterhood of women, man. I knew nothing except what I told you."

"Yeah, well. All of this is moving too fast. I don't want to see her. I'm too messed up." The admission brought an odd surge of relief, but it was short-lived.

"You'll go," Jeep said.

"You'll go," Adam agreed.

Shit. Bending, Mason slung his backpack over his

shoulder.

The smug bastards knew him too well.

Chapter Two

Priss stepped over the crack in the sidewalk. She wasn't superstitious, and her mother had been dead for over twenty-five years, but she couldn't afford any more bad luck right now. With shaking hands, she unfolded the note she'd found shoved under the apartment's door an hour ago. The letters were cut from a newspaper, giving the message the ominous look of a made-for-TV ransom note. That was freaky enough, but the words scared her even more:

Give us the Gutenberg or you and your husband will die.

Short and to the point. Was it Liam's work? God, she hoped not. It wasn't his usual style. He was an in-your-face kind of guy, and he always signed his work, but styles changed. And he was desperate. She wouldn't have left Mason if her brother's threats hadn't sounded as stone cold serious as a heart attack.

And yet the note didn't "feel" like Liam, which really cranked up the warning bells. Could it be from his buyer, the Bannion guy the Feds had asked about?

She rubbed her forehead. The whole situation, on top of all her crying jags, fueled a monstrous headache, but she couldn't turn off her brain. Not until it was clear who was behind what.

Months ago, when first Callie, then their mother-in-law, Minna, had been attacked, Priss had grilled Liam, who'd sworn on their mother's grave that the wheels she'd helped set in motion in Vegas were not, in any way, responsible for the attacks. He'd guaranteed his buyer didn't know anything except that there might soon be a Gutenberg for sale. Of course, in their own separate ways, they'd each made a career out of lying, so believing Liam was a jump ball at the best of times. However, regardless of the truth in the past, someone sure as hell had her number—and address—now.

Someone, that is, besides the Feds.

Despite her earlier protests, she wasn't that surprised to hear that her phone was being pinged. If the past was anything to judge by, the Feds took a few liberties where O'Briens were concerned, even with minor family members like herself. However, as the note in her hands proved, the fact that the FBI was keeping tabs on her whereabouts was the least of her problems.

So far, during the course of this Bible Hunt, two men—who'd worked for a person or persons unknown—were dead, and the note she thrust back in her pocket threatened more violence. Liam had sworn he wasn't behind the murders.

The question was, did she believe him?

The fact she couldn't answer that question with a resounding "yes," made her heart bleed. However, right now, her survival instinct was overriding all other emotions. She'd take the note at face value and apologize later, if need be. Calling Mason had taken Herculean effort, but he deserved to know there might be a price on his head.

Rounding the corner, she walked under the Macee's sign, a large, neon arrow that had been new about forty years before she was born. Tucked away on a lazy side street, the restaurant was a neighborhood hangout, just a few blocks from Callie's apartment. It was too early for the dinner rush and the place would be all but empty. *Perfect.* She didn't want any distractions when she spoke with her husband.

Her reflection in the diner's plate glass window made her pause. God, she was a hot mess. She'd lost weight, and the flowing, prairie-style dress she wore hung like a flour sack. Even the leggings she wore under it, her only nod to DC's schizophrenic spring weather, didn't add any bulk. Her hair was dull and lifeless, despite the shower she'd taken after the agents had left, while her eyes were puffy and underlined by dark circles. Make-up didn't factor into the equation at all.

A familiar, clean, woodsy scent tickled her nose moments before Mason's reflection joined hers in the glass. Turning, Priss drank in the sight of him. Damn the man. He wore clothes well, whether dressed to the nines or when sporting a more casual look, like now. His worn jeans and sage-green corduroy shirt hugged his lean, muscular frame in all the right places. The shirt matched his eyes, which were fringed with long, blond eyelashes any woman would envy. The down-filled jacket he carried over his shoulder only added to his rugged appeal, its navy color a stark contrast to his light, wind-tossed hair.

Priss glanced in the window again. The hottie and the dishrag. What a pair.

"Um. H-hi," she blurted out, after several awkward beats told her he wasn't going to speak first. Or maybe, considering his hostile look, at all. *No. Not hostile.* That wasn't him. Apathetic? Blank? *Cautious.* That was it. Like he was about to step into a pit of vipers. She couldn't blame him. The note she'd written had been pretty brutal, even if for his own good.

"So." She fixed her eyes on his left earlobe, figuring it was the least sexy part of him, but she hadn't factored in the adorable way his hair tweaked out. Shifting her gaze to his shirt collar, she tried again. "Thank you for coming. I wasn't sure you would."

He shrugged. "Jeep told me you said it was 'life or death.'"

After drawing in a shaky breath, she fished the note out again and handed it over. "I got this today."

He frowned as he scanned the page. "What the hell is this?"

She glanced down at her old-timey, lace-up boots. They had three-inch heels, which meant they weren't worth a damn in bad weather, but they looked incredible and gave her five-foot-four frame the boost it needed around the Hughes family. Callie had legs that didn't quit and her mother-in-law, Minna, skimmed six feet. There was another reason they'd become her go-to footwear, though. Mason had loved it when she wore them…and nothing else.

Shelving that thought, she met his questioning eyes. "Someone slid it under the apartment door today, while I was in the shower. I-I'm worried. I think it's the real deal."

He leaned forward in that familiar, unconscious way, as he re-read the note. "Probably just some weirdo who's seen our name in the paper." He gave the note back. "Between my grandfather, my father, and my mother, the police have a whole filing cabinet filled with these. Looks like we've joined the club."

She held the note between her thumb and forefinger,

as if it might bite. "I know, but…" She shook the paper. "This time, I really do think we might be in danger."

Because, although I haven't mentioned it before, my father was Seamus O'Brien. You know, the famous mob boss.

He raised a shoulder. "Okay. If it makes you feel better, talk to the police. They'll tell you the same thing. Just another weirdo."

Her tension level decreased by an ounce or two. His lack of concern was tempting. "You don't think it's serious?"

He smiled then, not with full wattage, but enough that her heart did a backflip. "I don't."

She allowed her shoulders to relax an inch. He was right. Anything the Hughes family did made headlines, and there were plenty of wackadoodles out there.

He flicked a finger toward the note. "Was that it? Because I have some place I need to be."

Was that impatience or awkwardness in his eyes? Either one was rare for him.

She refolded the piece of paper once more, hiding the menacing cutouts. "Um, yeah, I guess." Craving the comfort of sitting across a table from him, she'd planned on inviting him into Macee's for coffee. But Priscilla plus Mason equaled the poop emoji. It was better to quit while she was ahead. Bad luck always caught up to the O'Briens, guaranteed.

Another thought struck her, knotting her shoulders again.

"Wait." She spoke to his back as he headed down the sidewalk. "How did he know where I was?"

Still holding the coat over his shoulder, he swung around like the GQ model he'd once been. "What do you mean?"

Her boots clicked against the concrete as she closed the distance between them, waving the paper in her hand. "How did the author find me? You didn't even know where I was, did you?" Priss would bet good money that Callie hadn't spilled the beans.

"No." His eyes, now narrowed with concern, met hers. "You're right. I didn't know, not until you picked this neighborhood to meet. There's no way—" The rest of his sentence was lost as tires squealed and a car engine revved.

Priss peeked around his broad shoulder. A black SUV, its windows darkly tinted, roared down the road in their direction. One of the back windows opened, just enough for her to see…

"Gun!" Lunging, she slammed into Mason, and they fell to the ground as a haze of bullets pinged into the brick wall behind them.

****

Mason's ears rang with the echoes of gunshots. In the distance, he heard the faint screech of rubber, the roar of an engine accelerating. Then, silence.

Holy shit. Was he dead? Was Priss?

He slid his hands along her shoulders and back. She remained on top of him, thinner than he remembered, and freakishly still.

"Priss. Priss! C'mon woman, say something!" He swallowed the panic rising in his throat.

A small crowd circled around them. With a practice borne from both years in the spotlight and his career as a doctor, he tuned them out, training all his attention on Priss. Cradling her head, he rolled her onto her side and made a quick pass of her prone body with his free hand, checking for any obvious injuries. At last, she opened her eyes.

"Easy does it." With trembling fingers, he pushed her hair off her face, his motives not entirely altruistic. He had to touch and reassure. Her skin was warm, her pulse throbbed.

Thank God.

"Mmmph." Her violet eyes widened as she rolled onto her back and sucked in air. "I think…wind… knocked out."

After stretching his own kinks out, he grabbed his coat and shoved it under her head. "You're okay. Just give it a sec."

She inhaled again and splotches of color returned to her face, including the purple smudges beneath her eyes. Tired, unhappy eyes.

Well, duh. Someone had just shot at them.

"Holy shit." He said it out loud, as reality seeped in. "What the hell just happened?"

Priss' hair rubbed against the nylon of his jacket as she moved her head from side to side. "I don't know." She levered herself up on her elbows and he motioned for her to stay down as he pushed himself to his feet, reaching in his front pocket for his cell.

"I already called the police," a woman informed him. "They're on the way."

"Thanks." He pressed a speed dial number and raised the phone to his ear. His oldest brother answered after the first ring.

"You and Priss kiss and make up yet?"

Jeep's voice, calm and deep, steadied him. "Not exactly. We were just shot at."

"Shot at?" Jeep's laconic tone disappeared like

water on sand. "As in, with bullets?"

Mason scanned the face of the brick building. Gunshots had left distinctive divots high up in the masonry. "Sure looks like it to me."

Jeep swore. "Everyone okay?"

Mason turned his gaze back to Priss. She was sitting up, breathing deeply, giving a shaky "thumbs up" to a few bystanders. He wasn't buying it—her eyes told him she was as freaked out as he was—but it wasn't a bad effort, given the situation.

"Yeah, they aimed high, and no one was hurt. Cops are on the way."

"Okay. You still at Macee's?"

"Yep."

"I'm on my way."

Mason hung up and hunkered down next to Priss again. Without thinking, he slipped a hand under her mass of silky hair and squeezed her shoulder. Then, he pulled back. In the midst of the danger they'd passed through, he'd forgotten they were over. That he was respecting her right to call it quits.

"Jeep's *en route*. He'll circle the wagons. That okay?"

Priss rubbed an elbow. "I guess so."

He could guess what she was thinking. "Our business is our business. My family cares about you, but they won't try to fix anything," he said.

Except for his mother, of course. And Jeep, who couldn't help himself...Not that his father was too far behind. Then, there was Adam, and now Callie.

"Oh, fudge." He pulled out his phone again. "I'll text them. Call off the dogs."

Priss gave a weak chuckle. "Fudge? Come on. I

know we were shot at and everything, but is that the best you can do?"

He smiled back, both in relief at her apparent recovery, and at her teasing reference to the game he and his brothers still played. Since high school, they'd turned swear words into alliterative phrases to avoid their mother's expensive penalties for cursing. "Flipping flapjacks, then."

Her eyes went from pale lavender to a deeper violet, and his heart skipped a beat.

"That's better," she said, nodding. "I don't mind if Jeep comes, but don't bother everyone else."

He composed a long text to the family's group chat, finishing just as a pair of cop cars, lights flashing and sirens blaring, skidded to a stop at the curb. His back twinged as he rose to his feet once more, but he shrugged it off. Hitting the pavement from his height was bound to leave a mark or two. Leaning down, he offered Priss a hand and helped her to her feet, too. *Damn.* Those boots. They brought back memories he shouldn't be remembering right now.

Man, he sucked at this new status quo.

You've never had to fight for anything in your life.

His brother's words taunted him. Intrigued him. What if…what if he didn't make this easy for her? What if he tried to change her mind?

A line from the note she'd left for him paraded across his mind. *I'm sorry, but this isn't what I want anymore.* His gut twisted. Not a whole lot of wiggle room there.

He squeezed his eyes shut for a second and ran a hand along his forehead. His emotions were uneven before the shooting. Now, they were off the charts.

Escaping to the mountains was sounding better by the second, but he couldn't—wouldn't—leave if Priss was in danger. So, what if she came with him? They'd be safe at the cabin and buy themselves time to unravel the craziness that had just happened.

They'd also have time to talk about their relationship. Find out if they still had one.

She might agree. Or she might accuse him of being that Neanderthal he'd spoken of earlier.

Before he could weigh the pros and cons, two of the four police officers walked over. The older one tipped his hat, a gleam of recognition in his eyes.

"Dr. Hughes, right? I promise, we'll try and make this as brief as possible."

Much to Mason's surprise, it was. Firstly, because he and Priss didn't know what the hell had just happened. Secondly—it was made clear—because of their last name. The brawny, aging officer who'd recognized Mason, was A Fan. And In Charge. With all the tact of a drill sergeant, he dispatched the three other officers to interview the crowd and canvass the neighborhood while he interviewed Mason and Priss.

"Typical drive-by," the officer said. "They aimed high, missing you and the windows. I've seen it before," he added, with what Mason deemed a little extra swagger. "Most likely a gang initiation."

"So, you don't think it had anything to do with the note?" Priss stood ramrod straight, her arms crossed, hugging her thin frame.

Mason fought the urge to touch. To give and receive comfort. They were individuals instead of a couple. For now.

Maybe for always.

The policeman gestured at the pockmarked building. "I doubt it. People who send notes, write letters. They don't usually act." He patted his clipboard, where the note, safe in a plastic bag, was clipped. "We'll run it, though. See if it tells us anything."

Mason nodded, taking a discreet peek at the man's name badge. "Thanks, Officer Thompson. We appreciate it."

Thompson handed them both his card. "If there's anything you need, just give me a call." He inclined his head, as if bowing to royalty, before joining his co-workers in the crowd.

Mason checked his watch. Jeep should be arriving any minute now.

"We need to talk." Priss looked up at him. "There's something I need to explain, before I lose my nerve."

Mason raised his eyebrows. In all the months he'd known Priss, "nerve" had never been an issue. She tackled everything with an easy confidence. It wasn't arrogance, just a determination to face life, good times or bad, head-on and with a smile. As his father liked to say, she "rolled with the punches." But getting shot at was bigger than a punch—a lot bigger—and she had a right to be rattled. God knew he was.

She inclined her head toward the diner's entrance in an unspoken question. The fact that it remained open after the shooting told Mason a lot about the neighborhood. His urge to get her out of town climbed a notch.

"Come on. Let's grab a bite to eat while we wait for Jeep. We're safe now, with all these cops crawling around, and I promise this place looks worse than it is."

Mason remained where he was for a moment,

staring up at the restaurant's large, lighted sign. One of the "e's" had burned out, reducing the sign to "MACE." His nickname. A name Priss had shouted over and over again, in the throes of passion.

Shit. His brothers were right. He'd never fought for anything.

Until now.

Chapter Three

Getting shot at sucked. But, sitting here in an ancient diner, waiting to tell the man she loved that everything he thought he knew about her was a lie? That sucked more.

Waaaay more.

Priss wasn't surprised to find Mason acting...aloof. She'd expected it, deserved it, prepared for it. Yet, he was so far from his normal self it tore at her insides. Offering aid and comfort wasn't just his job, it defined him. He was indefatigable and never lost heart. An asteroid could be headed straight for Earth and he would see the bright side, in a sincere, non-saccharine way. Family lore had it that Jeep had called him "Sunny," right up to the day Mason had topped him in height.

Today, however, his empathetic optimism was MIA, and it was her fault. *She'd* done this to him, six weeks ago. No, correction. This train wreck had started six months ago, when she'd agreed to marry him. They'd been a bad idea from the get-go, but a tidal wave of love had slapped the common sense right out of her head.

Love. A condition she'd always intended to avoid. The O'Brien clan was unlucky in a whole host of ways, but love topped the list. Then, three wild days in Vegas with the captivating male now exiting the Macee's men's room had changed her mind.

Stupid Vegas.

The duct-taped, red vinyl seat protested as Mason slid onto it, and the table rocked on uneven legs. But, on the plus side, they were in a dark corner, away from prying eyes. The booth was horseshoe shaped, and six weeks ago they'd have slid to the back and cuddled together, unwilling to break physical contact even while eating. Now, the continent-sized table sat between them, he on his side, she on hers. The honeymoon was over. Do not pass go. Do not collect two hundred dollars. Instead, head straight to the divorce courts.

Typical O'Brien luck.

"Okay. Let's talk." Stretching a long arm across the back of the booth, Mason slouched against it, a picture of calm despite all the chaos that had transpired in the last half an hour.

It was one of his superpowers, shelving his feelings until he was ready to address them. She'd seen him do it after an unexpected death at the hospital and the ability made her a little jealous. Her family, her *life*, had taught her to shelve things, too. To be dealt with *never*.

"I'm not sure where to begin."

"The beginning's always good." The corner of his mouth twitched, and a flicker of compassion burned in his eyes. She took heart. Old Mason must be wounded but not dead.

Of course, that might change once she told him the truth.

"Right." She pulled in a lungful of the diner's stale air, which smelled of years of burnt toast and coffee.

"When we met in Las Vegas…I said I didn't know who you were, but that wasn't one-hundred percent accurate."

His shoulders tensed. Just a fraction, but enough that

she, ever in tune with him, noticed.

"Un-uh." He shook his head. "We'd never met before. I'd have remembered."

"No, you're right. We'd never actually met." *Arrgh.* She was making a hash of this. "Let me back up. I haven't told you much about my family."

Mason raised his eyebrows. "That's the understatement of the year. Always figured you would when you were ready."

She managed a weak grin. "Well, today's the day. I told you that I'm an orphan, that I have no family, but that isn't exactly, um…true."

Shifting forward, he set both elbows on the lino-topped table, sending it listing in his direction. The guarded expression he'd worn earlier had returned. "Okay."

"Both my parents are dead, so the orphan part's accurate now. But I wasn't orphaned as a young child. And I have a sibling, a brother."

He sat there, so quiet that she began to wonder if he'd heard her or not.

"That's a lot to take in," he said, after a lifetime. "Why would you…" He shook his head again. "Your brother is alive?"

The butterflies in her stomach spawned smaller, more vigorous butterflies. "Yes, he's alive, but it's complicated." Hell, nuclear physics were simple compared to her family history.

Mason studied the tabletop. "I disagree. Either you have a brother, or you don't. Why lie about it?"

"That will be obvious in a minute. My mother died when I was very young, just like I said, and my father ran the, um…family business. My brother, Liam, is eight years older than I am. Lee was a better parent than my father was on his best day."

His eyes met hers as he nodded. She knew no one understood tight sibling bonds better than he did.

"So why the lie?"

Priss was saved from answering that million-dollar question by the waitress, who picked that moment to set two glasses of ice water in front of them.

"Kitchen's closed, folks, at least until the police are done sniffing around." The well-seasoned woman gave them an eyeroll. "Don't know what this neighborhood is coming to. Gangbangers think they own everything, I guess. I can give you coffee and something cold."

Mason ordered coffee and a piece of peach pie, then gave the frizzled waitress the sympathetic smile that made him such a hit with his patients. Priss envied it. She'd been trained from birth to keep people at a distance. Maintain a permanent stiff-arm and the world couldn't exploit you.

"I'll stick with water, thanks," Priss told the woman, who then spun off toward the kitchen. Explaining the past was hard enough without adding any chewing to the mix.

"I idolized my brother. There was nothing he could do that was wrong in my eyes, right up until my fourteenth birthday."

Mason nodded once. "Okay. What happened then?"

"Liam came home from college and joined the family business."

He lifted a hand and ran a finger in a circle. "And that was a problem because…?"

Priss took another deep breath. This was it. The big-girl-panty moment. "Because I'm from Boston and my name—my birth name—is O'Brien."

Confusion clouded Mason's green eyes. "Boston. O'Brien. You don't mean…?"

Chewing her upper lip, Priss nodded. "Yep. *Those* O'Briens."

The vinyl seat squealed as he collapsed against it once more. "No. Fucking. Way."

In any other circumstance she'd be laughing. Mason almost never dropped the "F" bomb.

"You're telling me that your family is…that you're connected to…the most successful Mob family in the history of the United States?"

On the other side of the near-empty restaurant, the exit beckoned. *No. You can't run this time.*

"Not just connected. My father was Seamus O'Brien."

Boom.

Mason raised both hands to his head, as if to stop it from falling to pieces, before running his fingers through his longish hair. "I don't even know what to say to that."

He lurched forward again, until he leaned halfway across the table. "Are you kidding me?" he demanded, belying his words. "You're the Godfather's daughter?" A muscle in his jaw jumped. "Your father was Public Enemy Number One, right up until…" He gestured with a hand, apparently unwilling to get into her father's messy death.

"Shhh!" Priss glanced around at the vacant booths. "Mob rule number one: Keep your voice down."

"Again. You're the Godfather's daughter. How could you not tell me this?"

The hurt in his voice and eyes stabbed at her soul, like a thousand stickpins. "My father preferred 'skipper' to 'godfather,' but yes, you got it. Now, my Uncle Sean runs things. And I didn't tell you because…well, it's not an easy truth to tell." She shrugged. "My relationship with my family has always been complicated."

Mason said something too low for her to catch, before meeting her eyes again.

"All right." His hands flexed and fisted, like the close-ups in a movie before someone got strangled. "Let's set aside the fact that you've never told me, *your husband*, any of this. They've never said as much, but I can guarantee my family had you vetted six ways from Sunday as soon as we tied the knot. Jeep certainly did. How did you manage to hide all of this?"

She slid her water glass two inches to the right, then back again. This was somehow the hardest to admit. It made everything seem so…criminal. "Lee's good with computers. Over the years, he's become an expert at building false identities." She fingered the puddle of condensation her water glass had made. "Let's just say he took certain steps to make sure your family got a friendly report."

And has been using it against me ever since. God, what a family.

Mason whistled. "Wow…I'm almost afraid to ask but, what else don't I know?"

She flushed but didn't duck it. "Our meeting in Vegas wasn't exactly a happy accident."

"Meaning?" His tone indicated he'd beaten her to the punchline.

"Lee's been looking for a way out of the business, but he needs some serious cash to make it happen. He saw the magazine story about your family's rumored Gutenberg and…" Priss raised her hands. "Look, he's always been a bit of a dreamer, so I didn't think it would amount to much. I was living in Vegas at that time. He found out you'd be in Vegas that week and he sent me to meet you, to see if you'd say anything about the Bible."

A flush flooded Mason's face and, for a few seconds, she worried he might stroke out.

"I only agreed to talk to you, nothing else," she added, as if that would help. Heady memories of those first crazy days assaulted her, making her shiver. From the get-go, they'd been both compatible and combustible. "Everything that followed was *off script*. All *me*." If Mason took nothing else away from this conversation, she wanted him to understand that much.

"Why'd your brother ask you for help?"

She sipped some water, and wished for something stronger. Lying she could do with cold calm, but coming clean always made her sweat. "Because I'd helped him before, in similar situations. Just not with a Gutenberg's-worth at stake."

It gutted her, watching the light dawn in his eyes.

"Jesus. You're a scam artist!" He rubbed at his chest, as if her story had made a hole there. "My father. If this gets out, it'll look like he's in the O'Briens' pocket. And Grandpa… My family's entire legacy could be called into question. My God! Do you hate me? Is that it? No, wait. You claim to have a sixth sense about things. Did I offend you in a past life?"

That stung. She'd told him she got a funny feeling sometimes, like a tingle or twinge, but it was premonition, not time traveling or past lives or such. But she let the cheap shot go.

"That's why I buried it. I promise you I've never done anything illegal." Right up to the line, maybe. "And

Lee, he's never scammed anyone who didn't have it coming. He's…he's like a modern-day Robin Hood." *Or was, until he decided to fleece your family out of a thirty-five-million-dollar Bible.*

She shifted forward, her hands flat on the cold tabletop. "Mace, I fell in love with you. I didn't plan it—it just happened and, you know me. Act first, think later. It's never been my intention to hurt you, or your parents, or your grandfather, or anyone else. That's why I left. I'm only sitting here, telling you all of this, because I have reason to believe your life's in danger."

He started to say something, but pressed Pause when the waitress appeared at the table with his pie and coffee. After giving the woman about fifty percent of his usual smile—still impressive, considering the curve ball she'd thrown straight at his head—he stared down at his order as if he'd never seen food before. That reaction worried her the most. Mason led with his heart, but his stomach was never far behind. Instead of fiddling, he would have eaten while Rome burned.

"I'm not just talking about that threatening note," she continued, once they were alone again. "My brother's in over his head with a real bad dude. I admit that I'm partially to blame. Lee promised me he'd drop the whole thing when you and I got married and, like a fool, I believed him." Had desperately wanted to believe him. "I got a visit from the FBI today."

He leaned over the table until their heads almost touched. "And?"

"They asked me a lot of questions about some black-market dealer who doesn't play nice. Liam's promised him your Gutenberg, and if he doesn't deliver…" She broke off as a shadow hit the table.

"Hi, kids." Without waiting for an invite, Jeep Hughes squeezed his muscle-bound self into the booth next to his brother. "We've got a problem."

****

Mason took one look at his brother and knew Jeep knew. *Everything.*

"Thanks for the heads-up." Mason didn't try to hide his sarcasm.

"Yeah, well, things are never what they seem when you're dealing with the O'Briens." Jeep sent Priss a look that had made grown men cry. She raised her chin a notch, but other than that she stood firm. Mason had to hand it to her. She had guts of steel. It was one of the things he loved about her.

Or used to love about her, before a truck named O'Brien had come out of nowhere and flattened him. Now, he wasn't sure about anything.

"Someone knows somebody who's a Grade A hacker." Jeep kept his eyes on Priss. "Your fictional backstory's the best I've ever seen. If you hadn't run off without a word, I wouldn't have bothered digging so deep. Even then, it's a good thing I know a guy."

Priss opened her mouth.

"We can go into that later." As much as Mason might enjoy watching it, now wasn't the time for this to turn into a pissing match between his wife and his brother. "What do you know, Admiral?"

Crossing his arms over his chest, Jeep sat back in the booth, his hooded gaze still aimed at Priss. "Apparently, Liam 'The Lion' O'Brien has made an enemy out of man named Bannion. He's promised him our Gutenberg and keeps failing to deliver. In fact, it seems O'Brien began this deal long before the Bible was on our radar. Ballsy guy, your brother, selling things that, one, aren't his, and two, may or may not even exist."

The plastic-covered booth squeaked as Priss fidgeted, but she didn't mount a defense.

Jeep switched his attention to Mason. "My guess is Bannion's given The Lion a finite amount of time to hand over the copy, or else. That would be in keeping with Bannion's usual MO. In the meantime, there's been a recent uptick in web research on a certain doctor we all know and love. That's what initially got my attention."

Mason knew better than to ask how or why Jeep kept track of that sort of thing. He brought his fist down on the table, making his plate of untouched pie jump. "This is bullshit. I've played it safe my whole life, save for three straight days in Vegas six months ago." The self-pity was unlike him, but today, he was entitled—at least to thirty seconds' worth.

You know you've had a shitty day when a talk with your wife overshadows being the victim of a drive-by. When they got out of this mess, he'd check into becoming a hermit. If they offered medical, he was all in.

Jeep pointed to Priss. "I can't be sure who knows you're Liam O'Brien's sister. Like I said, whoever it was who built your cover did a bang-up job. Too bad they're not working for the government." He leaned back and stretched an arm across the top of the booth, behind Mason. "You, Dr. Hughes, are the easiest target out of all of us. Anyone could reach you when you're at the hospital."

Mason huffed. "I shouldn't be a target, easy or otherwise. I didn't *knowingly* marry into the Mob."

Jeep shook his head. "Oh, no you don't. I don't have

a dog in that fight. I'm worried about everyone's safety. Granddad is literally surrounded by armed guards and, after the security issues last year, Mum and Dad are locked up tight, too. Adam and Callie are about to embark on a European honeymoon, and me—" Jeep raised a smug eyebrow. "Well, would you fuck with me?"

Mason wouldn't, but he wasn't about to give his brother the satisfaction of telling him so.

"Don't get me wrong, bro." Jeep gave Mason a once-over. "You're in wicked shape for a stringy dude, and I know for a fact you pack a mean punch, but the hospital's not Fort Knox."

"It wouldn't be much good if it were," Mason pointed out. "So what you're saying is, I've got a target on my ass." He shoved the plate of pie into the middle of the table.

Jeep nodded. "Yep, that about sums it up."

"Shit." Once again, Mason tried to process it all. Had he dropped into some kind of parallel universe where things were the same but different?

"Okay," he said, after a beat or two. "It sounds like a bad movie, but I trust you." He kept his eyes on his brother's. "What do we do to get out of this mess?" His heart stuttered as he realized he was still thinking of "we" instead of "me." *Damn it.* God help him, he couldn't just throw her to the wolves, even if she was related to some of them.

Jeep withdrew his arm from along the seat back and shrugged his linebacker's shoulders. "You're already headed to the cabin. I still think that's a good plan. It's hard to find, both geographically and on the web. I double-checked. Since it's been in the family since the

45

Dark Ages, the county deed's engraved on stone somewhere, so it would be difficult for an outsider to connect the address to us." His gaze flickered between Mason and Priss. "As a matter of fact, in the name of safety, I think you both should head up there as soon as possible."

"Together?" Priss glanced at Jeep, her eyes wide and serious. And scared.

Mason checked an auto-response to reach for her hand. He cocked his head toward the front of the restaurant. "What about today? Do you think this shooting was connected?"

Jeep took a long sip of Mason's untouched coffee and pulled the wedge of pie over as well. "This is DC, so it's anybody's guess," he said, around a bite. "But, yeah, I think we should assume it is, for now."

"How would anyone know we were here?" Priss asked. Head down, she appeared to be taking excessive interest in the ring of water at the base of her glass.

Jeep forked another bite, chewed, and swallowed. "Bannion, The Lion, whoever, or all of the above—they're monitoring your cells. You'll have to hand them over. I have burners in my truck, but they're only to be used sparingly. Basically, I want you two completely off the grid until we find out what's going on and know you're safe."

Priss paled, the drain of color highlighting the blue smudges bracketing her eyes. Over the past several months, Mason had studied her face countless times, the way an art student would study the masters. Even now, he could sit there, gazing. Was he an idiot, or a man in love?

Both, damn it all.

"All right." At long last, she raised her head, but kept her bruised eyes trained on Jeep. "I just need to run back to the apartment to—"

"Nope," Jeep interrupted, around another mouthful of pie. "No detours. We're only safe here while the police are still sniffing about."

"But I'll need clothes—"

"Nope," Jeep repeated. "You'll have to make do with what's at the cabin. We'll take my truck."

"What about Sal? I'm not leaving her here." Mason had rebuilt his classic Mustang from the bottom up, to relieve the stress of medical school, and he wasn't about to abandon "Sally" to this crap neighborhood.

"Already on it. I've got a buddy who'll drive her back to your place."

Mason fished in his pocket and handed over his car key. "Sounds like you've thought of everything as usual, Admiral, and I appreciate it. But if I find one scratch on her…"

Jeep yanked the keys from his grasp and rolled his eyes to the ceiling. "Yeah, yeah. It's a fucking full-time job looking after this family right now."

Mason studied his brother. Jeep was a lawyer with the Judge Advocate General's Corps, better known as JAG. Lately though, everything from his brother's mercenary-ish "buddies" to his easy access to top secret intel had Mason wondering what else was in his brother's job description. However, he didn't prod. Even when they were kids, Jeep could keep a secret. If he was hiding something, it would remain hidden. The one thing Mason did know was that whether Jeep was a boring, old attorney or something more bad-ass, there was no one Mason trusted more, in or out of a tight spot.

Priss scooted out of the booth. "Well, if we're taking a road trip, I'm making a pit stop first." Her long dress flared around her legs as she headed for the restaurant's back hallway.

Mason set his head in his hands. "God. I'm such an idiot. She's never talked about her family. Not once, in all this time. That should have been a red flag."

Jeep grunted. "You could've had six red flags waving at you in a gale force. No one would have gotten to 'mob boss's daughter.' "

"Thanks." Mason accepted his brother's brusque words with a nod, even though they made him feel only a fraction better. "What else do I need to know?"

"No contact, like I said. I assume you can cut ties with work for a week or two?"

Mason nodded. "In truth, they'll probably be glad to see the back of me. I'm not on the rota for a couple of days, as it is." He pulled out his phone. "I'll arrange to take a few extra."

"Good. The mountains just got dumped on—about fifteen inches of fresh snow on top of what they already had—so you'll have some nice protection from Mother Nature. I've got snowshoes for both of you. I doubt we can make it up the drive, even in my truck. Should be plenty of firewood and canned food." Jeep shrugged. "Hell, knowing Mum, she's made enough frozen meals to feed an army."

Mason finished up the text to his superior and gave his brother half a smile. While you wouldn't know it to look at her, their eccentric, busybody of a mother ran a global empire, complete with her own nationwide television show, specializing in all things Home, with a capital "H," including cooking.

"Basically, you guys just sit back, relax, and let others do the heavy lifting." Jeep finished the last bite of pie before shooting Mason a sideways look. "Should have plenty of time to talk up there."

Mason sighed. "If that's your attempt at marriage counseling, let me stop you right there." He looked across the table at Priss's empty spot. "Given today's events, I think it's safe to say we've reached the point of no return."

Chapter Four

"Wow. When you said this place was remote, you meant *remote*," Priss said, as they rounded the fifth switchback in so many miles.

As far as she could tell, she was talking to herself. Throughout the two-hour-long trip into the heart of the Appalachian Mountains, the men in the front seats had exchanged maybe ten words with each other, and zero with her. That was normal for Jeep; unusual for her husband. She was trying her best not to let Mason's mood get to her. Just because she'd abandoned him for all the right reasons didn't make it hurt any less—for either of them—and he deserved some time for grieving. God knew, she was.

It all stemmed from trying to have her cake and eat it too. If she had walked away from Mason all those months ago, none of this would have happened.

But then she'd have missed out on all those nights in his arms.

Since the truck's atmosphere was one notch up from a funeral, she used the time to plan. It appeared she would be holed up in the cabin with Mason for several days, if not longer, so she had to stay on her toes. Even at his worst, her husband was frickin' adorable, with his innate sense of humor, good manners, and ability to turn just about anything into breakfast food, including pickles.

Remember the O'Brien curse. Unlucky at love, cards, and pretty much everything else, except running a national syndicate. That was a good mantra, although it hadn't helped her any all those months ago, in Vegas.

Vegas. It seemed a lifetime ago. A lifetime of fun and love and the family she'd never had. Oh, and great sex. Life-altering sex.

And now, poof! She'd destroyed it all.

All because she'd owed her brother one. Despite what Mason thought, she wasn't a con woman. Not really. Once or twice, she'd helped Liam by chatting up his victims. "Fact finding" he'd called it. She'd inherited her father's ability to set people at ease, whereas Liam's technique was less finesse and more bull in a china shop. His forte was choosing whom and where, and he chose well. His marks were the real cons—people who made a living using others. People who, frankly, had it coming and wouldn't go to the police when they lost.

Then the whole Gutenberg fiasco had begun. That was Liam getting greedy, another O'Brien trait.

And yet she'd agreed to help with that initial contact. Two years ago, when her oldest friend from Boston got sideways with the O'Brien gang, Priss had gone to Liam for help. He'd delivered, and then, in typical mobster form, sat back and waited. When payback took the form of talking to a handsome stranger in a hotel bar for half an hour, Priss thought she'd hit the jackpot. Her brother had promised no one would get hurt, and after that, she'd stopped asking questions. The less she knew about Lee's affairs, the better.

However, that half hour with Mason had turned into an hour, then two, three, and eventually, the whole damn night. And what a night it had been! They'd talked for hours. She'd never connected to anyone on such a visceral level, and never would again. What they had, right from the beginning, was magic.

"That's the turn off, there." Mason pointed to the left.

Shoulder-high piles of snow flanked the steep, ice-rutted, single-lane road. Jeep shifted into low gear and the truck's powerful engine roared in protest as they climbed.

"It's beautiful!" Priss gazed out at the tall pines, their skinny, dark green tops stretching toward the blue sky. A born-and-bred city girl, she'd travelled through mountain scenery before but had never spent any time in high country. It was a lovely vacation spot.

Or it would be, without the looming threat of her brother, Bannion, the Mob, and heaven only knew who else.

They went up, up, up, a good couple miles before Jeep pulled to a stop before a faded, wooden sign that announced "Hughes." Both brothers hopped out and, after a moment's discussion, began wrestling with the old, carved plank. Sliding across the seat, Priss opened the door but remained in the relative warmth of the truck.

"Is that necessary? I mean, who's going to find us way up here?"

With a final heave, the sign came away in Mason's hands. He tossed it into the bed of the truck with a bang. "Better safe than sorry," he said, his breath visible in the freezing temperature.

Jeep grunted his agreement before circling around to the back of the vehicle. He rummaged around for a few moments, then returned, carrying a puffy jacket and two sets of snowshoes. He waved the smaller pair at her.

"Here you go." He set them down in the snow.

Priss looked down at her boots.

"Uh…"

"Shit." Mason's curse said it all.

"That's a problem I didn't foresee," Jeep admitted.

Knowing she couldn't put it off forever, Priss slid off the seat into the snow, ignoring the rush of cold and wet that sank over the tops of her impractical footwear. Jeep handed her the down-filled jacket before he tossed the smaller snowshoes back into his truck.

She donned the coat as fast as she could and zipped it to her chin, thankful for its warmth. "In my defense, I didn't realize I'd be playing Grizzly Adams when I dressed this morning."

"Understood." Jeep released a visible sigh. "Guess you'll have to carry her, Mace."

Mason looked about as happy as a polar bear in the desert. "It's a quarter mile or more to the cabin."

Jeep shrugged. "You could go it alone, then come back for her, with a pair of Mum's boots and snowshoes. Either way, I've gotta head home. I want to get out of these hills before sundown."

Priss eyed the heavy woods surrounding them, her head suddenly filled with images of lions and tigers and bears. *Oh my.*

"I can walk. I'm a Boston girl. And I'm wearing heavy socks." Because the boots were too big without them.

Jeep reached between the front seats and withdrew a large, military-style backpack, which he handed to Mason. "Here's your gear. Remember. No contact. Turn the cell on every day at eight and again at 2100 hours—nine p.m.—each time for five minutes only. If I have anything to say, I'll contact you during one of those windows."

Mason slung the pack over his shoulder before embracing his brother in a masculine hug, complete with lots of backslapping. "Thanks, bro. I owe you."

Stepping back, Jeep rolled his eyes. "Yeah, that list started when you were two."

Priss took a few, unsteady steps forward. It was going to be a long walk. "Yes, thank you, Jeep. I can't tell you how grateful I am."

To her surprise, her brother-in-law pulled her in for a hug as well. "Use the time wisely," he whispered.

The cryptic comment might mean anything, but Priss drew encouragement from the glint of affection in Jeep's dark blue eyes. "O-okay."

His gaze dropped to her feet one more time before he headed around to the driver's side of the truck. "If you have to, Mace, put her on the pack and drag it behind you, like a sled," he called, over the truck's hood. "It's waterproof, unlike those boots."

Priss's cheeks burned. That would happen *never*, even if it took her three years and two frostbitten toes to get to the cabin.

The snow crunched under the truck's tires as Jeep drove away. Mason finished securing his snowshoes, straightened, and gestured with a hand. "After you." There was a decided challenge in his eyes.

Setting her chin, she took a giant step forward. Mason passed her in one effortless stride and kept on going. In seconds, she was ten feet behind.

"Show off." One step. Two steps. The snow came up to her knees and every time she lurched forward, more of it worked its way inside her boots. She was glad she couldn't see how ridiculous she must look, taking such exaggerated strides. The indentations of Mason's snowshoes didn't ease her way at all.

"How far is the cabin again?" she shouted, hoping the question would make him pause.

"About ten minutes' walk," he yelled back, without stopping.

"In rain or shine?" she muttered. Reaching down, she wrapped the long, damp skirt of her dress around her waist and kept on slogging. This was a metaphor for her life. She would be going it alone from now on.

Man. Did it suck.

****

He categorically refused to feel sorry for her.

There wasn't one speck of this that wasn't her fault and, regardless of the chivalry his mum had ground into him, Mason wasn't caving.

Except…she was so damn pathetic, in those ridiculous boots and that oversized coat.

Pausing, he adjusted the strap on the backpack Jeep had given him, certain it was filled with bowling balls. Of course, knowing Jeep, there was no telling what kind of gear it held. Night-vision goggles, bulletproof vests, flash bombs—all this and more came standard in one of his brother's go-bags. Mason wasn't sure whether to be comforted or terrified by the thought that he was now prepared for World War III.

He started moving again, his legs burning as he utilized muscles that didn't get a daily workout. After years in med school, followed by his residency, he'd forgotten how much he enjoyed the outdoors. Fresh air, hard exercise, amazing views. There were worse things he could be doing.

Like walking through two feet of snow on ridiculously high heels.

Sighing, he looked down at his own sensible boots and the attached snowshoes. To be honest, it was just dumb luck that he wasn't wearing his usual, day-off, casual footwear of choice—*flip-flops*. However, he was beginning to realize he'd always had good luck.

Until now.

He was still digesting the new information Priss had spilled. Might still be digesting it when he was ninety. When they'd found the Gutenberg, in a tin box behind the old blacksmith's forge at his parents' farm, it had been difficult to believe they'd really found it. It was surreal, even when he'd held the fragile book in his own hands. But this…this shock was bigger. Ran deeper. All this time, he'd thought he knew the woman he'd fallen in love with.

Marry in haste, repent at leisure.

A loud "oomph" sounded some ways behind him, and he turned to find Priss some twenty feet behind, nose first in the snow. Sighing, he retraced his steps.

She looked up at him, her face damp, her cheeks and nose blotchy with cold. Pushing back the jacket's overlong sleeves, she wiped at her face with trembling pink fingers, causing more damage than good.

"Here." Kneeling, he brushed her off as best he could. Her long, dark eyelashes fluttered down against her soft, pale skin as he swiped his thumbs under her eyes. The wind lifted wisps of her hair, and the long, snow-dampened curls ensnared his hands. She had the softest, fairest skin. Reacting out of habit, he leaned down for a kiss. He came within inches before pulling back so fast his snowshoes became tangled and he landed, butt-first, in the snow himself.

No surprises there. From the start, she'd drawn him to her like iron filings to a magnet, and he'd become lost in her, until he didn't know where he ended and she began.

"How much farther?"

Mason shook himself out of the past as she hopped to her feet, breathing into her cupped hands.

He stood too, and squinted up the narrow drive. It had been years since he'd been up here, but his grandad had placed a lamp post at the twisty halfway point. It was dead ahead. "Maybe five more minutes."

She uttered a word that paid double into his mother's swear jar.

"I can give you a ride on the pack, like Jeep suggested." He hid a smile behind his hand, knowing what her answer would be. The woman was tough as nails and stubborn to boot.

I guess she'd have to be, in her family.

If only she'd told him the truth when they met. But was that fair? He knew what it was like to grow up in a famous family, even if his was famously good instead of…well, *bad*. He was proud of being a Hughes, but in the back of his mind, the sense that people he'd just met were judging him never went away. It must be the same or even worse for Priss.

Hell, she'd even gone so far as to change her name.

He re-adjusted the backpack. There was no point in dwelling on what hadn't happened. He had enough to worry about without adding might-have-beens to the list.

"What was that?"

"What was what?" he asked, plowing forward again. "I heard a noise. Are there grizzly bears around here?"

He swung back around to face her. Her eyes, fringed with those beautiful lashes, were wide open, and she stood as if rooted to the spot. So much for courage. The damn woman was crazy—more worried about a wild animal attack than she was about the Mob.

"Black bears. No grizzlies. You'd have to go west to see one of them."

"Nope." Her shouted response was swift. "I don't want to see *any* bears, outside of a zoo. Not black, polar, grizzly, or teddy."

Mason grinned. "I've been coming up here since before I can remember, and I've seen a bear exactly once." He omitted the fact that once had been enough. As kids, he and Adam had startled a sleeping bear cub. While it had stared up at them, all cute and cuddly, the mama bear had prepared for an apocalyptic attack. Only their father's and grandfather's timely arrival—shouting and waving a couple of big sticks—had saved them from becoming that bear's chew toys.

"Gotta watch out for the bobcats, though," he said, over his shoulder. It was a cheap shot, but he took it.

"*What?*"

He doubled over with laughter. God, it felt good.

He laughed till he cried, and even then it took all he had to rein it in. After sucking in a few gulps of the bracing air, he peeked around the lumpy backpack. She still stood frozen—and unamused—about fifteen feet back. The stubborn bits of snow that clung to her hair made her look like a bedraggled kitten.

He would not give in. He would not.

"Mason Hughes—you're a rat!"

"Got those up here, too," he said, giving her a wide

grin.

He'd just resumed his trek when a loud thud hit the backpack. *Oh, no, she didn't.* Lowering the bag to the ground, he checked its outer cover. Yep. She'd wasted him.

"Don't start something you can't finish," he warned.

Her only response was to bend down and scoop up more snow.

Two can play this game. Shedding the pack, he armed himself.

The next few minutes passed in a frenzy of flying snow. All his anxiety, anger, and pain dulled as he focused on their battle. He freed himself from the alternate universe he'd lived in the past six weeks. Smiles and shouts of joy told him she was experiencing the same.

"Damn, woman! You pack a mean snowball." He ducked behind a tree that didn't even begin to cover him while he wiped snow from his eyes.

Her laugh tinkled out from behind another, more sizable evergreen. "For a guy who spends most of his time in scrubs, you're not so bad yourself."

He heard some rustling, then a snowball nailed him right on the ass.

"Bullseye!"

The little sneak had flanked him and was now doing a victory dance, seemingly oblivious to her damp skirt, red hands, and ridiculous boots.

Mason sucked in a lungful of frigid air as a wave of truth hit his solar plexus. Even now, after all the lies and with God knew who was chasing them, this woman calmed him, captivated him, and—most important of all—made him laugh.

He wanted her.

He needed her.

Hell, he *loved* her.

But he couldn't trust her. Not anymore. Which meant, despite his brothers' goading, he was sticking to his original plan.

Once this whole mess was over, he'd let her go.

"Okay. That's it. I'm done." He settled the backpack between his shoulder blades and turned toward the cabin again. The bag's weight was nothing compared to the heaviness of his heart.

Chapter Five

The city girl in Priss was relieved to find the cabin was rustic—but not *too* rustic. It had the three things she considered absolute essentials: indoor plumbing, electricity, and hot water. Granted, the heat was primitive, since it was limited to the massive stone fireplace in the great room, but she didn't mind sleeping under a mound of blankets. Five of the ten words Mason had spoken to her since they'd arrived were, "You'll be cold by morning."

She stood by the front door, useless as a chocolate teapot, while he brought in an armload of wood from the cabin's covered front porch. In less than five minutes, he had stacked a mix of kindling and logs on the grate and was coaxing a fire to life.

Well, yippee. At least one of them appeared to know what the hell he was doing.

Bending, she attacked the soggy mess of leather and laces that had once been her designer boots. It took five tries and a lot of blowing on her fingers to get them unlaced. After saying a word or two over their dead bodies and peeling off her wet socks, she headed toward the open kitchen. It was smaller and more countryfied than her mother-in-law's home kitchen, but it exuded the same efficient serenity. Somehow, the eclectic mix of knotty pine cabinets and sleek white marble countertops worked well together.

She wandered back behind the kitchen to the small laundry room and pantry. A quick glance inside the large chest freezer assured her they wouldn't run out of food anytime this century. No doubt Minna could turn the assorted canned goods and frozen meats into feasts fit for kings, but Priss would be pleased with "edible." Mason knew how to cook but didn't enjoy it, and with all his hours at the hospital, his eating routine was sporadic and non-traditional. She didn't mind making their meals up here in the back of beyond, but they wouldn't be five-star.

She grabbed a can of baked beans, dug out a rock-hard package of frozen ground beef, and set them, along with another equally solid lump labeled "brioche buns," on the island. Hamburgers were both easy and comforting. A can of peas would round out the meal.

Relishing a small sense of accomplishment, she skirted the wide pine dining table and chairs and stepped into the great room. The high log beams and the antler chandelier were beautiful, but they couldn't hold a candle to the sight of her husband's backside as he fed more kindling to the fire. Damn! He was One. Fine. Thing. Biting back a pensive sigh, she turned in a slow circle, taking in the rest of the room. The vibe was reminiscent of an English hunting lodge—or how she imagined one to be—with thick wool blankets, plaid throw pillows, and old dog prints hanging along the walls. She was admiring one of a group of beagles when Mason came up from behind, smelling of the woods and the fire.

"The room with the double set of bunk beds is where Adam, Jeep, and I always sleep. I'm happy to take it if you want the primary bedroom."

The thought of him jamming his length into a bunk bed was laughable. "I appreciate that, but I'm shorter. The bunkroom is fine with me."

He shrugged. "Suit yourself."

"I see your mother's touch here. How often do they come up here?"

"Mum and Dad? Whenever they can. They love it. Reminds Mum of childhood holidays in Scotland. We all enjoy it, but it's harder for my brothers and me to get away now." He pointed toward one of the south-facing windows. "There's a stream, maybe a quarter of a mile that way. In the summer, we'd fish or kayak, hunt frogs, all kinds of stuff. This time of year, we'd go cross-country skiing, build snow forts, have endless snowball fights. You know the drill."

Priss laughed and looked down at her hands. "Actually, I have no idea. We rarely left Boston, and the last place my father would have wanted to visit was a mountain cabin. His idea of roughing it was staying in a four-star hotel." She threaded her fingers together before lifting her head and meeting his steady gaze. It was awkward, speaking honestly about her past, but it was freeing, too. No longer any traps to fall into.

Mason quirked an eyebrow. "Really? No summer camp or anything?"

She shook her head. "Safety was always a concern. Both Liam and I spent most of our free time at home, where we could be protected."

"Home? Sounds more like a prison."

"Yeah, well…" *That's why I escaped as soon as I could.* Sidestepping, in more ways than one, she moved to the built-in bookshelves flanking the fireplace. They indicated a long history of family activities. "Wow. This is quite a jigsaw puzzle collection. And…" Chuckling, she pulled a VCR tape from a lower shelf. "I haven't seen one of these in ages."

His laughter washed over her, warming her far better than the fire burning in the hearth.

"It took us years to convince Mum to get the VCR. She liked having a television-free zone and, while we didn't mind reading and playing games, the tape player was a big upgrade."

Priss peered at the titles and whistled. "This is an impressive collection of Scooby Doo!"

Stretching an arm out, Mason tipped out another tape. "Yep. We do love our Doo."

She gripped the edge of a shelf. It would be so easy to turn into his arms, to snuggle up against his broad chest the way she had countless times before. But she didn't dare ruin the moment.

"I took some food out for dinner, but it'll take a bit to thaw."

He nodded. "That's fine. Thanks." Crossing to the other bookshelf, he cast an eye down the shelves. He pulled out a box and waggled it. "Up for a game?"

"Monopoly?" Her cheeks burned. "I, uh…I've never played."

His eyes widened. "Never? As in, never ever?"

She licked her dry lips. "Yeah. It was just me and Liam, and he's years older than I am. By the time I was old enough to play, he was off at boarding school." Under an assumed name, of course. They'd learned early how to be other people.

"So, you've *never* played Monopoly. Huh, I'm pretty sure that's a crime." He nodded toward the big, rectangular table. "Wanna learn? I warn you, I usually win."

It was an unusual olive branch, but she grabbed it with both hands. "Okay. What do I need to know?"

He gave her a crash course in the iconic real estate game, and they played until it was well past dinner time.

"When does this game end?" she asked, as her stomach began to complain.

Grinning, Mason got to his feet. "I'm not sure it ever really does. Basically, you play until someone is in hock up to their eyeballs."

She glanced down at her wall of hotels. "That someone would be you."

"Beginner's luck," he retorted, as he walked into the kitchen. "Do you want me to make some hamburgers?"

"Sure." She took his willingness to help as a positive sign. The board game had filled the hours, but they still danced around each other, afraid to disturb the elephant in the room.

The extra-large elephant named "O'Brien."

Joining him in the kitchen, she rummaged around until she found a couple of saucepans and a can opener and set to work on the beans and peas. Altogether, it took her less than five minutes. With her work done, she ambled over to the reclaimed wood shelves over the stovetop and surveyed the attractive assortment of dishes, spices, and other kitchen items.

"Only your mother would keep a supply of anchovy paste in a cabin."

Mason came up beside her and plunked a cast iron skillet down on the stove. "True. But I must admit, her Caesar salad dressing isn't the same without it."

Priss ran a finger along the row of copper spice jars. "Do your parents ever entertain up here?"

"Nope. This is just for family. Unwritten rule. My great-great-grandfather built it with his own two hands, and each successive generation has left its own mark. My grandparents added the electricity, and my parents' contribution was the indoor bathroom. They want to add on a third bedroom, too, but haven't found the time yet. Dad has some romantic idea about building it himself, like his forefathers did." He rolled his eyes. "Truth is, he doesn't know one end of a hammer from the other, so…"

"Your mom will do it," Priss said, smiling. Adding a room onto a cabin wouldn't daunt her intrepid mother-in-law. "Remind me to thank them for the indoor plumbing the next time we see them."

Mason's eyes narrowed, and she read the words he didn't speak in their green depths.

There might not be a "next time" because there was no longer any "we."

Her stomach cramped. The sense of belonging and trust she'd experienced among Mason's family was a rare gift, one she'd miss—almost as much as she'd miss him.

As usual, the O'Brien curse was biting her right in the ass.

****

Mason didn't hold grudges. Maybe it was hard-wired. Maybe it was the result of a lot of good-natured torture over the years, doled out by his older brothers. Most likely, it was a bit of both. Whatever the case, he was big on forgiveness, slid into it without noticing acceptance overtaking him. It served him well in his profession, where things happened every day that didn't make a lick of sense.

Right now, he would sell his soul to be able to hang

on to bitterness. To simmer in his own juices, pushing Priss farther and farther away from his heart.

Instead, he'd wanted to kiss her eighteen times during their Monopoly game. He'd kept track. Nineteen, if he counted her confession that she'd never played before. Even now, when they were skipping around each other like opponents in a boxing ring, he found her funny, smart, spunky...sexy.

And a first-rate liar. She'd built their whole relationship on false pretenses. He couldn't forget that.

He flipped two medium-rare hamburgers onto two plates and handed one to Priss before adding spoonfuls of peas and baked beans to his and heading toward the table. The food smelled good, and he was ravenous.

Priss took her time joining him, putting pans in the sink, returning spices to their rack, getting a glass of water. He watched her while he ate, amused by her obvious stalling. It was nice to know he wasn't the only one confused as hell by this whole situation.

"Come and eat, before it gets cold." He kicked the opposite chair out from under the table.

She complied, looking for all the world as if she wanted to bolt. Deciding it was high time he ripped the bandage off, he met her eyes.

"So, the fifty-two different cities you lived in before we met... After you finished a con, I guess you'd have to leave town."

He heard her indrawn breath, spied the bruised look in her eyes, and wanted to pull back the words. How had they gotten here? But a moment later, any chance for apologizing was gone, as a defiant tinge displaced the vulnerability in her features. His wife wore invisible Kevlar. Probably always had.

"First of all, it wasn't fifty-two. It was…" Lifting a hand, she counted on her fingertips. "Eighteen. And, no, the *cons*—your word, not mine—had nothing to do with it. I moved around a lot because I enjoy seeing new places and trying new things, just like I told you."

His hamburger had gone from greasy goodness to sandpaper. "Okay. That's fair." *You should shut up now and let it go. Or not.* Now that she'd started telling the truth, he wanted to hear all of it. "Earlier today, you mentioned your brother asked you to chat with me in Vegas. Why me?"

Priss set down her fork with a sigh. "You're determined to talk about this? Right now?"

"Yeah." He nodded. "I'm trying to wrap my head around it. Trying to understand why you…" He swerved away from the word *conned* with a small cough. "Did what you did."

She pulled a bit of bun off her hamburger and popped it into her mouth. "At the risk of sounding cliché, it's complicated," she said, after she'd finished the bite. "My brother is, at heart, a decent man—not a helpful trait for a mobster. For the most part, he's distanced himself from the more…unsavory side of the business and concentrated on the legit side."

Mason leaned back and folded his arms across his chest. His knowledge of mobsters was limited to the trio of Godfather movies, and there wasn't a whole lot of business in those he would term legitimate. "By that, you mean he's never whacked anyone?"

She let out a startled laugh. "Of course not! One, I just told you, he's a good person. And two, he's Seamus O'Brien's son." Her voice ran out of gas at the end, as if she brought her father into the discussion with reluctance.

"Meaning?"

She plucked another divot from her bun but didn't eat this bite. Instead, she placed it beside her burger. "In the Family—with a capital 'F'—there's a hierarchy, with the Skipper at the top. My dad was the third generation; my brother's the fourth."

Mason gave her an expectant look.

"In other words, he's too high up to be an enforcer."

"Oh." Comprehension dawned. "So others do his dirty work." When she started to protest, he held up a hand. "Never mind. If you come from such a long line of skippers, why wasn't your brother made Top Dog after your father died?"

Her wince told him he'd hit a sore spot.

"That's kind of a long story."

Did she have any other kind? Standing, he picked up his plate and walked over to the kitchen island. A glance outside the kitchen window told him it was snowing. It was almost dark, but the cabin's back porch light illuminated the falling flakes. "As it happens, I've got nothing but time," he said, more to himself than to her. On autopilot, he began to help himself to more beans, only to realize he still had plenty on his plate. Frowning, he returned to his seat.

Priss glanced around at the shadowy room, as if hoping someone would hop out of the woodwork and save her from telling her story. Fat chance. They were as alone as it got.

"My father was…tough." She wrinkled her nose, causing freckles to dance.

"Wasn't that part of his job description?"

She raised her eyebrows "Yeah, sure. *Duh.* He was

a mob boss. But in this instance, I'm not referring to the job. In Dad's eyes, Lee was never hard enough, ruthless enough, *man* enough." Sighing, she waved a hand. "I was a girl, and young to boot, so I didn't count, but Lee? Dad put an insane amount of pressure on him as his heir apparent. Still, Lee didn't give in, didn't let my father dictate his life."

She rubbed at a knot in the barnwood tabletop, a faint smile hovering on her full lips. "That's the irony of it. My father couldn't see that my brother *was* ruthless—*is* ruthless—in his determination to stay out of the more unsavory side of the business. Like I said, up until now, all his cons were payback, justice. Lee will only get his hands so dirty."

"Your dad didn't trust him." Finishing his last forkful, Mason pushed his plate aside.

"No, it wasn't that." Her smile was sad. "Both Lee and I proved ourselves in that department."

Mason was afraid to ask what that meant. Had *she* whacked somebody? He pushed aside the absurd thought. He might not know much about his wife, but he knew she wouldn't harm anyone on purpose. Hell, she didn't even kill spiders. Just trapped them and set them free outdoors.

"Dad felt Lee needed more time to grow into the skipper's role. He intended to pass the reins to Lee eventually, though."

"And yet your uncle runs the empire now."

"Yes." Her mouth twisted as she set her plate aside, too, although it was far from empty. Propping her elbows on the table, she set her chin on her fists. "I'm sure you know how my father died. It was all over the news."

Mason nodded. It had been a brutal way to go. He'd

been shot a ridiculous number of times, in the back, by the FBI, during a raid that had gone sideways. It had triggered some kind of internal federal investigation that, as far as he'd heard, had gone nowhere.

She leaned forward, as if about to impart a secret. "My brother and I aren't sure, but we suspect my uncle may have informed on Dad—told them where they could find him."

It was Mason's turn to raise his eyebrows. "That's a hell of a betrayal."

Priss rose and carried their plates to the kitchen sink, moving with the same fluid grace she always displayed—except when she was walking on high heels through two feet of snow.

"Yep. And it didn't stop there. After Dad's death, my uncle capitalized on the shock and repeated the doubts my father had voiced about Lee. He sowed so much confusion he was able to take over the reins within a week."

She faced him fully, hands on her hips. "Uncle Sean converted the faithful by promising to pass the reins to my brother when Lee turns forty, but that's a lie. It's obvious he's grooming his son, my cousin Patrick, for the job."

"And that leaves your brother where, exactly?" A man who ratted out his own brother wasn't likely to suffer any guilt over doing something similar to his nephew.

"Vulnerable, to say the least. Lee and I both agree that the chances of his reaching his fortieth birthday— he's thirty-six now—are slim to none. Which is where the Gutenberg comes in."

Mason scrubbed his face with his hands. *Damn it.*

Things always circled back to that book. Who knew something that old could cause so much trouble in today's world?

"Okay." He jackknifed around and propped his socked feet up on an empty chair. "Please. Go ahead. Explain how a Boston mobster gets tied into the Bible."

This ought to be good.

Chapter Six

Priss crossed to the nearby window, fingering the curtains apart by a few inches. Inky darkness now hid the miles of snow, rock, and evergreens. The sheer expanse of it was difficult for her to fathom, despite their trip through it earlier in the day. The isolation she understood. Her childhood, while privileged, had been a lonely one, stuck in a big house in the middle of a bigger city. But there had been constant action. Out here, the unaccustomed stillness made her edgy.

Or was it the company?

Her gaze flickered to the sky. The earlier snow had stopped, and the sky had cleared. The gasp that slipped from her lips didn't do the view justice. "The stars!"

Mason's chuckle came from close behind. "Yeah, you won't see a sky like that in Boston."

She shook her head. Nor in any of the other cities she'd lived in. "Not even close."

Hairs on the back of her neck tingled as he reached around her, revealing the long expanse of glass with one smooth pull on the curtain cord. The cabin had grown dark while they ate, and the orange glow from the fireplace was the only light within.

Mason traced the glass lightly with a finger.

"Big Dipper. Small Dipper. Orion. That's all I know." There was a smile in his voice. "Jeep and Adam can point out all of them, but constellations were never my thing."

"You were too busy reading," she guessed. All the Hughes brothers were readers, but according to Minna, Mason had devoured books faster than a chain-smoker smoked cigarettes.

"Yeah." The word was filled with his smile. "Too busy building worlds inside my head to notice what was going on in this one."

She took a deep breath, drawing comfort from their relaxed conversation. Snowball fights, Monopoly, stars, books…as long as they weren't talking about the O'Briens, she could pretend things were halfway normal. Mason was the softie of the family. Whenever something was bothering him, he tried to act icy cold, the way his brothers did on occasion, but it never stuck. He was wired to heal, not to hold grudges.

"And yet Adam's the writer of the family," she pointed out, prolonging the benign topic.

Mason glanced down at her, the firelight capturing the sparks of defiant humor in his eyes. "Give me time. I've been a little busy lately, but someday my Meanothos series will get written."

"Meanothos?"

He shrugged, while his killer grin worked its way across his lips. "It's a sci-fi world I made up as a kid. I've got journals full of stories about it. Someday, I'll do something with them. Young adult fiction, I think."

Huh. Priss stared up at him for a moment, digesting this new information. Wouldn't it be ironic if they finally revealed the hidden pieces of themselves right before they separated forever?

"That's great," she said, and meant it. "You'd be writing the same kind of books you loved as a kid."

He nodded, turning back to the night sky again. "That's the idea. Like I said, I'm a little too busy at the hospital right now, but I should have more of a routine in the future, as I gain seniority. Then, in my spare time, I'll write."

His tone was typical. Light and brimming with the confidence that was hard-wired into all the members of his family. It wasn't arrogance, just assurance that good ideas and hard work would pay off.

She envied it, his conviction that he would get things done and make change happen. Personally, she'd never stuck around in one place long enough to try making a difference. Until she'd met him. He'd been her first attempt at something real, something permanent.

And now they were a dumpster fire. Looking down at her stockinged feet, she smothered a sigh. Perhaps it was for the best. She'd let her heart overrule her head. They weren't meant to be together, never had been.

Shivering, she rubbed her hands along her upper arms and crossed to the fireplace, sitting down on the raised stone hearth. Mason followed, picked up some logs, and in seconds had the fire blazing once more. After brushing off his hands, he sank down on the dark brown leather couch, one long arm stretched across its back.

Prime snuggling position.

As if reading her mind, he dropped his arm, and his expression hardened. "You were going to tell me how the Gutenberg figures into things."

For the ninetieth time in the past six weeks, a familiar tugging began low in her belly. Just as The Force was strong in Luke Skywalker, the urge to run when things got tough was overwhelming in an O'Brien female. Her grandmother, her mother, her aunt—they'd all run, finding it impossible to be married to the Mob. Priss wasn't married to the Mob, but Mason was finding out *he* was, and the end result was the same: If she could have hopped a plane for anywhere but here, she'd already be at the nearest airport.

She straightened her spine and cast her butterflies to hell. When she'd met Mason all those crazy nights ago, she'd sent down roots. Despite her recent attempts to untether them, those roots were strong. And so was she. She'd persevere.

Plus, if she ran now, she'd wind up ass-deep in snow.

"About a year ago, Lee read the interview Adam gave to that magazine. You know, the one that started the whole Gutenberg hunt?"

His curt nod didn't convey much encouragement. *Fine.*

"Well, like I said in the diner, he's been looking for something big, something that will give him enough money to leave the family once and for all. As in, *poof!*" She snapped her fingers. "He's out of Uncle Sean's reach. Disappears without a trace. He has everything ready—papers, photo IDs, fake social—*everything* except the cash. When he read the article and found out how many millions a Gutenberg could bring on the black market, he couldn't pass up the chance."

Mason folded his arms across his wide chest and frowned. "If this is supposed to make me feel sorry for your brother, it isn't working."

Heat that had nothing to do with the flames at her back attacked her face. "I'm not asking for sympathy. My brother is a good businessman and a technical genius, but he has no common sense. In his…enthusiasm, Lee started sniffing around private collectors and running his mouth, talking about how maybe he could get his hands on the Bible. I don't know all the details, but apparently someone became very interested—obsessed, in fact."

"The Bannion guy?"

She shrugged. "I guess so. Lee never mentioned any names. Whoever it is, he's crazed—and he's only gotten worse since the book has been found. He's been threatening Lee." Which, in turn, had Lee breathing down her neck. She refused to believe that her brother would threaten her—and Mason—the way he had, if he didn't fear for his very life.

Mason's frown deepened. "What about the attacks on Callie and Mum, and the deaths of that security guy and Callie's kidnapper? Is your brother behind that? It sounds like the Mob."

"Lee swears he had nothing to do with any of that." *And I'm ninety-nine percent sure he's telling the truth.* Priss propped her feet on the hearth and hugged her knees to her chest. "He doesn't think it was Uncle Sean either, although I'm reserving my judgment, for now. Lee's strategy, from the get-go, was to get your family to start and keep the Gutenberg search going. He's always maintained that if anyone found the Bible, it would be a Hughes. Turns out he was right."

She watched Mason's handsome face as he connected dots. Again, the front door beckoned. Maybe it would be better to run. Sitting here, wishing they could get past it without accusations and blame, was agony.

"Forgive me, but I'm having a really difficult time believing you weren't some kind of inside informant."

Wow. That one hurt, and it looked like he knew it. "I

wasn't," she snapped, then took a breath. "Well, sort of."

His eyes shot daggers. "Sort of? What the hell does that mean?"

She raised her chin a notch. "I told you. I agreed to make your acquaintance in Vegas, have a half hour's chat with you, that's all. Just to see if you dropped any hints about the Bible. Lee wanted to find out whether or not you and your brothers were searching for it at that time. You weren't. I told him so and didn't talk to him again until after...after we were married." Her face flamed again, as memories of those heady early days and nights came flooding back.

Heat flickered in his eyes, telling her that he, too, remembered the instant connection of their first meeting, on both physical and emotional levels. Then his features altered again and hurt took over. Her heart ached.

Damn it. The O'Briens destroyed everything good and decent in this world. Maybe she should take the FBI up on their offer. She'd been away from the family for a long time, but she'd overheard at least a few conversations they might find interesting. Besides, working against her uncle would be cathartic.

Mason pinched the bridge of his nose with his thumb and middle finger. "I remember, you told me you'd read the article. We all considered it a family fairytale. I never dreamed..." Dropping his hand, he shook his head. "I walked right into it, didn't I? It must have given you and your brother some good laughs."

She swallowed hard and unfolded, propping her elbows on her knees. The move brought her closer to him, almost within arm's length. "I admit it. I pumped you for information that first night. But I *swear*, since then I haven't told Liam what you eat for breakfast, let alone anything about the Gutenberg. After that first night, I made it clear I was out."

He stared at her for a long moment, the firelight reflected in his eyes. "Maybe I believe that, and maybe I don't." His measured cadence revealed he was weighing every word. "Fact is, it doesn't really matter now. There are two things I can't get past. First, you said nothing to me about any of this and, second, you didn't do anything to try and stop your brother."

She opened her mouth, but no words came. There was no comeback to that. He was a hundred and ten percent right.

****

He had to move.

Pacing between the couch and the dining room table gave little satisfaction. He needed to stretch, to breathe, and just possibly, to punch something. Yanking open the closet door, Mason began piling on the layers.

"You know, you swept me away in Vegas. Blew. My. Mind." He climbed into a pair of his father's old ski bibs before shoving on his own boots. In his current frame of mind, letting words tumble out was dangerous. He'd probably say something he'd regret, but what the hell did he have to lose? Priss? Their togetherness was temporary. She was already gone.

"Now, I find out it was all about the frickin' Gutenberg."

She flinched, so he knew she'd heard him, but other than that, nothing. She did that sometimes, walled herself up. To be fair, he did, too. Always before, he'd assumed that, like him, it was her way of handling tough emotions. Now, he wasn't so sure. Maybe she didn't feel anything anymore.

Maybe she never had.

His heartbeat thundered in his ears. She'd placed the blame for the Gutenberg scheme on her brother, but what if she'd masterminded the whole thing?

He shook his head. What they'd had... It had been a lot of things, but fake wasn't one of them.

Or was it?

Dear God, he'd drive himself insane thinking so damn much. He needed to get the hell out of his head.

She rubbed her upper arms and her diamond-studded wedding band winked in the firelight. Mason thumbed his own ring for a second, before pulling on an ancient parka. Funny they both still wore them, meaningless symbols that they were.

"Look, I know I should have told you." Her expression was open, uncertain, vulnerable even.

He jammed a knitted hat on his head.

"Think about it!" Her voice rose. "I didn't want to lose you *or* put my brother in danger." She jammed a finger into her chest. "For the first time in my life, *I belonged.* I was afraid to rock the boat. As long as the Gutenberg remained a family legend, I could pretend. But once you and your brothers found the damn thing, it got crazy. Lee threatened you, and I panicked and did what I've always done before. I left."

She turned away, and he stood there, staring at her back, for a good long minute. The emotional roller coaster he was riding plummeted again as he reached out and squeezed her shoulder. She reached for him, covered his hand with hers, and he experienced the familiar sizzle of connection. *Shit.* He wanted to believe her. Wanted to believe in *them* again.

But he was too afraid.

The clock on the mantel gave him a perfect out. He withdrew, fisting his hands. "It's almost nine. I need to turn on the cell, see if there's any word from Jeep."

He shouldered the backpack his brother had given him and left the cabin.

The half-moon's light bounced off the snow, illuminating the darkness. Like a man possessed, he plowed through it, reaching the edge of the dense, surrounding woods in record time. He paused beside the dwarfing trees and dug out the cell phone. Turning it on, he was relieved to discover he had bars so far from the house.

He nearly jumped out of his skin when the device rang. Jeep was nothing if not punctual.

"Yeah. What's up?"

"Nothing good." The grimness in Jeep's voice carried across the miles. "I've been in touch with some buddies of mine."

Mason managed half a grin. His brother's legion of "buddies" was legendary. No matter what the situation, or how bizarre, Jeep knew someone who could help.

"And?"

"Rumor has it that Lion O'Brien is on thin ice with his Uncle Sean, a man you do not want to piss off."

Mason flexed his free hand, before shoving it back into his warm side pocket. "That fits with what Priss has told me."

"Yeah, well, that means he's a loose cannon, liable to do anything. Our game plan is to not do anything stupid, okay?"

"Unless you count teaching Priss how to play Monopoly as stupid, all is well here." He avoided any hint of his chaotic emotions. "Are Mum and Dad okay?

And Granddad?"

"Everyone's fine; we've upped security." As always, Jeep's clipped, confident answers brought comfort.

"Any word from the honeymooners?"

"Nope. But I don't expect any. They're en route to Europe as we speak, ready to see the sights, to hear them tell it. I have no doubt you're the main target right now—the weakest link."

Mason heard the smile in his brother's voice. "You've been waiting to say that all day."

Jeep chuckled. "Guilty as charged."

Mason smiled too. "Yeah, well… Knowing Adam and Callie, they won't leave their room for the next two weeks. Sightseeing in Europe, my ass."

"Right." The line hummed. "Look, I'll be honest with you. No one really knows who's on the O'Brien payroll these days. This might take a few days to unravel."

Mason kicked at some snow. "I was afraid you were going to say that."

There was a long pause. "Has it been rough?" It was as intimate a question as Jeep ever asked.

"Yeah. I want to strangle her one minute and kiss her the next." Mason sent another batch of snow flying.

Jeep sighed. "I'm sorry, man. If it helps, I think Priss really loves you."

"That doesn't help." Kick. Kick. "Not even a little." Well…maybe a bit.

"Right. I'll be in touch. In the meantime, watch your six."

Mason turned off the phone and slid it into the backpack before circling back toward the house. He wasn't ready to finish his walk, but heading into the woods at this hour was a great way to wind up lost. Or as bear bait.

He might be stupid, but he wasn't *that* stupid.

Chapter Seven

"Coffee?" Mason's question ricocheted off the cabin walls, shattering the still, cold morning air. His warning about the temperature had been right on the money. Despite several layers of blankets, Priss had awakened colder than a polar bear's toenail.

"Yes. A thousand times, yes." Shivering, despite the two oversized sweatshirts she wore, she padded across the wide-planked hardwood floor on sock-covered feet and grabbed the mug he offered like a lifeline. She wasn't surprised to find him already up, coffee made, fire roaring in the fireplace. Even more annoying, he looked flawless, dressed in jeans and a fishermen's rib sweater that had been tailor-made for his broad shoulders.

Priss sighed. Like the rest of his family, Mason was born for mornings. Herself? Not so much. She breathed in the coffee's rich aroma before taking a tentative sip, then glanced over at the battered tin percolator in appreciation. "Wow. This is good."

Mason laughed into one of the upper cabinets. "You sound surprised," he said, around the open cabinet door.

Relieved by his laugh, she ventured fully into the kitchen and tapped the glass knob on top of the coffeepot. "I am. This thing looks older than I am."

Still chuckling, he withdrew a box. "It probably is. Pancakes?"

"Ooh. Yes, please." She hadn't eaten much during

their charged dinner the night before, and her stomach was protesting. "Need any help?"

"Nope." He cracked an egg, one-handed, into a mixing bowl. "I didn't expect you up so early. Wander on over to the fire and warm up."

She did just that, wrapping her outer layer, a large, zippered hoodie, around herself as she crossed the room. It hit her mid-thigh and smelled like Mason did after a shower. Turning to warm her backside, she eyed her husband as he worked.

She'd always enjoyed the sight of Mason and his brothers in a kitchen. Whether they enjoyed it or not, all three were uber competent and confident cooks. Today, however, the scene struck her with extra "oomph."

Was there anything sexier than a big man making pancakes?

Spinning, she faced the flames. *Stop it. That way lies madness.* "I'll do the dishes."

"Deal."

His upbeat tone threw her off-kilter. It could have been any morning before their breakup. For a long moment, she stared at the flames, watching as they threaded their way up through the lattice of stacked logs. The fire was beautiful, but she could think of a better way to stay warm. *If only...*

If only what? It was time she came to terms with the fact that she couldn't change who she was. She'd tried for years, and now the sins of the fathers had come home to roost.

Sighing at her mixed metaphors, she sat down on the raised hearth. "Where'd you go last night? I got a little worried. You were gone a long time."

Mason paused his whisking. "No need. I know

where not to go up here, especially at night, in the middle of winter. I stuck to the perimeter of the woods." He began stirring again. "Spoke to Jeep last night. He's trying to get a handle on what's going on. Sounds like we might be stuck here for the better part of a week, if not longer."

She couldn't tell whether this bothered him or not. As a doctor, he'd perfected the art of relaying news in a non-threatening manner. In truth, she wasn't sure how she felt either. On the one hand, staying at the cabin meant more time with Mason. On the other hand…it meant more time with Mason. Leaving him the first time had almost killed her. Spending time together in this secluded hideaway wouldn't make her second exit any easier.

Once or twice, during her frigid, fitful night's sleep, she'd convinced herself that, after the bad guys were caught—and she was realistic enough to know that included Liam, among others—there might be a teensy-weensy chance she and Mason would find a way through. Then, the dream popped like a balloon. His father was the Chief Justice of SCOTUS. Hers had been Skipper of Clan O'Brien. The adage about opposites attracting could only stretch so far.

Restless, she left the fire's heat and wandered over to the windows, her half-finished coffee still cradled in one hand. The sun on the newly fallen snow made her blink. Everything was sparkling and bright and beautiful.

"You look like you want to run away. Again."

There was no heat in his words, so her hackles remained retracted. He was so good at reading her. "The O'Brien women are good at running," she admitted, tracing the window lock with a finger. "My grandmother left long before I was born. Then, when I was about four, my mother left, only to die a year later of cancer. Soon after that, my aunt took off." Looking down, she picked a piece of lint off the front of her sweatshirt and watched it drift to the floor. "She went to Florida, I think. I remember my father and uncle whispering about it. That left me surrounded by men." Turning, she gave him a wry smile. "I didn't really mind. It meant I was pretty much left alone to do what I liked."

"That's why you're such a free spirit." He walked over to the stovetop and switched on a burner. Then, without any wasted motion, he oiled the pan and set it on the heat.

She took a long sip of her coffee and shuffled over to the breakfast bar. "Yeah, maybe. Lee was there when I was younger, but once he left for college, there was no one to tell me what I could and couldn't do, that kind of thing. At my request, Lee—I told you he's a computer genius—created a rock-solid new identity for me before I was out of high school. I graduated early and left home soon after. You know the rest. I flitted from one thing to another, going wherever life took me."

"Did it ever get old? The constant moving around, meeting new people, learning new things?"

Priss shook her head. "No. I loved it. I might not have stayed in any one place very long, but I gave a hundred percent while I was there." She'd given him her all, too, before everything had come crashing down.

Mason tested the pan like a pro, flicking a few sprinkles of water into the pan before pouring out a few pancakes.

Yum.

"I called Dave at Traxx when you left. He said you'd

just called and quit, without notice." He hunched over the pancakes, as if he suspected they might take flight.

Or because it gave him an excuse not to look in her direction.

Draining the last of her coffee, she entered the kitchen for a refill. "I thought it best, until I figured out exactly what Liam had gotten himself into." She'd been managing the record store since moving to DC, after they'd married, but she wasn't a vital employee. "I think he was relieved. His cousin had been bugging him for a job, but he didn't want to push me out." She poured another steaming cup and spooned in some powdered creamer from a glass jar on the counter.

"I thought you really liked it there."

"I did." She stirred until her coffee was more khaki than brown. "I've loved all my jobs. But that doesn't mean I won't find another place I like just as much."

Although his back was to her, his movements told her he was flipping their pancakes, the batter sizzling as it hit the hot pan. The aroma made her mouth water.

"It's funny," he said.

"What is?"

His shoulders lifted, stretching the worn fabric of his sweatshirt as he pulled in a deep breath. "I've always known you had an unorthodox childhood. I just didn't know how unorthodox until now. I don't agree with what you did or how you did it—in fact, it cuts me to the quick." He half-turned, meeting her eyes. "But, as much as it pains me to admit it, I understand the *why*."

Priss stared at him for a long moment. Damn it. This man was the direct opposite of every man who'd come before. Decent and honest to the core. He might hate her. At the very least, he was trying to, but it didn't overrule his sympathy and compassion. They were his touchstones, making him a great doctor and an even better human being.

She crossed to his side, tilting her head back so she could see his face. His expression was, if not friendly, at least not openly hostile. Good. It would be a bonus if they parted as friends, the way they'd agreed to all those months ago in Vegas. Not that they'd expected it to fall apart.

"It sounds like we're going to be up here for a while. How is this..." she waggled a finger between them, "going to work? One minute we're playing a board game, the next minute we're at odds. It's a rollercoaster ride and I, for one, want to get off."

Instead of answering, he slid their pancakes onto plates and stepped around her, carrying their breakfast to the table, where he'd set two places. Unlike her family, who'd only shared a dinner table at holidays—if then— his family always shared meals together. Even, it appeared, when hiding out in a cabin far removed from the rest of civilization.

He took the same spot he'd sat at the night before and spread a napkin on his lap. "I don't have an answer for you," he said, at long last, meeting her eyes. "I'm kind of emotionally all over the place right now. I think we just have to take it as it comes. How about this— When I'm not feeling very social, I'll stick to my room or take a walk, okay?"

She slid into her seat as disappointment settled in her stomach like a lead weight. She wasn't sure what she'd been hoping he'd say. *All is forgiven; let's go to bed?* Yeah, right. The thought that he might spend most of their time here holed up in his bedroom was depressing as hell but, like he'd said, she'd have to wait and see.

"Fair enough." Although her appetite had once again fled, she slathered her pancakes with butter and a heavy pour of maple syrup before taking a large bite. A person had to eat. "I promise to do the same," she added, after swallowing. "If I feel out of sorts, I'll head for my room." It was a big concession for her, since she'd gotten in the habit of sharing every thought she had with him—well, *most* thoughts, anyway. She'd grown so used to hiding the truth about her family, keeping those thoughts private hadn't seemed like an omission.

The fire popped and hissed while they ate, Mason with his usual gusto, Priss with a little less enthusiasm. The pancakes were perfect—golden brown on the outside, pale and fluffy on the inside, but the tenseness between them robbed each bite of its flavor.

"Last night, you said your brother threatened you. How, exactly?"

Priss washed down a mouthful of pancake with coffee as she forced herself to remember the difficult phone calls with her brother. "It wasn't anything super specific. For the most part, he just…insinuated things—you know, as scare tactics. I don't think, if it came down to it, that he would hurt me or anyone else."

She could see the unasked question in his eyes. *So, why'd you leave?* Running was so hardwired in her, it had never occurred to her to stick around and see whether her brother was bluffing or not. She'd wanted Mason safe, and leaving seemed like the best way to guarantee that.

Coward.

"Do you think he's responsible for the shooting yesterday? I mean, the gunman aimed high—sounds like a scare tactic to me."

"I don't know. I'm conflicted. I don't want it to be Lee. More than that, it doesn't *feel* like him. He doesn't like violence—never has. But, no, I can't say for sure it wasn't him."

He smiled his sympathetic smile, which, in that moment, warmed her as much as a joyous high five would have. He had two brothers of his own and, without a doubt, he understood how difficult that admission had been.

"I have to ask. His threats—are they the only reason you left?"

Priss stared down at her half-eaten breakfast, weighing her answer out word by word. This was the new and improved version of herself, and she'd be honest, even if it killed her. "I wrote a lot of things in that letter. All of them were untrue. These past months have been the best of my life. You and me…" She swallowed, and the simple reflex thundered in her ears. "I've never felt that way before. The connection, the acceptance…it was amazing. But it was built on shifting ground—my fault, I admit. Lee's threats were a good excuse. I ran because I was afraid…afraid that what we have had won't survive my reality." Tears threatened and she blinked them back. "The truth is, I don't see a scenario where we stay together, given who we are…who our families are."

He picked up his empty plate and stood, looming over her in silence. At long last, he shook his head. "Given all the time that's passed, I… Marriage is about trust, Priss. I fell in love with you, not your family. I wish you'd told me the truth right from the start. I'd like to think that maybe, given what we had, we'd have found a way. Now, I guess maybe you're right. We can't really get out ahead of it anymore."

After setting his plate on the kitchen counter, he headed to his bedroom.

Priss continued to stare down at her plate. Teardrops fell onto her pancakes.

That went well.

****

The alarm on Mason's watch bleeped, reminding him it was time to turn on the burner phone. He reached over the side of the bed and dug it out of the backpack. Talking to anyone, even his brother, was the last thing he wanted to do right now, but he couldn't skip the call. The phone vibrated right on time.

"Yeah."

"I didn't want to do this, but she insisted," Jeep said.

Mason rolled his eyes. He knew what that meant.

Sure enough, his mother's voice came through, loud and clear and properly British. "Mason, darling. Do tell me you're okay?"

He couldn't hold back a grin. There was something about his mother that added color to the blackest of days. "I'm fine, Mum." *All fucked up, but otherwise fine.*

"And Priscilla? Poor girl."

"She's fine, too," he said, with less enthusiasm.

"Oh, my dear. Remember what your father always says: The road to love is paved with good intentions."

"I thought that was the road to hell."

"Oh, it's one and the same in a relationship. Two sides of the same coin."

Sighing, Mason raked a hand through his hair. He needed a haircut. And a shower, he amended, catching a whiff of himself. What he didn't need was his mother's usual obtuse logic. "Okay, Mum. Whatever you say."

"Everything works out in the end, my love. Always."

Again, he grinned. "We're going to have that engraved on your tombstone."

Three hundred plus miles away, his mother laughed. "That would be rather fitting, don't you think? Do you have plenty of food? There's a rib roast in the freezer. Makes marvelous leftovers, that."

"Thanks. I'll keep that in mind." Only his mother would be thinking of leftovers right now.

"Do be careful. And let us know if you need anything. John can be up there in two hours, the way he drives." His mother always referred to her eldest son by his given name.

A few smothered sounds came from her end.

"My turn," Jeep said.

"I love you both," was shouted somewhere in the background.

Mason shook his head. "I love her, too."

"Yeah. She knows."

Mason heard a door closing before the telltale static of wind hit the microphone on his brother's end. Jeep had stepped outside.

"Someone broke into your house last night. Trashed it," Jeep said.

Mason punched the bedclothes. "Why? The Gutenberg is at the university."

"Someone's sending a message. They want you to know they're looking for you and they mean business."

For the fifth time in as many minutes, Mason's mind hopped to Liam O'Brien. Was the mobster behind this, too?

"Anything taken?" he asked.

"Doesn't look like it. But it's more important than ever that we be careful. I'll make a trip up later today with some clothes, a couple of new phones, and some other gear. After that, you're on your own."

"All right." He didn't remind his brother to be careful. Jeep always was.

"I'll be there by fifteen hundred hours." Jeep clicked off.

Mason turned off the phone and continued to lie there, torn between staying in bed or getting up and doing something constructive. After a long minute, he rolled to his feet, albeit moving at a snail's pace. Wallowing wouldn't get him anywhere, and there was at least one bad guy after them. Before he so much as showered, he needed to get the lay of the land. He'd been up here a thousand times but had never considered it a fortress before. If any reinforcements were necessary, he'd rather make them right away. When he was halfway through cramming on a second pair of socks, Priss knocked on the door.

A small chunk of his heart decayed into dust. Now, they were knocking on separate bedroom doors. He sighed all the way to his toes. How far the totally-nuts-for-each-other had fallen. "Yeah, come in."

"Any news?"

He tried not to notice her red-rimmed eyes, concentrated on lacing up his old snow boots instead. "Yes. More from Mum than from Jeep, though."

She gave a watery giggle. "Sounds about right." Fondness for his mother filled her voice. "Is everybody okay?"

"Yeah. Everyone's fine."

"Going somewhere?" Priss pointed toward his boots.

He shrugged. "I want to know how safe we are up here. How easy it would be to sneak up on us, that kind of thing."

She wrinkled her nose, causing those damn freckles to dance. "Do you think it'll come to that?"

"I sure as hell hope not, but better safe than sorry. Someone broke into our house. Wrecked it, according to Jeep."

Her eyes widened as she shook her head. "I don't understand. The Bible's at the university. Why search our house?"

He caught the "our" and realized he'd used it, too. So far, they were pretty damn bad at this separation thing. "Jeep thinks it's a warning, to let us know they're coming for us."

She removed a throw pillow from the plaid-covered armchair in the corner and sat, hugging the pillow to her chest.

He stretched his arms over his head, trying to loosen his trapezius muscles, which were knotted like pretzels. Was it only twenty-four hours since they'd met at Macee's, or a lifetime? "I guess they were afraid shooting at us wasn't enough."

"This whole thing is crazy.

He didn't respond. Whether it was her brother or someone else who was behind all of this, "crazy" was an understatement.

She leaned forward and tossed the throw pillow onto the bed, frisbee-style, before tugging on the string of the wide window blind. As the wooden slats separated, sunlight spilled across the pine floor. "Are there any wild animals out there? You're not going to go off and get eaten, are you?"

Mason swallowed a grin. "Yes, there are wild animals out there. No, I'm not going to get eaten."

"What about bears?"

He rolled his eyes. "Geez! What is it with you and bears? If a bear decided to attack us, he could get to us inside just as easily as out. They can rip a door right off its hinges if they feel the need."

The blood drained from her face. She launched herself out of the chair and headed toward the door.

Shaking his head, Mason grabbed an extra sweater and followed her out into the great room. As he tugged the sweater on over his other layers, he could hear her muttering from within the large closet by the front door.

He ambled over and leaned against the closet door jamb. "What are you doing?"

She paused, her hand on one of his mother's puffy jackets, her face still pale, eyes big as saucers. "I'm going with you."

"Like hell you are. I'm not in the mood for company right now."

She slid into the jacket and stepped into a pair of his mother's furry-topped snow boots. They were clown shoes on Priss' dainty feet.

"Forget what I said." He grasped her upper arms but felt nothing but jacket. "You're perfectly safe right here. It would take one seriously pissed-off bear to breach this cabin. Besides, they hibernate, remember?"

She yanked a heavy scarf off a hook and began wrapping it around her neck. "Nope. I read somewhere that the whole hibernation thing is misunderstood. Turns out, bears only sleep *intermittently* through the winter.

That means there might be a few out there that are awake and hungry." After three wraps, she tied the scarf tightly under her chin.

He expelled a resigned sigh. She wasn't giving in. Reaching around her, he grabbed his own jacket and slipped it on while she jammed a hand-knit hat onto her head. He recognized it as one his mother had made for a long-ago Christmas. It was at least a foot long, with navy blue and gray stripes and a giant green pom-pom at the end. Priss pulled the tail around so that the pom came to rest along the slope of her left breast. Or, rather, what he pictured as her left breast, underneath all those layers.

His mother called that type of hat a "toboggan." Who knew it could be so damn stimulating?

He shook his head at his own depravity.

"Where are we going first?" Her slick jacket made swooshing sounds as she fumbled around, trying to zip the parka while wearing a pair of red mittens.

He flattened her arms to her sides and took over the task. He was a doctor. To him, a human body was nothing but another day at the office.

Except for *this* body. He knew this one. So. Damn. Well.

He rushed through the job and gave her his back, busying himself with the lanyard full of keys that hung on a nearby hook. "I'm headed to the garage. I'm going to shovel a trench around the cabin. If I pile the snow into tall drifts, it will be harder to get through." And, between the cold and the physical labor, he just might get himself under control.

"Okay. I'll help."

Accepting defeat, he waved her out of the closet and followed her outside. The morning was clear but cold, and he was glad they'd both piled on extra clothing before leaving the cabin. Their breath vaporized as they battled their way through the heavy snow to the garage. It took him only a few seconds to unlock the padlock and shove open the large, upswinging single door.

"Wow." Priss peered at the jumble of old furniture, lawn games, and tools. "Don't show this to Callie."

Mason laughed—a real laugh—thinking about his sister-in-law's penchant for turning old junk into new treasures. "True that."

Entering the musty structure, he blinked a few times, until his eyes adjusted to the dark. A collection of snow shovels wasn't hard to spot. He thrust one at Priss. She'd said she wanted to help, and there was a lot to do.

Turning toward the view, Priss shaded her face with a mittened hand and gazed out at the rolling hills, enrobed in virginal white against a bright, sapphire sky. "It's so beautiful up here."

Mason nodded. The garage sat on the property's highest point, and the scenery was hard to beat. Then he looked down at Priss. Her cheeks glowed and her nose shone bright red in the freezing temperature.

That way lies insanity.

Putting all his effort into it, he began to shovel snow.

Chapter Eight

Liam stared at the blinking dot on his phone. So, Priss was somewhere in the Appalachians. The thought of his city-bred little sister stuck in the back of beyond should have made him laugh, but he wasn't in a laughing mood.

For the first time in his life, he was scared. Really scared. Terrified, in fact. Somehow, he'd made an enemy out of two of the most powerful men in America. And they didn't bat for the good guys.

His Uncle Sean had never liked him, not even when Liam was a kid. From the start, his uncle had seen him as competition, a possible threat to the power Sean carefully cultivated while serving as his brother's number two. And Liam could have been a rival, if he'd lived up to the "Lion" moniker his father had forced upon him. But he didn't have the stomach for the seedier side of the family business. Toying with men's lives, letting them dangle on strings until they choked themselves, that wasn't his idea of fun. He had a good head for business and could sell a dog a fur coat. Yes, he'd put a few people out of business, but they'd deserved it. Jones had made a career out of exploiting his underpaid employees, and Rystrom was an embezzler. They'd walked away with nothing because of their own greed—but they'd walked on sound legs, free of cement shoes.

Then his father had died. Ever since, Sean had tested

him, poking and prodding, gauging how deep Liam's loyalty ran, dropping hints to others about The Lion's so-called "betrayal." This Gutenberg Bible deal had seemed like the perfect way to get Sean off his back. Sure, it was illegal, but in a nice and tidy, white-collar kind of way. The Hughes family was doing just fine without a multi-million-dollar artifact. Liam had figured he'd toss Sean a generous portion of the loot, for goodwill's sake, keep an even healthier share for himself, and disappear forever. He'd laid the groundwork long ago. All that was missing was the cash.

From the start, nothing had gone according to plan. First, starry-eyed Priss refused to play. Then, he'd gotten entangled with Bannion. The guy was a first-class psycho. He frightened Liam more than Sean and his minions ever had. Bannion had been obsessed with the Gutenberg long before they'd known for sure one even existed. When the ancient text had surfaced, the man had grown rabid. His threat to lower his buying price was one thing; kidnapping and murder—that was a different enchilada all together.

Sighing, Liam eyed the blinking dot again. The time was coming when, with or without money, he'd have to run.

And for that, he'd need his sister's help.

****

Priss wanted to run.

Hurt, confused, weary, done. She was all of that and more. But the fact of the matter was she was stuck in this cabin, with no escape in sight.

She yanked on the bundle of blankets she'd spent the night tossing and turning under, bringing them up and over her head, welcoming the darkness as well as the additional warmth. It was well past dawn and the day's light, grey and uninviting, filled her room.

Getting up, however, meant facing Mason. Once Jeep had left, they'd passed the previous evening in near silence, obeying courtesy, but otherwise keeping to themselves.

In other words, sheer hell.

Wimp, she mouthed into the bedclothes. It was time to get off this roller coaster. She set her own course, played by her own rules. People could take her or leave her, their choice.

That applied to her husband, too. She'd screwed up. Handled this whole thing poorly from the start. But, despite her secrets and her flight, she was still the woman Mason had fallen in love with. He'd promised to love her through good decisions and bad, and if he couldn't forgive her, fine. She was done apologizing and feeling sorry for herself.

And she was done running.

Invigorated by her self-talk, she hopped out of bed and pulled on the heavy gray sweatshirt she'd worn the night before. It smelled faintly of woodsmoke, but nothing worse. Thank goodness for the pack of new undies Jeep had brought. They were granny-style, but clean. Lastly, she pulled on her black leggings. They weren't as warm as the sweatpants she'd found, but she was more comfortable wearing something of her own.

There was no sign of Mason when she ventured into the cabin's main room. Maybe he was sleeping late. Heaven knew he deserved the rest. His schedule at the hospital was insane.

An ache rose in her throat. She needed to stop thinking like a wife.

After a quick stop in the bathroom, she headed into the kitchen, pausing to marvel at the perfect stillness of the day. In the city, motion and noise was a constant. Motors, horns, construction and—due to their townhome's proximity to the hospital—sirens, formed the white noise of her day. Up here, all was silent, as if the world was on hold.

If only.

A sudden stomping rang out from the front porch and, in seconds, Mason shouldered through the front door, his arms stacked with firewood. Despite the bravado she'd summoned minutes before, Priss held her breath.

"Brrrrr." He didn't quite meet her eyes, but one side of his mouth lifted.

She relaxed a fraction.

Snow clung to his hat and jacket, and she realized for the first time that it must be snowing. She tugged on the string of the nearest blind and saw nothing but white.

"Oh, wow! Is it a blizzard?"

"Not quite. But it's coming down pretty hard right now. I'm going to see if I can get a weather report on the radio." Piece by piece, Mason filled the firewood section of the large hearth.

"A radio, huh?" Priss searched the room for a telltale antenna. "You do kick it old school up here."

Mason gave her a real smile and nodded toward a bookcase on the far side of the room. "It's how Dad stays connected to football."

Following his nod, she walked over to the shelf and removed an ancient transistor. "Holy cow. I haven't seen one of these since the dinosaurs passed." She blew on it, removing a thin layer of dust before turning it this way and that. It had a large, luminous dial and could be powered by batteries or electricity. "Hmm. Are you sure it still works?"

"Think so. One way to find out."

She turned the power knob and staticky speech flooded the room. The sound took her back to her youth. One of their "housemen"—the quaint term her father used for the men who'd protected their home—always had a transistor radio playing. A sweet, grandfatherly type named O'Malley, he'd occasionally allowed Priss to join him. They'd huddled around the kitchen table, listening to the ups and downs of the Boston sports teams.

She'd been twelve before she realized having armed men hanging around your house was unusual. But kindness was kindness, and she'd enjoyed the time with the old man.

A twist of the dial brought her to a station playing light rock. "Guess we haven't left civilization behind completely." Setting the radio down, she hummed along to the familiar tune. Priss was certain she'd been a singer in another life, but not in this one. She couldn't carry a tune in a paper bag.

Mason and his family shared her love for music. Minna was a halfway decent pianist, Adam sang country in a deep bass, and even Jeep, on a good day, could be coaxed into riffing some blues guitar with Patrick. Mason was the hard rocker of the family, and he played along on his drum set with both great enthusiasm and an instinctive sense of rhythm. But there was one thing that made the Hughes family play-and-sing-alongs unforgettable: They made up their own lyrics. Every one of them, from her mother-in-law on down, purposely mangled the words to even the simplest of songs. Caroling with them this past Christmas had nearly made Priss pee her pants. She smiled at the memory.

"What's so funny?" Mason tossed the last piece of wood onto the flames and stretched. His long, strong arms almost reached the lowest of the rough, dark, wooden beams crisscrossing the ceiling.

"Nothing, really. I was remembering some of your family's more inventive Christmas carols. *God rest ye, Merry Gentlemen/Let nothing come your way.*" She giggled.

Mason made a finger gun and fired in her direction. "That's a classic. But don't forget our rendition of *Little Drummer Boy*." He pulled in a breath. "*Come, they told him/Da trumpets are one,*" he sang, in his pleasant baritone.

"No, the best is your dad singing *simply having a wonderful breakfast crime.*" Priss burst out laughing. "That doesn't make any sense at all."

"Sure, it does." Mason crossed to her side and frowned down at her with mock seriousness. "I hear violence against waffles and pancakes is on the rise."

She laughed harder, savoring the moment. Right from the start, they'd shared the same humor, and as always, it sent that crazy chemistry pinging between them. Their eyes met and he leaned toward her, one quarter of an inch, then another. She licked her dry lips, eager to experience the rush of his mouth on hers.

The fire popped, and they both jumped. Priss glared at the flames, as if they'd acted on purpose. Mason muttered something she didn't catch as he picked up the radio and stalked into the kitchen. The clanging sounds of shifting pots and pans soon followed, and she wandered across the room to see what he was doing.

"I'm gonna nuke one of these frozen meatloaf meals. Do you want one?"

She glanced at the large clock on the far wall. "It's eight forty-five in the morning."

Mason turned and gave her that sexy grin of his, with one eyebrow cocked. "And your point is?"

Despite the residue of tension hanging between them, she laughed. "I'll pass, thanks." But she walked over to the island, watching as he pulled a small glass casserole dish out of the freezer and removed the plastic top. Meatloaf with a side of homemade mac-and-cheese with roasted green chilies. Delicious, but not for breakfast.

"I can't believe I've never asked you this before. Have you always had such strange eating habits? Or is it an offshoot of the wild hours of your residency?"

Shrugging, he placed the dish in the microwave. "Yes, to both, I guess. As you know, Mum's always in the kitchen whipping something up, sometimes without rhyme or reason. I mean, they'll tape a Christmas show in October, or a Halloween show in July, and Mum always tries out her recipes on the family first. Growing up, we ate Thanksgiving dinner at least ten times a year. Not that I ever complained." His harsh tone softened as he remembered.

"So your menus were kind of screwy."

He nodded without turning around. "Beef Wellington and a *bûche de Noël* in June, pumpkin soup for the first day of school, that kind of thing. We never complained because, well…" He gave her a backward glance. "My mother's Minna Hughes."

His words were simple but sincere, his pride

evident. Minna had built up her company the same way she made cakes—from scratch. Her sons might complain about her meddling, but each was more than a little in awe of their mother. Priss was, too. It should have been difficult being daughter-in-law to the Maven of Make and Do, but Minna's warm, accepting personality had won Priss over from the beginning. What her mother-in-law thought about her today, Priss couldn't say. Like their youngest son, neither of her in-laws held grudges, but leaving Mason the way she had couldn't have won her any points.

Not that it mattered now. She was who she was.

And one thing she wouldn't be for much longer was Mason's wife.

Chapter Nine

Mason had hoped chopping more wood would exhaust both his body and mind.

He'd been wrong.

This morning, Priss had rocked that "just rolled out of bed" sexiness that he'd have to be superhuman or dead not to notice. Then there was the constant thrum of synchronicity, of rightness, between them. If not for the well-timed crack from the fireplace, he would have kissed her until they were both senseless.

He'd have to be as dumb as the logs he'd chopped not to realize this relationship was doomed. But—and he wasn't talking from his shorts here—part of him still wanted a miracle, a magic bullet that would save his marriage.

Therein lay the big *what if.* What if he took his brothers' advice and fought for her—asked her to stay. How on earth would they ever make it work? Seamus O'Brien's daughter and Patrick Hughes' son? He didn't need a bookie to tell him the odds were lousy.

Besides, what if, over the course of the past few weeks, she'd gotten used to the idea of being single again? It would eviscerate him if what he felt was one-sided. He wasn't talking about their off-the-charts physical attraction. He'd bet a million that was still there, on both sides. But you could want someone without wanting a relationship. You could leave someone who attracted you like a fly to honey.

He finished stacking the rest of the wood and plowed his way back to the cabin. His unorthodox breakfast meatloaf hadn't withstood the heavy exercise, and he needed more fuel. Entering, he spied Priss tucked into a corner of the couch with her journal. Except for the scratching of her pen, all was silent. It was one of the first things he'd learned about her, once they'd settled down after Vegas—Her doodle journal was always at the ready in case inspiration struck. When she was sketching or writing in it, the rest of the world melted away.

Fine by him. The less she talked, the less he looked at her kissable mouth. A win-win.

Part of the problem with being stuck up here was…being stuck up here. He understood the danger, but at least at home, he could be part of the solution. He wasn't used to being inactive, powerless. They were hiding out, holding their breaths, waiting to hear the coast was clear. If Priss wasn't constantly turning him on, he'd be feeling damn impotent by now.

After sticking a big bowl of frozen beef stew into the microwave, he pulled out the drawer that stored a half-dozen decks of cards and a mess of poker chips. He and his brothers had spent plenty of time by the fire upping each other's ante, but poker wasn't a game you could play alone. Solitaire struck him as mighty pathetic. He glanced back at Priss. Six weeks ago, he'd have suggested some strip poker to pass the time, but now…

Sighing, he grabbed a deck and his warmish soup and sat down at the table, where he inhaled the soup in no time and began dealing out a game of solitaire. In a matter of minutes, he'd lost five games in a row, which seemed about right, given his mood. He was setting up the sixth when Priss joined him.

"If looks could kill, those cards would be goners."

He tossed her the evil eye and continued dealing.

She fiddled with the ribbon page marker of her journal before yanking out a chair and taking a seat. "I, um, have come to a few conclusions and wanted to share them with you."

That got his attention. He ditched the cards and forced his achy shoulders back. "Okay. Just what have you concluded?"

"I've decided to accept the FBI offer. I'll tell them everything I know about the O'Brien organization and go into Witness Protection. A new identity sounds...safe. Plus, hopefully, it will put all this craziness to bed and keep any embarrassment I might cause your family to a minimum." Her long lashes fluttered, veiling her eyes.

Mason's stomach lurched, and it had nothing to do with anything he'd eaten. He reached for her hand, covered it with his own. A masochistic move, but he couldn't help it. "Are you sure? I mean, it's a pretty drastic step." Their relationship might be over, but that didn't mean he wanted her disappearing. A future of never seeing her, never talking with her again, loomed large and solitary.

You've never had to fight for anything in your life.

He pushed his brother's words aside. Right now was about her, not him.

She nodded, still staring down at the tabletop. "Yeah, it is. But I think it's my best option."

He rubbed the back of her hand with his thumb. "You've been away a long time. Do you still know where the bodies are buried?"

Priss winced. "That's a very unfortunate turn of phrase but, yeah, I know a few of Uncle Sean's secrets."

That info didn't give Mason a warm and fuzzy feeling. "I didn't mean it literally... You said, 'a few decisions.' What else?"

She flipped her hand over and laced her fingers with his. "I want us to spend the night together. One last time."

An image of the condoms his brother had sent 'in case of emergency' flashed in Mason's head, followed by other, more X-rated images. Even the innocent touch of her hand triggered shafts of desire. The thought of having her pressed against him, naked and willing, almost reduced him to a puddle at her feet.

"I don't know," he said, hoping he didn't get this wrong. "Seems like that might muddy waters that are already plenty brown."

With her free hand, she tucked a stray strand of hair behind an ear. "It might. Or, it might relieve this tension between us, get us back to a good place, so we can end things like adults."

He freed his hand and slumped back against the chair's hard frame. Its reassuring solidness was a stark contrast to his whirling thoughts. No matter what his answer was to her request, there was no way forward for them. Could he accept what she was offering under those terms?

"No regrets, you mean? I'm not sure that's possible." He already had a million regrets. But then, seeing as that was true, what was one more?

"No, I know. It's just that, right now, everything is so packed with emotion. Sex might release the steam a little. Bring everything back down to a simmer, instead of a boil."

It might at that, and it was sure as hell more entertaining than chopping wood, but still, he hesitated.

"Can I think about it?" He caught the flicker of disappointment in her eyes but refused to cave.

"Sure." She stood with another shrug. "I wonder if it's stopped snowing yet? I'd like to take a little walk, maybe build a snowman, if you think it's safe out there?" Doubt deepened her voice.

"From all the wild beasts and whoever's chasing us? Yeah, I think you're safe." If anything pounced on her, it would be him. Maybe. *Probably.*

She raised a shade, filling the room with blinding sunlight, and giggled. "Yep, it stopped snowing. Looks like I'll need some shades." Crossing to the door, she snagged hers from the small entry table and stuck them on top of her head.

"Looks like," he agreed, blinking. "You weren't serious about building a snowman, were you?"

Turning, she met his gaze head-on and with total seriousness. "Absolutely. I never joke about snow people. I'm a master craftswoman."

He pursed his lips. "Is that right?"

She grabbed the puffer jacket from the coat rack. "Sure is. Used to make entire families of them when I was growing up. Mom, Dad, babies, you name it."

Perfect little snow families to substitute for the messy one she had in real life? Mason didn't ask. Standing, he stretched instead, happy to press Pause on the billion-dollar question simmering between them. A little lighthearted fun never hurt anybody. "You know, I don't want to brag, but I have a bit of a reputation myself when it comes to building snowmen."

She stepped into his mother's wool-lined snow boots. "Don't say things you might regret." There was a decided challenge in her eyes.

He laughed. This might be dangerous, but after the past few shitty days, he didn't care. "Oh, I won't. Prepare to be amazed." Gathering his own snow garb, he followed her out the door.

The freezing air invigorated him as he once again waded into the fresh snowfall that had blanketed his redoubts overnight. The mounds he'd built capped seven feet in spots, walling the cabin away from things that went bump in the night, be they two-legged or four. It wasn't invincible, but anyone who breached their hideout would have to be one determined SOB, with one hell of a good GPS.

When he was about ten yards from the cabin, he bent down and tested a fistful of snow. Heavy and wet, it held its shape like clay. Across the way, he watched Priss begin rolling a snowball. She was smiling, her delight growing along with the bunch of snow she pushed and patted. Her long hair flowed out under her hat, glinting red in the mountain sunlight, while her cheeks took on a pink glow.

She was beautiful—inside and out. And she was still his wife.

Fluttering fireflies. He'd told her he needed to think about her proposal, but he'd lied. If one more night with this woman was all that was left to him, he'd take it in a heartbeat.

And make it last a lifetime.

Chapter Ten

Holding her breath, Priss lifted the perfectly chiseled, medium-sized snowball onto its larger base…where it immediately fell into pieces.

Smothering a curse, she brushed away the snowy bits with her mittened hands and began again. This snowman was becoming a perfect metaphor for her life: Sometimes fun, sometimes frustrating, and currently in smithereens.

Earlier, everything had seemed so clear. As often happened while doodling, she'd envisioned a plan. It wasn't the best plan, because it didn't involve Mason—at least not in the long run—but it was one she had a shot at living with. It put the O'Briens in the hot seat, but her loyalty to her uncle had disappeared long ago. Her main concern was that taking the FBI deal made things better for the Hughes family. They didn't deserve any of this. For the first time in six weeks, things appeared to be, if not peachy, at least settled.

Then Mason had turned her down. Flat.

Okay, so that was a slight overstatement. But a "maybe" was as good as a "no," wasn't it? Especially from a man, whenever sex was involved. Mason was more sensitive and solicitous than most, but he'd always come running when she crooked a finger. It hit her psyche below the belt in more ways than one.

She shouldn't be surprised. Lousy O'Brien luck was

always followed by more bad luck. It reinforced what she already knew—it was time to re-group and move on. Witness Protection wasn't something she'd ever envisioned. She'd left the Mob and its secrets behind a long time ago, but if the Feds wanted to set her up with a new life on their dime, why should she turn it down? A new adventure, that's what it was. The identity Liam had set up for her years ago had been a sort of trial run.

The price was high, though. Leaving Mason and his family…

No. She'd already started cutting that cord. Better to sever the remainder with one giant swing of the machete.

Catching sight of her husband several yards away, she experienced a twinge of envy. His zest for life was the by-product of a carefree childhood. Studying him as he whistled while playing in the snow, she caught a glimpse of that child. He already had three snow people completed, large, medium, and small. Granted, they listed drunkenly and weren't very round but, in usual Mason style, he'd gotten the job done with his upbeat, can-do attitude. As she watched, he closed his eyes and lifted his face to the sun, spreading his long arms wide.

What she wouldn't have given for a camera right then.

Yearning to get out of her own head, she circled her rounded base. Nine times out of ten, she was a free-spirited, roll-with-the-punches kind of person, but where snowmen were concerned, she was a perfectionist. It might take her more time to complete her snow family, but they'd be a true work of art.

"You know it's taking everything in me not to run right through that." Mason frog-marched through the snow until he stood only a few steps away, staring down at her snowperson-in-progress.

"You wouldn't dare."

Mason's lips slid into a naughty-schoolboy grin as he raised a booted foot. "Wanna bet? We've been out here for twenty minutes and that's all you have to show for yourself?"

Hands on hips, she stepped in front of her snow mound. "I'll have you know that I've created a perfectly symmetrical snowman bottom. Much more impressive than those," she pointed a disdainful finger toward his snow folk, "whatever-you-call-them over there."

"Ha!" His breath came out in a puffy cloud. "You're just jealous. My—" He broke off, one finger raised in the universal wait-a-moment signal.

"Shit!" He gripped her elbow and began tugging her toward the trees.

"Hey!" She stumbled in the deep snow. He righted her in seconds, and they kept on going.

"What the hell?" And then she heard it. The unmistakable sound of a helicopter.

They made it to the protection of the woods scant seconds before it passed overhead, slightly to the north of where the cabin stood.

"Shit," Mason said, again.

"I take it you don't get a lot of helicopters out here?" Priss couldn't quite keep the shakiness out of her voice. Pressing her head against his chest, she felt rather than saw his head shake.

"Never. It didn't even occur to me." Beneath her head, his chest rose and fell. "With all these footprints and snowmen, this cabin looks anything but unoccupied from the air. I hate to sound paranoid, but…"

She snaked her arms around his middle, seeking his

solidness under the squishy layers of down they wore. "That's okay. We've been threatened and shot at. Go for paranoid."

"Right." Their jackets whispered together as he ran a hand up and down her back. "I'll need to let Jeep know about this right away, see if he can trace the helicopter. Hopefully, it's nothing. In the meantime, I'm afraid we're stuck inside."

He squeezed her once, hard, then stepped back. Despite the hug, the frowning concentration on his face told her he barely registered her presence. In fact, it surprised her when he grabbed her hand.

"Let's go, while the coast is clear."

Together, they made a beeline for the cabin, although running in the snow was no easy feat. The cheery, welcoming warmth that enveloped Priss as she stepped into the great room struck her as false security. In the midst of this quaint setting, so far removed from everything familiar, it was easy to forget the danger that had led them there in the first place.

The helicopter had reminded her in the worst way.

Mason headed straight for his bedroom and Priss dogged his footsteps, unwilling to be left behind. Perhaps sensing that, he pressed the phone's speaker button after he'd dialed.

Jeep's deep voice flooded the room on the second ring. "What's up?" His concern transcended his usual brevity.

"We just had a helicopter fly over. No identifying marks."

"Military?"

Mason glanced over at her as he shook his head. "Definitely not. It was black with a yellow belly and tail.

Looked like a bumble bee."

"Fuck."

Priss's fluttering stomach sank. Jeep always managed to say more with that one word than most people did with a paragraph.

"Directly over, or some distance away?"

"A little to the north, but too close for my comfort…I've never seen one up here before."

Jeep grunted. "I'll see if I can track it. In the meantime, you need to shut it down up there. Make it look deserted. I'm talking no fire, blinds shut. Lights at a minimum. There should be a portable heater up there somewhere but, even with that, prepare to be cold. If I need to contact you, I'll come to you. That's safer than emitting any technical footprints right now."

Mason sat on the edge of the unmade bed and hunched forward, elbows on knees, jacket straining at the shoulders. Priss longed to rub a hand over his back but remained where she was instead, giving him space but unable to leave.

"Will do. How long before you know anything?"

"Not sure. In the meantime, be ready. Load that gun." With that ominous phrase hanging in the air, Jeep clicked off.

"Gun? What gun?" Still wearing her mittens, Priss pointed a finger toward the living room. "That ancient blunderbuss over the fireplace? The only person it might kill is you, if you dare try to fire it."

Mason scrubbed his hands over his face. "No. Jeep gave me another gun. A pistol. I meant to tell you. You know how much I hate guns."

She nodded. He'd worked in an ER too long to be a fan. "Do you even know what to do with one?"

Reaching out, he lowered the window blind, throwing the room into near darkness. "Yeah, we all had lessons. Practiced up here, in fact. But I'm a lousy shot."

Priss sighed. "So I'm in charge of the gun, then. Where is it?"

Mason stiffened and met her eyes with his. "Wait a sec. What do mean, you're 'in charge of the gun.' Can you shoot?"

She rolled her eyes. "I'm a mobster's daughter. What do you think?"

For a moment, Mason gaped like a goldfish. In any other situation, she'd be cracking up with laughter.

With obvious effort, he shut his mouth and swallowed. "How well? I mean, are you a good shot?"

Priss rolled her head around, trying to loosen her shoulders and neck. She really didn't want to get into all this. "I can hit what I aim at." She'd once had all kinds of ribbons and plaques to prove it.

"But you hate guns, too."

She sighed, seeing no way around it. "That's true, but it won't surprise you to learn my father was a crack shot. A long time ago, I took up prize shooting, in a silly effort to please him. Needless to say, it didn't work."

The gleam of compassion that crept into his eyes rankled. For her money, it was too close to pity. "Look, it was a long time ago. It doesn't matter. Didn't then either, in fact."

His gorgeous blues widened. "He was your father. Of course, it mattered."

Priss stripped off the wet mittens, sending a shower of snow to the floor. "God, I hate it when you do that."

"Do what?"

"Get all sympathetic and sweet. It makes my heart

melt." *Crap. Why did I say that?*

Mason stood and crossed over to her. He placed a hand on her shoulder, then slid it down the slick surface of her jacket until he grasped her fingers. "Priss. Things between us are…complicated." He grimaced, as if he hated that overused word as much as she did. "I'm not a machine. I've tried, but I just can't turn off my emotions at will. I know it's cliché, but when I met you, I thought I'd found my other half. My better half."

No, no, no. Not now, when I'm already in emotional overload. She'd be blubbering like a baby any second now.

"You know I'm angry—'hurt' might be more accurate. All the good stuff between us…" He looked down at their linked hands. "I don't want to let it go, but I also don't know if I can trust it anymore. It's like I'm on a seesaw or something, sometimes up, sometimes down."

The words peppered her heart with little shards of emotional glass, the pain unlike any other. She bit down hard on her lip.

With a shake of his head, he let go of her and took a step back.

"I'm rambling. The point is, I've always known your family life was different from mine. Now that I know *how* different, despite the mess that is our marriage, I can't help feeling sad for you. I grew up with all the good, fun, family stuff you missed, and I won't apologize for being empathetic."

Mustering a smile, she reached out, patted his chest through the layers of padding before withdrawing again. He wasn't the only one on a seesaw. "No, you shouldn't apologize for that, ever. It's essential to who you are.

Truth is, I tend to overreact when it comes to my childhood, my father. I've worked hard to get past it and, for the most part, I've succeeded. It just rears its ugly head sometimes. Frankly, it really pisses me off," she added, going for the easy humor.

He nodded. As usual, the large, high-ceilinged room seemed smaller with him in it. And that bed was a big bad invitation.

Get a grip, girl. He doesn't want you anymore.

"I'm gonna go smother the fire and knock down our snowmen. They may have been spotted already, but it won't hurt. I'll leave our fortifications intact. A helicopter can't land that close, because of all the trees, and friend or foe, the harder it is to reach us, the better."

Jeez. It sounded like they were awaiting a fricking invasion.

Duh. Because we are.

"Right." She squared her shoulders, knowing she'd have plenty of time to dwell on her emotional battle after they won this war. "Show me where that gun is, first."

****

Mason nudged the heater's ancient cord with a socked foot. "Good thing we have a lot of blankets, because this thing is toast."

Priss, wrapped to her neck in an old quilt, nodded beside him. "Looks like it's ready for last rites." Kneeling down, she peered at the plug. "Did something chew on that?"

The alarm on her face made him laugh. "I won't lie. We have been known to have mice up here."

She rose with an obvious shudder and readjusted the quilt. "Super. Bears outside, mice inside."

He bit back a grin. Her newfound fear of critters was

adorable. In another life he would have wrapped her in a ginormous hug and vowed eternal protection.

She moved to the hearth, where the final embers of the smothered fire slowly blinked in the darkness. "Brrr. The temperature in here has really dipped since the sun went down. My bedroom's freezing."

Mason set the old heater aside. He'd add it to the junk pile in the garage at some point. Right now, the last thing he wanted to do was open the door and let in more cold. Straightening, he faced the one outcome he'd hoped to avoid.

"We'd both better plan on sleeping in here tonight. Even without the fire, it's the warmest room in the place." Moving to the couch, he picked up a small throw pillow his mother had embroidered with the phrase "Life's better at the cabin," a sentiment he wasn't vibing with right now. "You take the couch. I'm too big for it, plus I've slept on this floor a couple of times." He and his brothers had spent a few youthful Christmases strewn about in sleeping bags, trying to stay up to meet Santa Claus.

"Oh." Priss frowned at the wood-planked floor while running a stockinged foot along the fringe of the colorful but thin throw rug. "It doesn't look too comfortable."

As far as he could remember, it wasn't.

She shot him a hesitant sideways glance. "You know…we'd generate more body heat if we snuggled together."

Mason gulped down a bubble of panic. He was a doctor, and this was simple science. He could handle it. *No. Big. Deal.*

"We could drag your queen mattress in here and

share it. We don't have to," she waved a hand, "you know, do anything. Survival mode only? It's up to you."

His stomach clenched. Spending the night together, lying inches away from her, it wouldn't be difficult to convince himself that his survival depended on them doing *something* several times over again, at the risk of decimating what was left of his heart. However, if he said "no," he'd be denying them their best chance at comfort.

"Okay." He hoped his shrug conveyed a nonchalance he didn't feel. "Let's get dinner taken care of, and then we'll move everything."

Nodding, she rose and padded into the kitchen, the quilt dragging along behind her like the train on a wedding dress. The vise in his stomach tightened at the thought. They'd planned on having a real wedding, with all the trimmings, on their tenth anniversary. No chance of that happening now. They hadn't even made it a year.

She pulled a frozen pizza out of the freezer and gave him a questioning look.

"Yeah, sure." For once, he wasn't hungry. A burst of the fidgets propelled him over to the table. After glancing at the wall clock, he flipped on the radio. The top-of-the-hour news and weather should be on. Reception wasn't great, but he pieced enough news together to realize he hadn't missed much. He turned up the volume when the perky Southern accent of the meteorologist came on.

"It will be a cold one tonight, y'all, with temperatures dropping into the mid-twenties, but it's the windchill that will really sting. The real feel temp will hover somewhere in the teens. More snow's expected in the high country, with increased wind and lower temperatures overnight. After a cold night, tomorrow should be chilly but clear."

Mason switched the dial to the "off" position and whistled. "Damn. We picked a bad night to go without heat. That's about as lousy as it gets up here."

The oven beeped and Priss lowered the glass door. "Hunh. Makes me wish I could slide in here along with this pizza."

He moved to a window and peeked outside. The yellowish-gray glow of the sky verified the forecast. There was snow in those clouds. An image of himself and Priss twined together on the queen mattress sucker-punched him with the force of a Mack truck.

The phrase "cold night in hell" came to mind. Things were bad enough before he knew she was willing. Now, all bets were off regarding whether he could keep his hands to himself.

He flipped a mental switch and refocused, a trick he'd learned working in the ER. He'd be all right if he kept to boring, inane subjects. "Dad has talked about putting in a solar-powered heating system. I just might volunteer to help him after this." *Perfect. Nice and snoozy.*

Priss smiled at him from the kitchen. "Why? Are you envisioning another time when you'll be forced to hide up here without heat?"

Mason winced. "Good point. I sure as hell hope that kind of luck only strikes once."

Despite the distance between them, he spied the shadow that crossed her face, and wondered what she was thinking. She'd worn that expression before, but he'd never been able to decipher it. While she was usually optimistic, he sometimes sensed an unwillingness or, at least, a hesitancy, deep within her, to trust the positive. It made some sense now. Life with the Mob must have taught her that Lady Luck was fickle. If television shows were anything to go by, you could be Number Two one day and swimming with the fishes the next. On the heels of that thought, he wondered how many people had been in and out of her life, growing up. No wonder she'd developed a "grab it while you can" philosophy.

The innate desire to comfort surged again, but that way lay insanity. Instead, he walked into the kitchen and grabbed a couple of plates, plunking them down with more force than necessary at the large kitchen island, before plopping himself down on one of the stools.

"Have you ever watched my mother eat pizza?" he asked, in another attempt at the mundane.

She placed one of his mother's homemade pumpkin pies on the counter to thaw. "I don't think so, why?"

"She uses a knife and fork. Cuts her slice up into tiny, ladylike bites."

Priss goggled. "You're kidding. They have pizza in England, don't they?"

He nodded. "Of course. And it's finger food over there, too. But Mum always uses utensils. She'll even ask for them at a restaurant. Used to drive my brothers and me nuts as kids."

She rolled her eyes. "I can only imagine. You guys are still pretty good at giving your mother grief."

"Hey," Mason said. "She gives as good as she gets."

"Yeah, out of desperation!" Priss countered. "She's completely surrounded by testosterone. Probably needed a whip and a chair when you guys were younger."

He mimicked the cracking of a whip. "Wa-toosh. Yeah, we pulled some crazy stunts. There was a constant stream of bloody noses, broken arms, chipped teeth. You name it, we tried it."

Priss threw her head back in a full-throttle laugh, drawing his eyes to the graceful curve of her throat and the wispy strands of hair that escaped the messy topknot she wore. His fingers itched to explore, to caress.

He clenched his fists. *Damn it.* Being safe and boring with this woman was harder than climbing Everest. He grabbed another deck of cards from the junk drawer. Cards were harmless, right? But, no. Immediately, his treacherous mind conjured images of a particularly erotic game of Slap Jack they'd played on their three-month anniversary.

Biting back a curse, he dealt another game of solitaire.

He really sucked at mundane.

Chapter Eleven

Priss couldn't sleep, and it had nothing to do with the cabin's frigid temperature. Between the load of blankets they'd piled onto the mattress and the steady warmth of their shared bed, it was halfway to comfortable.

The cause of her insomnia slept about six inches away, his broad back to her nose. Lying there, trying not to move, she was intoxicated by his clean, woodsy smell. It didn't help that she could envision each curve and angle of his muscular body.

She'd hoped they'd climb into bed together and nature would take its course. After all, he knew she was willing. Instead, Mason had issued a perfunctory "good night" and turned over. If he wasn't asleep, he was doing a bang-up job of faking it. He hadn't moved an inch in the last hour.

Meanwhile, she tossed and turned, oscillating between her visceral need for this man and a mix of anger and hurt over the obvious fact that he didn't want her anymore.

Those good old O'Briens, one hundred percent unlucky at love. No, two hundred percent unlucky at love.

Sighing, she rolled over again.

"For the love of God, will you please be still!" Mason's voice bit into the silence.

"I'm sorry. Did I wake you?"

"No," he snapped. "It's impossible to sleep next to a tornado."

Priss counted to five before answering. "Sorry," she repeated. "I can't sleep."

Moonlight or snow light—she didn't want to get up to find out which—snuck around the edges of the blinds, giving the room a silvery glow. Mason's shadowy form rose and sank as he inhaled.

"That makes two of us," he whispered into the gloom.

She flopped onto her back right as he did the same and they overlapped each other like falling dominoes. As she flailed around, her hand brushed his stomach and lower still, before she jerked away.

Hmmm. Now, there was food for thought. Her husband sported an erection of mammoth proportions. Should she act casual and pretend she hadn't noticed? Or should she offer to help with that particular problem?

"Screw it," Mason said.

It was the only warning she got before his mouth found hers with laser-like precision. His mouth was hard, punishing, and arousing as hell while his hands found every hot spot, coaxing embers into a five-alarm blaze.

She alternated between wiggling out of her layers and tugging at his. He pulled away and allowed her to tug his heavy sweatshirt over his head, before meeting her eyes in the murky light.

"You'd better be okay with this."

She paused as the knot in his sweatpants stymied her. "I'm more than okay with it." Running her hands up his bare abdomen, she memorized every inch. They fit together like jigsaw pieces, but he was hard where she was soft. Reaching up, she bracketed his unshaven face with her hands. "I want you. Right here, right now. Whatever you can give, I'll take."

Her words opened the floodgates. Taking a deep breath, she dove in and let the current sweep her away.

****

A scratching sound from the front porch dragged Priss from a dreamless sleep and sent her clutching at the blankets. Was it a squadron of mice, ready to attack? *Don't be silly.* Beside her, Mason slept on. As a busy doctor, when he could sleep, he did so like a rock, and since this was just her imagination running wild, she didn't want to wake him. She'd do that after she peeked out the window. That way, she could enjoy their next bout of lovemaking without wondering what was scampering about outside.

However, after worming her way back into her sweats and easing out of the blankets, she retrieved the loaded gun from where she'd stashed it under the couch hours before. She might be silly, but she wasn't stupid.

Halfway across the room, she realized she was hugging the wall with the gun pointing toward the floor, like cops did on television. Clearly, she'd been binge-watching way too much *NCIS* lately. Forcing herself into a more relaxed approach, she reached the window beside the front door in a few silent steps.

She lifted the edge of the blind half an inch, but it was enough.

There, working steadily at the lock, stood Liam.

"Son of a bitch." She sent a silent apology to her mother as she glanced over at Mason. Still no signs of life. Before she could talk herself out of it, she slid on her boots, grabbed her jacket, and flipped the deadbolt.

"Holy f—"

Priss launched at her brother, smothering his words with her hand. "Shut up." She pulled the door shut behind her without so much as a click.

The element of surprise was all hers when she flashed the gun.

Throwing up his gloved hands, Liam fell back a step. "What the—? Have you lost your mind? I'm unarmed. At least, I mean, I'm not here to hurt you."

That appeared to be true. The only thing he held was a credit card. Nothing she'd ever seen on television indicated that could be turned into a lethal weapon.

"What about Mason?"

Liam nodded. "He's safe, too. I promise. C'mon, it's fucking freezing out here." He gestured toward the door. "Let's go inside and talk."

Priss hesitated. Freezing was an understatement. The wind bit right through her sweatpants, and a glance at the porch railing revealed that at least six inches of new snow had fallen. But there was no way in hell she was letting Liam into the cabin. This was as close to Mason as he would get.

"Hang on." She opened the door a few inches and slid her hand inside, feeling for the ring of keys hanging on the wall.

Bingo. She withdrew the bunch and eased the door closed again. Waving the gun toward the looming shape of the garage, she took a step forward. "Come on. You first."

The large backpack he pulled from the shadows sent a ripple of fear through Priss. Chances were good it hid something a lot more deadly than a credit card. "Nope. That stays here."

He shot her a look chock full of disbelief, so she punctuated her words with a wave of the gun. God, it was like a scene from one of the Hughes' old VHS collections. All that was missing was Jimmy Cagney. *You dirty rat.*

Sighing, Liam propped the pack back against the wall and headed toward the garage, frustration clear in every stomped step. "I'm telling you, you can put that gun away," he hissed, over his shoulder.

"And I'm telling you, if we're attacked by a bear, I'm shooting you right after I shoot it." She double-timed it to keep up with his longer strides. "How the hell did you find us? And is more company coming?"

Under his breath, Liam swore. It was an old, Gaelic oath her father had used often, and despite herself, a stab of nostalgia attacked her midsection.

Damn it. Now was not the time to wax sentimental.

"No. I'm alone and I wasn't followed."

She snorted, wincing as the cold air invaded her sinuses. "Like I believe you!"

"I promise. It's just me. As to how I found you? Remember that fountain pen I gave you for your birthday?"

Priss remembered it well. She'd met him for coffee several months back, against her better judgment, and he'd surprised her with the beautiful "birthday" gift, even though that date had come and gone much earlier in the year. It was an expensive brand, one she had a weakness for—as he well knew. Giving him a hard, sideways glance, she answered her own question. "Holy shit. You've been tracking me." *Unbelievable.*

He shrugged but kept moving. "For your own protection." His tone rang with a smug arrogance that heightened her annoyance.

"Yeah, right. Here Mason and I were thinking we were being so careful, and you knew where we were the whole time!"

"Hey." He bulldozed through a large snowdrift like it was made of feathers. "I didn't turn it on until it became absolutely necessary."

She kicked out at the snow, wishing it was his shin. "Oh, gee whiz. That totally makes it okay, then."

Liam whipped around, his brawny, six-foot-three-inch bulk stopping her in her tracks. Gun or no gun, he wasn't afraid of her. "Go ahead, sis." He spread his arms. "Act as snotty as you want. Don't you understand? We're playing with the big boys, here. I'll drop a thousand more trackers in your purse if it helps keep you safe."

Oh, how she wished she had a comeback for that. Instead, she had a go at her father's old curse, finding the guttural word oddly satisfying.

By unspoken agreement, they resumed the trek to the garage in silence, although Priss's thoughts were deafening. After months of bullying her about the Gutenberg, Liam now claimed he was trying to protect her. Whose side was he really on?

After wading through one more snowdrift, they arrived at the garage. She waved her brother back several steps, then double-checked the safety before placing the gun on a handy ledge. The last thing they needed was an accident. A full moon shone from the now cloudless sky and reflected off the snow, but even with the helpful light, it took her a minute to find the right key. She unlocked the solid door, pushed it wide, and retrieved the gun. At her prodding, Liam preceded her into the dark, windowless building. She stayed hot on his heels.

Shutting the door with her foot, she flicked on the bare lightbulb overhead and they stood facing each other, blinking in the light. Once her eyes adjusted, she made her way over to an old canvas lawn chair, removed the toolbox sitting on it, and plopped down, setting off an explosion of dust.

"Ugh," she choked out. "Find a seat."

Liam waded through the snow shovels, skis, and other miscellaneous clutter to a chippy wooden barstool. As he sat, he folded his arms across his padded chest. The move reminded her of Mason. *Please, God, let him stay asleep.*

Both the flimsy chair and her oversized jacket made sitting upright difficult, and after a few moments of fighting gravity, she gave in and slouched. "Intimidating" wasn't a look she wore well anyway. She checked the gun's safety mechanism once more before setting it on the arm of her chair.

"Why are you here? How did you get here? Were you followed?"

Liam raised a hand. "Calm down. I rented a chopper. And, yes, I made certain I couldn't be traced. I lost my tail days ago, used a fake name, paid in cash. Trust me, I know all the tricks."

Priss pursed her lips. There was a lot there to unpack. "Wait a minute. Who's tailing you and why are *you* hiding, too? You're working *with* these guys, right?"

Liam's gray eyes darkened. "Yes and no."

Priss shook her head. "Un-huh. You can't have it both ways. Spill."

He pulled off his gloves and wool beanie and ran a hand through his hair. The strawberry-blond tones, so similar to her own, glinted in the garage's LED light. Five or six feet full of garage junk separated them, but she heard his sigh. An aura of failure emanated from him, something she'd never before associated with her confident, sometimes too-cocky brother.

In short, he had the appearance of a man in trouble, and it threw her off stride.

But, before she had a chance to follow-up, the garage door was yanked open. She grabbed for the gun moments before Mason entered, holding the ancient shotgun and looking ready to slay the bear she feared so much.

This time, Priss went with a good, old-fashioned, American curse.

****

No question about it. He was the dumbest son-of-a-bitch who'd ever lived.

Stupid. Stupid. Stupid.

He'd fallen head over ass for Priss again—ready to fight like hell for her—only to have his heart trampled on once more. That knowledge made it a little easier for Mason to keep the shotgun trained on the other man in the room.

Built like Jeep physically, this man was a formidable foe. Or would be if Mason wasn't holding a gun. There was no mistaking his identity. His face was a slightly older, masculine version of his sister's.

"Lion O'Brien, I presume?"

The man winced and gestured at the shotgun. "Liam, yeah. Could you put that thing down? I promise, I come in peace."

Mason weighed the pros and cons of setting his weapon down. The damn thing probably wouldn't fire, but O'Brien didn't know that. Sitting down on the top of an old metal cooler, he placed the gun across his lap, figuring that was a good compromise. It no longer pointed at anyone, but its presence lent him a measure of security, even if it was false. Priss, he was happy to note, had already lowered the pistol.

"Liam was just about to explain what he's doing here." Priss glared at her brother.

Mason rocked back and forth as the frigid temperature of the metal cooler breached the thin fabric of his pants. "Like you don't already know."

Priss whirled toward him in her low seat, sending dust motes flying.

"I have no idea what he's doing here."

He laughed. "Un-uh. I'm not falling for that wide-eyed, innocent look of yours anymore."

A flush appeared above the collar of her jacket and flooded her high cheekbones. She wore a similar, rosy glow when they made love—a glow he wouldn't be seeing again.

Because he wasn't falling for any more mind-melting sex, either.

"Look, I realize I'm not calling the shots here, but could we go over to the cabin? It was quite a hike from the chopper, and I'm freezing. That wind's a bitch." O'Brien cocked an eyebrow in Mason's direction.

"You were in the chopper?" Even as he said it, Mason realized it was the only thing that made any sense. He doubted the roads were clear enough for a car yet. "Alone?"

"As good as. Like I told Priss, I made sure we weren't followed and the pilot's a trusted friend. Luke set her down, I hopped out, and he was ten miles down the road in less than five minutes."

"You didn't use the family's bird?" Priss asked.

She appeared surprised by that, but Mason didn't trust his instincts at the moment. He'd been dead wrong too many times of late.

Frowning, O'Brien turned to his sister. "Uncle Sean and I aren't exactly on friendly terms."

She raised her eyebrows. "That's why you're here? You've finally gone *mano a mano* with Uncle Sean? Damn it, Lee. You're insane."

"Lee" stamped his feet in the manner of anyone who'd been walking miles in below-freezing temperatures.

"Shit on a shingle," Mason said, under his breath. At this rate, he'd owe a fortune to his mother's swear jar. No matter what, he couldn't stop himself from thinking like a doctor. This man had hiked in the elements for several hours. Resigning himself to his fate, Mason shouldered the shotgun and stood. "Ok. Let's move this touching family reunion to the cabin." He nodded at his brother-in-law's boots. "You'll need to soak your feet in warm water. If you manage to convince me that you're not a threat, I'll even consider starting a fire." Besides, his own ass was numb with the cold now.

Priss removed her bare hands from her pockets and rubbed them together. "Yes, please." She glanced sideways at Mason, then rolled her eyes. "I can see I'm now *persona non grata*, but, for what it's worth, I'm one hundred percent surprised he's here." Turning, she gave her brother another glare.

With a sigh, Mason waved them ahead of him into the night.

****

135

"You're lucky." Mason let Liam, jeans rolled up to his knees, step back into the bathtub of warm water. His toes were beginning to turn a nice healthy pink. "I don't see any signs of frostbite. You were smart to wear wool socks and use heater packets in your boots and gloves."

Liam's wide shoulders lifted. "I'm a Boston man. I have a healthy respect for the cold." As if on cue, a blast of wind hit the side of the cabin, rattling the bathroom's small window.

"All the same, you'd be whistling another tune if you'd been out there much longer."

Holding onto a towel bar, Liam sloshed around until he faced Mason. "I know, man. And I appreciate it. The weather's far worse than predicted."

Mason nodded. At this point, he was wary of committing to much in front of his brother-in-law, even about something as benign as the weather. Turning, he ran straight into Priss, who blocked the door.

"How is he?" The concern in her eyes belied her flat tone.

"Fine. No hypothermia nor frostbite."

"That's too bad." Brushing past him, she charged at her brother and punched his upper arm, hard. The big man didn't move.

"What were you thinking, hiking all the way out here in the middle of winter? You might have died!"

"I had no choice. I need to disappear, but that takes money. Lots of it." Liam flashed a cocky smile. "Fortunately, my sister married into one of the richest families in America."

Okay. Now, Mason wanted to punch him, too.

"Oh my God! You're here for a loan. Why am I not surprised?"

"A loan?" Mason raised a skeptical eyebrow and looked at Priss. "As in, he'd pay it back?"

She pushed both her hands through her long hair, pulling it back into a ponytail before releasing it to fall down her back. "No. Not a chance."

Mason gave her props for at least one honest answer.

Liam lifted his head, and the two siblings stared at each other for a long moment, appearing even more alike than they had before, their faces filled with the same combination of distrust and stubbornness.

A pang of pure sadness stabbed Mason, at this glimpse of what it meant to be an O'Brien. He trusted his brothers with his life and couldn't imagine the loneliness of growing up without anyone in your corner. He wasn't ready to forgive Priss for helping her brother, but he understood why she still sought a connection with her only sibling. Family was as vital as breathing.

None of that helped him at the moment, of course. Liam's sudden arrival changed things, and not for the better. The mobster said he wasn't followed, claimed he only wanted money, but Mason didn't trust that answer without a polygraph test. It might be a trap, designed to lure them into false security so Liam could get his hands on the Gutenberg. If it came down to their lives or the Bible, Mason's family would hand the damn thing over, but then what? Didn't he and Priss already, in words straight out of a bad mobster movie, "know too much"?

You can't go back, you can only go forwarder. His mother's favorite old saying had never been truer. And while he still argued that "forwarder" shouldn't be a real word, that was exactly what he'd do—press on. Carefully.

Priss lowered her hands to her hips as she transferred

her attention to him. Her distrust was gone, but the stubbornness remained. "So what's next?"

I have no fucking idea.

Another gust of wind rattled the windowpanes. It would be dawn soon, but the roads would be unpassable for hours, if not days. "For the moment, we can't do much of anything. With all that new snow, even a polar bear couldn't get through." He tilted his head toward his brother-in-law. "Much as I'd love to haul his ass to a police station."

"Hey!" Water dotted the floor as Liam took a step out of the tub. Mason had to give it to him. The man had a mean glower, but Mason had two older brothers, so this wasn't his first rodeo when it came to intimidation tactics.

"I came here for help." Liam poked Mason in the shoulder as he wiped his feet on the bathmat. "You're my only shot at getting out of this mess, at finally escaping the family and living my own life."

Mason took a step forward. "I don't give even a flying—"

"Please," Priss interrupted Mason with a hand on his chest. "Don't go to the police. Not yet… Not until we weigh all our options."

Mason frowned. Liam could go to hell, but the miserable look in Priss' eyes made him pause.

She kept her gaze trained on her brother. "For what it's worth, I believe him."

Mason ran a hand through his hair. *That makes one of us.* "I'll call Jeep at the usual time and get his take," he relented. "After that, no promises."

Priss gave him a half smile. Then she stepped back until she leaned against the bathroom wall. "I need you to know I had nothing to do with this. He dropped a tracker into my doodling pen. That's how he found us."

Exhaustion washed over him. Did he believe her? He understood family loyalty, but he and she were family, too.

Or had been.

He plucked the shotgun from its perch by the door. "I'll go start the fire." *Before my head explodes.* Shouldering the weapon, he looked past Priss to his brother-in-law. "I'll be keeping this bad boy close, so don't get any ideas."

Liam fired up his glare again.

"No worries. I'll make sure he behaves."

Mason caught the flash of steel as Priss withdrew the pistol from her sweatshirt's large front pocket.

She shrugged. "I said I believed him. I didn't say I was stupid."

Chapter Twelve

Priss frowned at her reflection in the steamy bathroom mirror. One of her favorite memories from childhood was of Saturday morning television, watching ancient Laurel and Hardy shorts with her father, who otherwise had little to do with his daughter. While many of the punchlines slid past her, the black-and-white footage of the duo never failed to make her father laugh. There was one line of Oliver Hardy's that resonated with her now: *This is another fine kettle of fish you've gotten us into, Stanley.*

Except Liam hadn't gotten them into a kettle of fish, he'd tipped them into the damn ocean. He'd been on thin ice with Uncle Sean ever since their father's death, but he'd always been smart enough to maintain his usefulness, ensuring his own safety. Now, given his open betrayal, all bets were off.

The sudden gurgle of the tub emptying drew her gaze back to her brother. Perching on the side of the bath, he slipped on the thick pair of socks Mason had provided. Finished, he rested his hands on his knees and gave her an expectant look.

She rubbed a hand along her forehead. "Don't look to me for any answers, because I've got nothing."

It was the plain, unvarnished truth. She, who'd reinvented herself more than once, had no idea how to help her brother do the same. His past was too murky, and there were too many people who wanted a piece of him—not just their uncle, but that Bannion guy, the Feds, and heaven knew who else.

It was a formidable group.

Sighing, she pushed away from the vanity and walked back into the great room, leaving Lee to follow or not. The cabin had warmed up, thanks to the fire crackling away in the hearth, but there was no sign of Mason. The door to his bedroom was shut and the shotgun's spot above the mantel remained empty. Relief swept through her. More than anything, she needed to think, free from snarky comments and talk of notifying the authorities.

She hadn't ruled that out. The Feds had offered her Witness Protection, and they might extend the same to Lee. After all, he knew more than she did. However, her father's brutal death had taught her one thing. Until they knew who they could trust, they needed to steer clear of both the cops and the Feds.

The weight of the gun in her pocket stretched her sweatshirt uncomfortably and she longed to set it aside. In her heart, she didn't believe her brother would hurt her or Mason and, as she'd noted earlier, Liam appeared more desperate than threatening. In fact, his crushed vibe was borderline freaking her out. No matter how tough the times, a lifetime of training had always meant he managed to at least *act* like a tough guy.

However, the weapon gave her the upper hand, a position she'd rarely experienced when it came to her brother. She wasn't quite ready to relinquish that yet. Starting toward the couch, she changed course to the kitchen. The tangled bedclothes on their makeshift bed conjured up memories she needed to avoid just now.

Making coffee wasn't much of an escape, but at least it gave her something to do.

Liam followed, filling the cramped space in the same manner the Hughes men did. No wonder she'd been so at home with her husband's oversized family.

"So you're on Uncle Sean's shit list. What else is new?"

The question didn't appear to faze him. "Sean's the least of my worries right now."

She spooned some coffee into the basket of the percolator before glancing his way again. "Bannion?"

He nodded. "I've managed to get sideways with the world's most ruthless black-market antiquities dealer." Cursing, he folded onto one of the island stools. "None of this was supposed to happen."

She twisted on a burner. "The good old O'Brien luck strikes again." Although, to be fair, this was more of an O'Brien bad choice. "I hope to hell no one knows you're up here."

"I told you. I wasn't followed."

He ran a hand through his dark hair. It was longer and shaggier than when she'd last seen him, and his face was haggard, his cheeks hollow beneath a couple of days' scruff.

"When did you last sleep?"

Mason's door banged open, and the sound reverberated in the high-ceilinged room, swallowing her brother's answer. Liam straightened on his stool as the level of testosterone flying around shot into the stratosphere.

Reaching across the counter, she patted her brother's forearm. "Save the pissing match for when this is all over. Right now, we have bigger things to think about."

Liam's lips flattened into a frown, but he nodded once.

Mason gathered up the mess by the fireplace and heaved the mattress back into his room. A minute later, he reappeared, the old shotgun in tow once again.

"Everything okay out here?" he asked. His stance mirrored the tension in the room. No cat had ever looked so ready to pounce.

"We're fine." She took a good look at both men. *Geez. If looks could kill.* Figuring Mason was the least hardheaded of the two, she shot him a pleading look. "May I have some time alone with my brother?"

"I don't know." Indecision hovered in Mason's stormy blue eyes. "Do you think that's wise?"

Liam slid around on the stool. "C'mon, man. I'm not going to hurt her. She's my sister."

Mason remained silent, his gaze locked with hers. She touched the bulge in her sweatshirt. "Please."

After an eternity, he nodded. "Okay. But I'm leaving my door ajar." He headed back toward his bedroom, then reversed course, his attention on Liam. "If you harm one hair on her head…" Mason patted the shotgun. "I'll shoot first and ask questions later."

Priss rolled her eyes so hard it hurt. *Enough of the machismo already.* "I promise. We'll just have a harmless sibling chat." She shooed Mason away with her hand.

He retreated into his bedroom where, good as his word, he left the door open about six inches. Grabbing a pair of mugs, Priss plunked them down next to the stove, desperate to keep her hands busy and her mind off her husband. Despite all the drama, it hadn't escaped her that, if they hadn't been so rudely interrupted, she'd still be snuggled up with him, basking in the afterglow of their lovemaking and pretending that maybe, just maybe, their relationship could survive this test.

Instead, she was standing here staring at the man who'd brought six kinds of trouble raining down on their heads.

Damn it, Lee.

She should have run from the start. High-tailed it to Whereverville when Lee first suggested chatting up Mason Hughes. Instead, she'd snatched at a happiness she'd understood, deep down, wasn't in the cards.

Within minutes, the percolating coffee's rich aroma mingled with the scent of the burning wood in the fireplace. A cozy setting, except for the thundercloud of danger hanging over them. She poured the steaming brew into the waiting mugs and placed them, along with the jar of powdered creamer and a few sugar packets, onto a metal tray decoupaged with large cabbage roses. Recognizing it as a craft her mother-in-law had demonstrated on a national morning show, the tray's cheeriness clashed violently with her mood. Ignoring the bold colors, she carried it over to the island and sat down on the empty stool.

Inches away, Liam doctored his coffee in silence. He took his java the way their father had, with extra sugar.

Priss took a cautious sip of unadulterated coffee before clearing her throat. "So how'd you manage to get wrapped up with Jonathan Bannion in the first place?" The name alone made her hair stand on end. "Wait. Before you answer that, did you know the FBI tracked me down, back in the city? Bannion's on their radar, big time."

Three short days ago. She'd lived at least six lifetimes since then, and in one of them, she'd made glorious love with Mason.

Not helpful.

Liam set down his mug with a sigh. "Yeah, I know…" He shook his head. "I guess I'd better back up a bit. From the moment I showed Sean that interview with your brother-in-law—the one that mentions the Gutenberg—he was obsessed. Rabid. He wanted that Bible. It started me thinking."

Only by biting her tongue, hard, did Priss avoid making a smart-aleck comment about his thought processes.

"The Gutenberg was the perfect leverage. Since Dad's death, the family's been losing capital. Uncle Sean's more muscle than businessman, and he's desperate for cash right now. If I got to the Bible first, sold it to a private collector for an obscene amount, I could buy my way out. I talked to Sean, and he agreed. For half of the take, he'd let me go, free and clear."

Priss stared at him. "And you believed him?"

Liam laughed. "Of course not! That's why I had him agree to the deal in front of the Council."

"Oh."

The Council was a brainchild of their father's, a sort of watchdog group he'd set up in his will that, to some degree, had Lee's back. Comprised of the five men Seamus O'Brien had been closest to, excluding both Liam and Sean, the Council held a great deal of power. In short, they knew where the bodies were buried and, in case of emergency, they could make or break anyone in the family, even the Skipper himself. And Sean O'Brien knew it.

"Did the Council have any issues with your exit strategy?"

Liam shook his head. "No. I think, in a way, they were relieved. No one's said anything, but I think they've been worried about Sean's ambition. Worried about me. If I'm out, it simplifies things."

Priss thought for a moment. "That makes sense. But if you made it legit with Uncle Sean, why's he so angry now?"

"That's where Bannion comes in."

A bad feeling came over her as she gave her brother the side-eye. "Oh no. You didn't…"

Liam grimaced. "I sort of contacted Bannion without telling Uncle Sean. And I sort of negotiated a deal that was more, um…personally beneficial."

"You cut out Uncle Sean?" Priss shoved him with both hands, almost knocking him off his stool. "Do you have a death wish?"

Once he'd reseated himself, he raised his hands. "I know. Stupid. But it's so much money, Priss! I'd be set for the rest of my life."

"Yeah, with a price on your head!"

Liam shrugged. "I've had a fake identity in the works for a long time. It's rock solid, completely untraceable. And, let's face it, not being an O'Brien isn't all bad. Look at you."

She shook her head. Of all the asinine things her brother had ever said, that took the cake. "You're wrong. If there's one thing I've learned, it's that you can't outrun the family name. It always comes back to bite you in the ass."

****

Mason couldn't believe what he was hearing. Or overhearing. He tiptoed away from the wall of his closet and stretched out on the unmade bed. He and his brothers had discovered long ago that there was no privacy in the cabin. It was a cinch to eavesdrop on anyone if you knew where to place your ear. The kitchen backed up to his closet—he'd heard everything Priss and her brother had discussed. Underworld crime kingpins, mob bosses…the freaking Council. He had a first-class imagination, and he couldn't have made this up if he tried.

Yet Priss was in there talking about it like it was just another day. From the start, they'd been polar opposites. It was a large part of why they'd clicked. But this? This went beyond opposite. This was that crazy parallel universe again.

It pissed him off. But, at the same time, it made him ache. Not in a physical way, although the red-hot attraction was always there, simmering away like his mother's Sunday gravy. This ache was soulful. He longed to correct the wrongs of her past, give her a sense of safety and belonging that her messed-up childhood hadn't. He wanted to believe in the commitment they'd made a few short months ago and recapture the conviction that what they had was a forever kind of love.

These wants, though, were mixed with a healthy dose of fear. He was afraid of the bad guys, sure. Who wouldn't be? But he was also afraid to let Priss in again, only to have her lie to him, leave him, or both. He was still reeling from the last six weeks. To put his heart in jeopardy one more time would be as foolish as crossing a street without looking both ways.

It has nothing to do with whether I know how to fight or not. I could, but I choose not to. Self-preservation was a good thing, right?

Speaking of which, just how the hell were they going to shake free of the walking liability that had turned up on their doorstep?

It was Liam who really fueled Mason's ire. How dare he put his sister in danger like this? Of all the idiot moves! Snow or no snow, the man deserved to be dumped at the nearest police station. With him in custody, the whole mess went away. But Priss might never speak to Mason again if he acted on this impulse.

Which shouldn't matter to him if he was ending the relationship.

If. Uttering something between a curse and a sob, Mason rolled onto his side.

Shiny silver snowflakes. Right now, he could either work with Priss or against her. It was one hell of a choice.

****

"Listen to me. Mason's a good man, the absolute best. He won't throw you to the wolves. I'll make sure of it. And with the Council on your side, you've now got a measure of protection."

"Yeah…" Folding his arms across his chest, Liam shot his sister a doubtful look. Bless her little hippie-dippie heart. She never stayed down for long. Somehow, he had to make her understand how bad things were.

"That might have worked a few years ago, but I'm pretty sure Uncle Sean has lost it. I don't know what's behind it, but these days…? He's completely paranoid. He's got the old-timers jumping through hoops. In fact, a few of them have disappeared entirely."

Priss inhaled. "What do you mean?"

He ran a hand over his three-day stubble, which was just beginning to itch. "I don't know what I mean. Paddy

Walsh supposedly moved back to Dublin, but I haven't been able to trace him, and God only knows where Mick O'Connor is."

Dismay glinted in Priss's eyes. Good. Maybe he was getting through.

"But they were Dad's closest friends. Paddy taught me how to ride a bike."

Liam nodded. "Exactly. Sean's systematically getting rid of everyone left over from Dad's reign. And rumor has it that he's expanded into drugs."

"No!" Now Priss appeared well and truly shocked. "He wouldn't. What about Uncle Kelly?"

Liam shook his head. Their father hadn't been a saint, but he'd drawn the line at drug running after his youngest brother, Kelly, died of an overdose before Liam was born.

"Sean has no problems with it. He's mad for money. For all I know, he might be making a new deal with Bannion as we speak. The Gutenberg in exchange for my ass. Then there's the Feds…" Liam bit his lip. On the one hand, Priss deserved the truth. On the other, the less she knew, the better.

Reaching over, she grabbed his forearm and shook. "I'm not five years old anymore. Tell me. Everything!"

Grunting, he gave in. "I overheard a couple of phone calls. I think Sean's drug supplier is in law enforcement. Maybe FBI."

"Are you kidding me? That's crazy. The Mob and the law don't mix, unless…" Her eyes widened, and he knew she'd completed the math.

He shifted closer, a lifetime of caution making him lower his voice. "Remember when Dad died I told you I thought Sean might have tipped off the authorities?"

"Yes, but it's a big jump from arranging for your brother to be arrested to—"

"That's the thing. I think it may go deeper than that—deeper than we ever dreamed. At Dad's wake, Paddy took me aside and swore Dad had moved away from the gun business, which was in line with everything I'd been told. The crates at that warehouse were supposed to be filled with microwave ovens, not an army's worth of AK-47s. Paddy said he would swear, when Dad pried the top off one, that the guns inside were a surprise. Within seconds, the Feds came out of nowhere and blasted him, claiming he was armed and dangerous." He raised his brows. "Dad was seventy-six years old and facing away from them. If they'd announced themselves, told him to put the gun down, he would have. There was *no reason* to use the kind of force they did." He tapped the counter for emphasis.

"Are you saying what I think you're saying?" she asked, after a long pause.

"Yes. I think Sean used the Feds as his own hit squad."

Priss blew out a long breath. "That's…terrifying. And you screwed him over. Genius."

"Believe me, I wish I'd never heard of the damn Gutenberg. I'm sorry for what it's cost you. What *I* cost you." Meeting her eyes, he willed her to believe him. If life offered do-overs, he needed about a hundred.

She waved her free hand, as if shooing aside his words. "Like I said, we've got bigger things to worry about right now. What about Witness Protection?"

He shook his head. "Un-huh. Not until I'm positive Sean doesn't have a couple of agents on the payroll." He pointed a finger at her. "You should stay clear of the Feds too, until we know they're not in Sean's pocket."

Priss ran her hands along her upper arms and gave an obvious shiver. "Shit, Lee. I'm not sure I'll ever feel completely safe again."

Chapter Thirteen

Priss ran a hand along the chinked logs of the outside wall. She'd been tucked into the bottom bunk, listening to her brother's steady, deep breathing, for more than an hour. After their long talk, Liam gobbled down a giant helping of microwaved lasagna, brushed his teeth, and crashed face first onto the top bunk in her room. He'd been asleep within seconds. She, not so much.

Witness Protection.

She'd grown up believing those were the two worst words in the English language. Yet she was still convinced that it was her best option, even if it meant severing contact with Mason forever. A tear welled, then zigzagged down her cheek and plopped onto the pillow. Like it or not, their relationship was over. Whatever hope their night together had spawned, Lee's unexpected arrival had snuffed it out in no uncertain terms.

But now there was a new doozy of a wrinkle in her master plan. If Uncle Sean had agents on his payroll, choosing WITSEC wasn't just a rash decision—it might be a downright dangerous one. There was no Rogue Agent Hotline she could call to find out if the Feds she'd be dealing with were on the up-and-up.

Then, of course, there was Lee. If the Feds got their hands on him, rogue agents or not, there was no telling what might happen. When a bona fide mobster—which, regardless of his intentions, Liam was—"turned state's," as her father used to say, it was the ultimate betrayal. Even stealing from the family didn't have the same kind of stigma attached to it. There was an almost grudging admiration when one member of the clan outsmarted another. Her father had proved bulletproof during his reign, until that final round the Feds had fired, but she'd seen shake-ups happen in other families over the years. In each case, the overall view was that if the house was in that kind of disorder, the family got what they deserved.

She rolled away from the wall and blinked into the room's inky darkness. Lee had been all kinds of stupid, but what did he deserve? At best, a clean getaway. At worst… She shivered under the heavy pile of blankets. Living on the run was better than not living at all. But, with Uncle Sean and the Feds on his tail, how long could Lee stay safe?

She'd been where her brother was now, convinced that the edited version of her past would withstand the future.

It hadn't.

Shelving her what-ifs for a moment, she propped herself up on an elbow and lifted the corner of the plaid curtain that covered the bedroom window. The wind had died down, leaving behind the utter stillness of a snow-covered world. Despite some warmth wafting through the open doorway, the bedroom remained chilly, and the bottom of the window was etched with a million tiny snowflakes. Against the yellowish-gray light of predawn, the frost resembled nature's own version of stained glass. Absently, she scratched her initials in the ice, wondering if Mason was awake and whether he'd continue to hole up in his bedroom, with only the ancient shotgun for company.

P.H. + M.H.

Sighing, she let the curtain obscure what she'd written—what her *heart* had written—on the glass. The ache she'd stiff-armed for the past several hours returned with a vengeance. Lying back, she tugged the mussed covers up to her ears and curled up in the fetal position.

There was just no hope for her brother. Unless…

The rap on the door jamb was so soft, she wondered if she'd dreamt it.

"Priss? You awake?" Mason's whisper carried across the darkness.

"Yes." She kept her answer short, not quite trusting her voice.

She heard the soft scuffs of his socked feet as he advanced into the room. "If the plan was for you O'Briens to murder me in my bed, you've missed your chance," he whispered, *sans* malice, before kneeling beside the bed.

A whiff of minty toothpaste and lemony soap sent her heartbeat skittering. First thing in the morning, her husband was hard to resist.

And midmorning, lunchtime, midafternoon…

"No one's getting murdered, in or out of bed," she said, around a yawn. *Although if Uncle Sean sends one of his goon squads after us, all bets are off.*

"From your lips to God's ear, as Mum says."

The pep in his voice increased her urge to retreat under the covers again. A consummate morning person, he sounded as if he had slept the whole night away, instead of a mere few hours. Raising a hand, she checked her own breath while smothering another yawn. *Ew.*

"So what's the plan?" she asked, into her palm.

"I'm due to speak with Jeep in about an hour. In the meantime, give me the gun and I'll take over the watch. I'm recharged now."

Uh-oh. Priss bit her lip. Apparently, Mason was still operating under the assumption that her brother was dangerous. She, on the other hand, had ruled that out hours ago. Halfway through their chat, he'd admitted he would have exposed her true identity to the Hugheses, but that was where he drew the line. Of course, it stung that he'd been willing to torpedo her happiness. However, when she held that in comparison to the actions of the previous generation, she had no real complaints. Lee'd sworn up, down, and sideways that he would never, *ever* hurt her, Mason, or anyone else, which put him one up on Uncle Sean.

Shoving aside those thoughts, she refocused on Mason. "You hate guns and are a lousy shot."

"True. However, courtesy of my well-trained mind, I slept like a log the past three hours. Did you?"

Despite herself, Priss grinned. He was adorable. "I'm not sure mastering the art of sleeping anywhere and under any condition makes for a 'well-trained mind,' but I get your point. No, I haven't slept."

"Who could, with a snoring mobster in the bunk above them?" Once again, the teasing tone took the sting out of his words.

"I assume *you* could, given that well-trained mind of yours."

His smile flashed in the grayness. "Touché. But my point still stands. Loaded guns are not for the sleep-deprived. Now, hand it over. I'll keep an eye on your brother while you get some sleep."

"Mace." The nickname slipped out, suggestive of the intimacy they'd shared last night...and would never share again. "I understand why you're cautious where Lee is concerned, but believe me, he has no desire to hurt either one of us. In fact, it's just the opposite. We're his only chance."

"That doesn't make me feel better." He still whispered, but all teasing had left his voice. "If we're his only chance, it doesn't sound like he has much to lose."

Okay, he had her there. She covered her face with both hands before kicking aside the bedclothes. "Oh, damn, it's cold." Feeling around, she grabbed the extra sweatshirt she'd stashed under the covers and tugged it on. "We need to talk."

In one fluid motion, he stood. That innate gracefulness of his only made it hurt more when she banged her head on the bottom bunk. *Screw it.* No one had, or would ever, accuse her of being graceful. She withdrew the gun from the bedside dresser before following Mason out into the great room. He gestured toward the open bedroom door behind her, and she pulled it shut, smothering the sound of her brother's snores.

Crossing the room, she made a show of setting the gun behind a stack of books on the mantel. Mason nodded in approval. The weapon was out of sight, but within easy reach. Not that she expected to need it unless they received uninvited visitors. "What's the plan?"

Lips pursed, he placed a bigger log on the fledgling fire, then another, seemingly oblivious to the angry pops and spits he stirred up. If it was his intention to get a rise out of her, he was succeeding. She was ten seconds shy of screaming in frustration when he turned and met her gaze.

"I think we need to return to civilization. And I think we need to involve the authorities." He raised a hand before she could protest. "Jeep will vet them in advance and make sure they're clean."

His words pricked, like a thousand little blowgun darts, but could she blame him? She released a measured breath, reminding herself that in his world, good and evil had always been stark contrasts.

He plopped down on a wing chair and sat, leaning toward her, elbows on his knees, hands clasped together. "I know it's tough, turning in your brother, but by his own admission, he's a hunted man. What other choice do we have?"

"Ha!" Hugging herself, she stared up at the ceiling. Rough log beams crisscrossed each other, lending support to the cabin's tin roof. *Support.* For all those years, Liam was the only support she'd known. He wasn't perfect—not by a long shot—but he'd given her his best effort. She'd do the same in return.

All she had to do was convince Mason to go along with her crazy-ass plan.

She sank down on the couch and stared into the fire. "Liam wants protection, and if half of what he says is true, he needs it."

Mason nodded. "I agree, and the Feds can provide that—it's what they do. They offered you Witness Protection and you've been away from the family for what? Ten years or more? They'd be winning the lottery with your brother."

Priss clenched her fists. He just didn't get it. "You're assuming he'd live to tell them anything."

Mason waggled his head in something between a

shake and a nod. "True. But if—and it's only an 'if' right now—there are rogue agents connected to your uncle in the FBI, they're few and far between." He straightened in the chair and glanced at the fire, which answered his look with a few staccato pops. "Look, Priss, I understand. Regardless of what he's mixed up in, Liam's your brother. You love him and you don't want to see him hauled away in handcuffs. But the truth of the matter is that's where he's headed, what he deserves, and frankly, where he'll be the safest." The steady glint of sincerity in his eyes told her he really believed he understood.

"In all fairness, you don't know how the Mob works. With or without rogue agents, going anywhere near the Feds is a death sentence. If Lee throws himself on the agency's mercy, my uncle will find a way to get to him. Guaranteed." She stretched her double-socked feet toward the hearth, fear for her brother freezing her from the inside out. Given their tattered relationship, she wasn't certain how much she should share with Mason, but she decided to risk it. She didn't have much choice. "Don't make fun, but I'm getting another one of my feelings. You know, like my women's intuition is kicking in."

He looked down at his hands and flicked a speck of dirt off a finger. "Yeah. You got one the night Callie was kidnapped. Felt certain she'd be okay, and you were right." As he cleared his throat, his gaze met hers once again. "You also got one the night we met. Said we'd be together forever."

Ouch.

She waved that pain off. "I'm not saying I bat a thousand, but I'm more right than wrong. From the moment Liam showed up last night, I've known he was in danger. Not thrown-in-jail kind of danger. *Mortal* danger."

His brow furrowed. "What do you mean?"

"My brother has to die."

Mason had been speechless numerous times in his life, but this time took the prize. He opened his mouth, but no words came.

"Oh, my gosh." Priss laughed until she was bent over and breathless. "If you could see your expression right now. Don't tell me you took me literally!"

Gritting his teeth, he silently counted to ten. "We're hiding from the Mob and an underworld criminal mastermind. Forgive me if I'm having a little trouble separating fact from fiction right now."

"You're right. You're…right." Her expression sobered as she wiped tears away. "All three of us are in the middle of a nightmare, which is why I think Liam has to go." She raised a hand. "Not as in we kill him. As in we help him fake his death."

It was fortunate he wasn't drinking anything or he'd have spewed it everywhere. "Fake his death?" He shook his head. "This isn't a television show. People don't fake their deaths. Besides, I'm a doctor. Helping someone fake anything, even the common cold, would ruin my career."

Understanding dawned in her eyes.

"Yeah." He paused a moment, letting that truth sink in. "I was born to be a doctor, and I won't do anything to jeopardize that."

She tucked her feet up under her sweet little ass. "No, of course not. I hadn't thought—"

"No kidding." He added a heaping dose of sarcasm

in his voice.

Pouting, she rearranged the couch cushions and wiggled into a straighter position. "Don't be such a jerk. At least I came up with an idea."

"Sure." He propped his sock-covered feet on the coffee table. "A bat-shit crazy one."

"Maybe, maybe not."

Crap. He recognized that look. She was going to ride this train all the way into Crazy Town.

"Hear me out. Liam's managed to get himself on the wrong side of both the family *and* Jonathon Bannion. That translates to trouble—swimming-with-the-fishes kind of trouble. Okay." She held up both hands. "I get it. Faking his death would be a problem for you, given the oath you took. But that doesn't mean we can't help him *disappear*." Excitement flooded her face until she nearly glowed with it. "Don't you see? It's his only chance! I don't trust the Feds. It's not in my DNA. Or Liam's."

That much Mason did understand. They'd killed her father, after all. But the Feds had the resources and the manpower to unravel all of this. "Priss…Liam is a grown man. His choices will land him where they land him. My family knows a lot of people in the Justice Department. We'll put him in the hands of good people. But the chips will fall where they may." He sat back, linking his fingers over his stomach, hopeful she'd recognize his offer for what it was: generous.

Her thick, dark lashes didn't mask her skeptical look. "Let's say we turn Liam over to the Feds—the 'good' Feds," she added, with air quotes. "You know how much time they take! Liam would spend months sitting in jail, with a gigantic target on his head. I'm telling you, he has to disappear *now*."

Shifting toward the fire, Mason watched the flames lick at the dry, fat logs. By the time his brother-in-law woke up, the cabin would be nice and warm.

Didn't that just figure.

He stood up, only to realize there was no place he could go. God, hiding out was getting old.

Damn it. He owed Liam O'Brien nothing. But Priss…he owed her something for the best months of his life.

Or, maybe, he was just a sucker.

He ran a hand over his unshaved face. "I shouldn't even ask, because there is no way in hell I'm agreeing, but what exactly do you have in mind?"

Her face relaxed into a dazzling smile. It propelled him a step forward, like a moth to a flame. The sizzle between them was inescapable. Always had been, always would be.

The word "destiny" flashed into his mind with the force of a thunderbolt, leaving him shaken. So shaken, he sat back down.

Sweet heaven. He got it now.

Some things are worth fighting for.

Priss was worth fighting for. Liam? Not so much. But he couldn't have one without helping the other.

"Slimy stuttering salamanders," he muttered.

Her eyes widened in mock surprise. "Goodness! Do you kiss your mother with that mouth?"

Despite his internal chaos, Mason laughed.

"That kind of alliteration from you or your brothers is the equivalent of another man's f-bomb." She gave him a wide grin. "What prompted it?"

Right now wasn't the time to reveal that he'd figured it out. To share how, despite everything, he was still hers, body and soul. He'd fight to save their relationship *after* they figured out their Liam problem.

If it's not already too late.

He shrugged away his fear. "Nothing. Go ahead. Tell me your plan."

"It's not entirely mine. Lee helped. I mean, I'm kind of copying him. First, we get rid of all his stuff. He found me because he dropped a tracker into my doodling pen. We need to make sure someone hasn't done something similar to his gear."

Mason shook his head. His thoughts must have showed clearly on his face, because the set of Priss' chin grew even more stubborn. "I'm helping Lee, with or without you." She folded her arms across her chest.

Sighing, he rested his hands on the chair's arms and counted to ten. "Go on."

"Everything belonging to Liam O'Brien goes, until he's down to his undies." She glanced toward the fireplace. "Maybe we burn it. We probably don't have to scrub this cabin. I doubt the Feds will search it for DNA, plus I don't think it matters if they find out he was here."

Mason raised an eyebrow. "Have you been binge-watching *NCIS* again?"

Her shoulders lifted. "Maybe."

He took that as a solid "yes."

"Okay, maybe we don't have to be that extreme, but we'll need to cover our tracks from here on out. We leave here as early as possible, go back to DC, and check into a hotel somewhere. Nothing fancy. Somewhere in the suburbs, where we won't attract any notice."

She made it all sound so simple.

"And then?" He didn't quite succeed at keeping the sarcasm out of his voice.

"Then, we give him some cash and he flies away to Bora Bora or wherever. Using the identity he's been perfecting all these years."

He stared her. "Is that all?"

"There are two old friends of my father's who would help, if we can find them." Her eyes grew cloudy. "Mick and Paddy. I'm worried about them. Liam says they've disappeared. They were very kind to me when I was growing up." The corners of her mouth twitched. "They always made time for me, no matter how busy they were."

Good gravy. She'd had her brother and a couple of old mobsters for company during her childhood, and that was it. No wonder she was so loyal to her douchebag brother.

"What about a compromise? We follow your plan and hole up, outside the city, with your brother in tow. But from there, we lean on Jeep's expertise, follow his advice." Even as he said it, he knew Jeep would never consent to letting Liam escape the law, no matter what feelings were involved. He never minded being the bad guy.

That sounded like a win-win to Mason.

She narrowed her eyes. "He'll just turn him over to the authorities."

Mason made a face. She'd seen right through that plan. "Maybe. But he's the expert. I don't see a way out of here without his help."

For a long moment, she stayed silent, gnawing on her bottom lip. "Yeah. I guess we need Jeep to get us out of here, so there's not much choice. But promise me— no police and no Feds. Not until we know who we're dealing with and we *all* agree to the plan."

Now he hesitated. He wasn't keen on giving his brother-in-law any breaks. But he knew this woman, inside and out. If he didn't promise, she'd dream up a different plan—no doubt a dangerous one—that would put Hollywood writers to shame. He was prepared to fight for their marriage, but he couldn't do that if she was dead. Her safety came before anything else. If that meant making a promise he might not be able to keep, so be it.

"Deal."

She stood. "Thanks. I'll go wake Lee and share the plan." Rounding the couch, she headed toward the bedroom door, but paused with a hand on the doorknob. "Your help means a lot, Mace. I'll never forget it."

He nodded once before kicking the leg of the coffee table.

Fifty ferocious felines.

Chapter Fourteen

Liam's rhythmic snuffles still filled the air when Priss re-entered the bedroom. Dawn glowed around the curtains and she had no trouble seeing her way across to the bunks. Now that she and Mason had made some plans, the comfy pillows and tangle of blankets called to her. She stretched out on her bed, drifting back in time as she listened to her brother sleep. When she was young, middle-of-the-night thunderstorms had sent her fleeing to her brother's room in terror. Thunder would rattle the windows while lightning flashed like a strobe, and still she'd have to shake him awake. Yet he'd never uttered a word of complaint when she woke him. Instead, he'd folded back the covers, allowing her to climb in beside him, his reassuring words melting her fears and sending her back to sleep.

He'd been a good big brother, before family pressures had squashed his dreams and soured his perspective. Because of those early years, she forgave him for this mess. He deserved another chance, a shot at living his life free from Uncle Sean and other bad influences.

Thank goodness Mason had agreed to help. It made everything easier—and not just because of his family contacts. With him, she felt stronger, surer. And maybe, just maybe, when this was all over, he wouldn't despise her quite so much. He wasn't made for hate, and she wanted peace for him much more than for herself.

As a "seize the day" kind of woman, she'd never worried much about the end of things, just took it as part of the journey and kept on paddling. Mason, though, would be her first and possibly her only regret. She'd given up her oars for him and started sending down roots. Over these horrible recent weeks, those roots had dried and withered, leaving her prey to a wild, scattering wind.

She wiggled around, burrowing deeper into the blankets. Falling into a funk right now was so not helpful. Above her, Liam turned over and sighed.

"Priss?" His voice was groggy with sleep.

She moved to the edge of her mattress. He leaned over the edge of his. "Yep. I'm here." It was a curious role reversal, playing the protector when he'd held that job for so long.

Grunting, he rolled out of sight. "What time is it?"

She could just make out the luminous hands of the old alarm clock on the table beside her. "It's early. Six-oh-seven. It'll be a while before we can go anywhere, so we might as well go back to sleep."

"Go? Where? It's nice and safe here. As long as there's food and firewood, I'm in no hurry to leave."

Priss lifted her legs in the air, covers and all, and rammed the middle of Liam's mattress.

"Hey!"

She didn't apologize. It hadn't been much of a jolt, and it had felt good. "You don't have any say in the matter. Mason and I have made plans. We're going back to DC."

He hung over the edge again. "Are you crazy? I told you, Bannion is a bad dude. We're talking a psycho-killer, and he seriously wants to find my ass."

"I know. I think he's the one who shot at Mason and me. Arranged it, anyway. I guess it could have been Uncle Sean, but it lacked his signature…tidiness. It was impetuous, wild. I think it was Bannion."

The bunk protested as Liam climbed down the ladder and plopped down at the foot of her bed. So much for a nap.

"I agree. It was Bannion. That proves my point. We're better off staying up here until the Feds get him and I have a clear escape plan."

Priss shimmied upright, fluffing the pillow against the headboard before she leaned back. "Now who's talking crazy? That could take months, maybe longer. Besides, you don't trust the Feds any more than I do. Neither does Mason." That was stretching it a bit. Her husband had no beef with law enforcement, but the moment called for some poetic license. "Besides, we're tired of waiting. Sometimes you have to make things happen. And we're going to make you disappear."

Liam nudged her with his foot. "And just what does that mean?"

"Just what it sounds like. We'll go back to DC and help you escape without a trace."

He shook his head. "I'm a dead man the second I leave this place."

She waved off his negativity. "Not if we do this smart. It might be WITSEC, if we can vet the Feds, or it might be smuggling you out of the country. I don't know yet. But you have my promise—and Mason's—that nothing happens without your approval." Her weary muscles protested as she leaned forward. "Think about it, Lee. Either way, you get a fresh start. New name, new life, a chance to thrive on your own, for the first time."

Liam picked at the top quilt. "First of all, I can't believe your sainted husband and his family have agreed to help. Second, what about cash?"

This time, Priss kicked out, nailing him in the thigh. "Ouch!"

"You deserved it. Cash, my hiney. You'd better kiss any dreams of a life of leisure goodbye. Your head will stay attached to your shoulders, and that's more than enough. As for the Hugheses, you'd be amazed at what that family can make happen. They're the most generous, genuine, warmhearted people I've ever met. They'll help you because family is everything to them." A lump rose in her throat as she realized, once again, how close she'd become to her in-laws. Their wholehearted acceptance had increased the sense of rightness and belonging she'd experienced with Mason.

Liam shook his head. "They may be the best thing since sliced bread, but your father-in-law is Chief Justice of the Supreme Court. I don't care what your husband says. Helping Seamus O'Brien's son will not look good on his dad's resume. Face it, sister dear. We're on our own."

The words hit her with the force of a semi. Was he right? Had Mason simply told her what she wanted to hear in order to keep her from going rogue? She couldn't deny it—every now and then, his overdeveloped desire to help morphed into an attempt to control, prompting her to call him on it before things got too far. She hadn't willingly taken orders since she was sixteen.

"No." She shook her head, putting more force behind the word than she felt. "Look at me. Six hours with you and I'm already distrusting everyone's motives. Mason's not an O'Brien. He's trustworthy. This will go down without law enforcement. Unless we know they're legit and can guarantee your safety."

But, in a tiny corner of her mind, a question played on repeat.

Are you sure?

****

"You promised *what*?"

Mason lifted the phone away from his ear. Jeep was a loud talker at the best of times. When pissed, he was downright deafening.

"I told her we'd keep law enforcement out of it for now." Mason's words vaporized into the cold air as soon as he voiced them. He sat on the old porch bench, enjoying both the privacy and the feeble sun.

On the other end of the line, Jeep whistled. "Well, you've already fucked that up. I *am* law enforcement, or the next thing to it."

Mason toed at a patch of ice and zipped his jacket up to his chin. He was freezing, but he preferred to have this conversation outside the cabin. "As an attorney, you're an officer of the court, but you're not exactly law enforcement. Besides, you're family, so you don't count."

Jeep grunted. "That's both semantics and wishful thinking. I've already been in contact with the Feds. As soon as weather permits, we're storming the cabin."

Mason shot to his feet. "No way. That sounds like a great way for someone to get hurt, or worse, plus I promised Priss. No Feds until we say so. Once we're in the city, we can huddle up and figure out the next step. I think Liam might be open to Witness Protection if we know the Feds are honest—"

"Yeah, about that," Jeep cut in. "I'm not sure I buy

the whole dirty-agent bit. At least, not on Liam O'Brien's say-so. I've done some homework, and everyone connected to this case looks clean."

Mason pinched the bridge of his nose and sighed into the freezing air. Life wasn't supposed to be this complicated. "Okay. I guess that's good news. Priss and Liam seem convinced, but they're predisposed to hate all Feds. Not without reason, I might add. Their father's death was brutal, to say the least."

The sound of papers being shuffled came over the line. Was Jeep at his desk in his office? That was impossible for Mason to picture, and not just because Jeep was, to his core, a man of action. No one in the family knew exactly what he did. He evaded questions about his job, citing security issues, and the exact place and scope of his work remained vague. Mason and the rest of his family assumed it was at JAG's Virginia headquarters, but it could be at the Pentagon or on the moon, for all they knew. Once again, Mason was struck by just how cagey his oldest brother was. Adam wrote about a spy while Jeep acted like one.

Jeep muttered a string of curses that would have set their mother's hair on fire. "Yeah, that was a shit storm and a half. Tell you what. I'll give you twenty-four hours to come up with something we can present to the Feds, starting now."

Relief swept Mason from head to toe. That was twenty-four more hours than he'd thought Jeep would agree to. "Thanks, I owe you one."

Jeep laughed. "As I've said before, I'll add it to your tab."

"I hear you. What time do you think you'll be here to pick us up?"

"We're going to try and get a helo in there by sixteen hundred hours."

Mason rolled his eyes at his brother's use of military time and did some quick math. "So, ten hours from now." It was a little longer than he'd hoped for, but it would have to do. "Wait, why a helo? And who in the hell are 'we'? The fewer people who know about this, the better."

"Number one, the snow's up past my ass and it's not safe to drive. Two, me and a few other guys. Washington and Adams. And three, they are completely trustworthy."

Mason laughed. "Washington and Adams. Seriously? You and your nicknames."

"It's no joke. Jamal Washington and Bryce Adams. Good guys. Former-SEALs. They've helped me out before."

"Let me guess, their call signs were 'George' and 'John,' " Mason said.

Jeep's bark of laughter had Mason lifting the phone again. "Nope. 'Buzz' and 'Nutter,' but I won't say why. Collectively we call them 'The Beatles,' so you're kind of right."

"The Beatles?" It took Mason a moment, then he chuckled. "Right. George and John." Sometimes he envied the camaraderie his brother enjoyed with his Navy friends. Then he imagined the hellish situations that had forged those friendships, and his jealousy vanished.

"Once we've picked you up, we'll fly to a small, private airport just outside DC. I'll set you up in a hotel that's remote, but not too remote. I imagine you're tired of eating out of a can by now. Mum made her signature chicken last night and I ate three helpings, plus dessert."

That was easily the longest string of complete sentences Mason had heard from his brother in years. "We haven't exactly been eating out of can, but I wouldn't say no to a good burger. Just to be clear, you aren't bringing any Feds with you, right?"

"Copy that. But I'll say it again. Chances are O'Brien will wind up with the Feds before nightfall. I think it's his best chance."

Mason didn't argue. Priss' hopes aside, he understood there was no fairytale ending to this story. "As of right now, I want it to be Liam's choice." Unless his brother-in-law did something stupid—something *else* stupid. Then all bets were off.

Jeep grunted. "I'll call you at fifteen hundred with details. Phone off until then."

"Will do," Mason said, but the line had already gone dead. He powered down the phone and leaned forward, resting his forearms on the porch railing, soaking up the sun's warmth. His chest tightened as he gazed out at the postcard perfect view.

For thirty-plus years, life had been black-and-white for him. Do good. Steer clear of bad. Like his brothers had said, it had always been that easy. But now, his love for Priss had him leaning into that gray area, if not crossing into the black, with zero assurances he'd get the girl in the end.

What did he know about Liam O'Brien? That he was a mobster and a con man. Not the greatest of recommendations.

Someone could get hurt.

He sure as hell hoped it wasn't Priss…or himself.

Chapter Fifteen

Priss had never ridden in a helicopter before, but she could learn to like it. It was a small craft, cramped in the back seat, but she was by a window. Mountains, towns, cities. In a helicopter, you enjoyed a unique view of them, and she welcomed the sense of insignificance the expansive view of the countryside triggered. She was one human being in an ocean of billions, each warring against life's undertow. Granted, most weren't battling a mix of O'Briens, Feds, and underworld art dealers, but she embraced the feeling of solidarity anyway.

Beside her, Liam radiated stress. He hadn't been too excited about meeting another Hughes—especially one who happened to be a former SEAL—and remained worried that the whole thing was a trap. As she studied her brother-in-law's rugged profile, Priss admitted it could be. Jeep bent the rules, but only when it led to a by-the-book outcome. Had her desire to get her brother out of harm's way caused her to jump the gun? Sighing, she looked down at her wedding band. It wasn't the first time she'd dived in headfirst. "Impulsive" was her middle name. But she trusted Mason, and it was too late to pump the brakes now.

In front of her, a soft-spoken man Jeep called Buzz sat in the pilot's seat. Jeep sat next to him, on a jury-rigged jump seat with a harness seatbelt that had been bolted to the floor, while their co-pilot, a smiley man called Nutter, sat in the passenger seat on Jeep's right. All three wore headsets, so they could communicate over the loud hum of the rotors. Not that they had said much. By her count, each man had spoken all of five words total in the forty-five minutes they'd been in the air. However, that was typical of her brother-in-law, who never spoke three words when two would do.

Priss was still hazy on what the plan was once they reached their hotel. Liam needed money, and he needed a destination—as far away as possible. Someplace overseas would be ideal. The long arms of Clan O'Brien stretched throughout the U.S., but even her ambitious uncle had yet to make inroads internationally. If Sean was really running drugs, it might be best to avoid a couple of countries, but for the most part, Liam could take his pick. Extradition wasn't a huge concern since he swore his cover was rock solid. She didn't know how he created aliases and backstories that could withstand background searches, and she didn't want to know. Her own whitewashed history had passed scrutiny for years, only breaking down under Jeep's bad-ass, military-grade digging.

In fact, given that she was difficult to trace, it was possible that, with Liam holed up somewhere safe and the bad guys neutralized, she wouldn't need Witness Protection. Despite herself, she couldn't shake the feeling that there was something suspicious about Young and Peters. Was that just her long-standing distrust of law enforcement, or something more? From the mists of memory, another one of her father's rules floated to the surface. It was short and sweet and had given her plenty of laughs in the past: *Know who you climb in bed with.*

She stole a glance at Mason. *If only climbing in bed*

was an option. It would make for one hell of a tension breaker.

The persistent fear that the bottom was going to fall out at any minute was giving her a first-class headache. She leaned back against the seat and tilted her face toward the window again. She'd be better off sticking to sightseeing right now.

Before long, pastureland morphed into the unmistakable web of interstate leading into DC. Another few minutes and she spotted the pyramid-shaped tip of the Washington Monument, pointing toward the dusky spring sky like an arrow on a giant weather map.

"There's the city," she yelled to her fellow backseaters.

Liam and Mason simply shrugged, then eyed one another with suspicion. Again.

She rolled her eyes. *Men. Such children.*

Leaning forward, she began ticking off buildings. "There's the Capitol's dome, the Supreme Court building, and…is that the *Statue of Liberty*?" She glanced back at her husband and brother once more.

Nothing. They were still too busy glaring at each other.

Idiots.

Good thing she didn't mind entertaining herself. The nearer they got to the city, the more she recognized. Seeing it from above was truly something, with the entire grid of DC stretched out before her like a giant quilt.

But her tour didn't last. In another minute, the helicopter banked, drawing away from the city, toward the suburbs. They were headed for the Maryland side, but that was all she could decipher.

As the aircraft turned, the pounding in her head

pulsed faster. For a split second, she fantasized about running again. Skipping the painful goodbye. Why not? Liam would be gone in a few short days. The Gutenberg was, as her mother-in-law would say, "safe as houses," a British expression that never failed to make Priss smile, since houses were broken into all the time. Would it really be a big deal if she left right after her brother did?

Out of the corner of her eye, she spotted Mason stretching his arms over his head, something she'd seen countless times since they married. The simple movement assured her she'd stay right where she was. A week, one day…hell, even one hour… She'd take whatever time she got with him by her side.

The decision didn't calm her nerves. Instead, she couldn't quite shake the feeling that, like a character from an old Saturday morning cartoon, someone was lying in wait, ready to drop a piano on her head.

O'Brien luck. It always had her waiting for the other shoe to drop, even when both her feet were well shod and there wasn't a shoe store in sight.

"Almost there," Jeep shouted from the front while pointing at the ground. Buzz spoke into his microphone a time or two and, after a moment or two of heart-racing hovering, set the mechanical bird down in what appeared to be a small airfield. Beside the helipad, various runways crisscrossed one another, dotted here and there with small planes. The only buildings were a couple of huge hangers, a smaller terminal building, and an ancient, glass-topped tower that sprouted from the end of one runway like a giant mushroom.

They remained where they were while Buzz and Nutter busied themselves with numerous switches and the rotors slowed to a stop. Then, as if by some unspoken signal, Jeep and the pilots removed their headphones and fist bumped each other before Jeep turned and gave them the thumbs-up signal. In seconds, Priss had the copter's door open. A gust of cold wind welcomed her back to civilization and tugged at her clothes and hair as she jumped down onto the pavement.

Her teeth chattered as they stood in the twilight, chatting with the pilots. Both men had relaxed into an unexpected friendliness now that they had returned to earth. Must be that military training, Priss figured. No socializing while on the job. Finally, after another round of smiles and thanks, they headed into the terminal. The building was old and redolent with the smell of recent meals, but Priss welcomed the blast of central heat. However, in less than five seconds, she decided that, aside from the temperature, things didn't feel right.

In less than five more seconds, she understood why.

Four men and one woman, all wearing the prerequisite dark suits, fanned out before them, blocking their path. Two of the men were familiar: Peters and Young. The other three were unknown, but it was clear they shared the same occupation.

Whirling around, she shoved Mason back a step. "You bastard! We had a deal."

He encircled her wrists before she could shove him again. The look of surprise that he and Jeep exchanged didn't fool her one bit.

"Priss, I swear—"

Lee's string of Gaelic curses drowned out the rest of Mason's words. The stricken look on her brother's face tore at Priss' heart. *Know who you climb in bed with.*

She yanked free of Mason's grasp.

Peters stepped forward, a pair of handcuffs dangling

from one hand. "Liam O'Brien, you're under arrest for suspected money laundering, tax evasion, and wire fraud."

"Just to mention a few." Agent Young laughed at his own joke.

Lee shot her an "I told you so" look as Peters turned him around, cuffed him, and read him his Miranda rights. His dejected image seared itself in her brain.

"Lee... Come on. Is this really necessary?" Her brother wouldn't run now, not when he was surrounded by agents with guns. He wouldn't want to end up like their father.

Peters didn't spare her a glance as he grabbed Liam by the shoulders and perp-walked him toward a side exit.

Utter helplessness swamped her as she watched her brother being led away. It was unreal. A nightmare. A complete betrayal.

But by whom?

"Follow Agent Peters, please," Young said, spreading his arms to usher them toward the same set of automatic glass doors. "We've got vehicles ready to take us down to headquarters."

"Priss—" Mason set a hand on her shoulder.

She waved him off and they were herded through the exit doors and out into a large parking lot. Two huge black SUVs stood at the fire curb, doors open, drivers at the wheels. Peters and Liam climbed into the second vehicle while Young waved Jeep, Mason, and Priss to the first one.

"I'm going with my brother," she said, on a wave of false bravado. She jutted her chin toward Mason and Jeep. "You two Judases can ride together."

"Damn it, Priss," Mason began, running a hand

through his hair. "You've got it all—"

But she didn't wait to hear the rest. Instead, she hopped into the back of the second car and shut the door.

As she fumbled for the seatbelt, Liam sat rock still next to her, staring straight ahead.

"Lee, I—"

The cuffs jangled as adjusted his hands. "Please, spare me the apologies."

Sighing, she clicked her seatbelt into the buckle and lowered her head into her hands. Another bit of her father's wisdom drifted back to her with a vengeance.

Just when you think it can't get worse, it will.

****

The only thing that would make Mason feel worse right now was if one of the stoic FBI agents in the front seat opened fire. Short of getting shot, there was no way his pain level could get any greater.

He skewered his brother with a nasty stare across the expansive back seat. "What in the hell just happened?"

Jeep met his gaze with a brief shake of his head. "Un-uh. This isn't me. I gave you twenty-four hours." He glanced at his watch. "You still have eleven and a half left."

Mason studied his brother's face. As far as he knew, neither of his brothers had ever lied to him—not when they were kids; not even when it hurt. "Then, I repeat, what in the hell just happened?"

Jeep tugged at his seatbelt before shifting sideways. "Don't know," he whispered, into Mason's ear. "My guess is our friends here," he flicked a thumb toward the front seat, "have been tracking Liam."

Mason shut his eyes against the pain that stabbed at his midsection. "Priss will never believe it wasn't us…*Me*."

Jeep rested a heavy hand on his shoulder and squeezed. "I guess you'll have to fight to make her believe it."

Opening his eyes, Mason met Jeep's calm, unblinking gaze. His brother had a way of making the most difficult of tasks seem easy. Hands down his most annoying quality.

"If it makes you feel any better," Jeep said, with the air of one who knows it won't. "I think Liam will be able to cut a deal. If not, he made his own bed."

Mason drew in a lungful of air and let it out in measured seconds. "Yeah. I know we were probably headed here anyway. But knowing doesn't stop me from wishing things were different."

Jeep squeezed his shoulder once again before straightening in his seat. "I'm sorry, man."

Mason nodded twice and swallowed around the sudden lump in his throat. "Thanks for all you've done," he said, and meant it. Family was important, precious even. He shifted in his own seat as razorlike stabs of guilt, fear, and sadness shredded his midsection.

Once upon a time, he and Priss had been a family. Liam was part of that, too. Mason might not have known that going in, but when you loved someone, you took the good and the bad. That was Marriage 101.

"So what comes next?" *Besides my divorce.*

"Questions, I imagine. Lots of 'em."

The female agent swiveled in the front passenger seat and flashed her badge. "I'm Agent Gutierrez. I'm the lead on this investigation. We play fair, Dr. Hughes. Your brother-in-law has nothing to fear if he tells us what we want to know."

Mason held back the pithy retort that jumped to his lips. He would have believed her, hook, line, and sinker, a few short days ago. However, he'd been schooled since then. Sean O'Brien was a powerful man and there was no love lost between him and his nephew. As Priss had said, all that it would take was an O'Brien-connected prison insider, and…bye-bye Liam.

Or a rogue FBI agent.

Mason shook his head. He wouldn't have believed it. Three days in a cabin with a couple of O'Briens and he, the son of a jurist and brother to—whatever Jeep was, now doubted law enforcement. He eyed the agent again. The woman's competent and professional demeanor inspired confidence. But of course, a bad apple wouldn't exactly be wearing a sign.

Fancy French fries. When had his life become so complicated?

The moment I met Priss O'Brien, that bundle of intelligence, excitement, and sass that currently hates my guts.

Clearing his throat, he leaned forward in his seat. "I assume you'll provide Liam with plenty of security. My wife, too, for that matter."

Gutierrez's head bobbed once. "I can assure you, sir, we've taken all that into consideration."

Huh. That reply was a little too vague for his liking, but Mason could tell by the agent's tone that it was the best he'd get. He glanced over at Jeep for his take, but his brother's nose was buried in his phone screen, both thumbs typing away. Behind them, in the third row of seats, one of the other two agents who'd met them in the terminal had yet to make a sound. Glancing at the man, Mason pegged him as a rookie. Tall, skinny, with a prominent Adam's apple that bobbed a lot, he looked like he was about fifteen. No doubt the Mob ate guys like him for breakfast.

Traffic was heavy, and it took them over an hour to reach the J. Edgar Hoover FBI building in downtown DC. Mason had toured the large, iconic building once, back in middle school. As they entered the building, all he could remember, ironically, was that the public parts of the building featured displays relating to the agency's most famous cases, many of them involving mobsters. He struggled to wrap his head around the fact that today's visit was due to his own connection to the Mob-with-a-capital-M.

That truth was evident, though, as the SUVs parked beside one another in a gated, guarded lot beneath the building. There was no time for a tearful reunion as they were shepherded through a back entrance and into an oversized elevator.

"No talking, please," Young warned, as he punched the button for the third floor. Once they exited, the agents led them down a rabbit warren's worth of hallways into a nondescript, government-issue holding room, complete with threadbare orange carpet and tailbone-busting, unpadded black chairs. At that point, Peters, Young, and two newcomers led Liam away, still in handcuffs.

"Wait. Where are they taking him?" Priss's stance and tone indicated her high alert. "He has the right to an attorney."

Jeep stepped forward. "She's right. I'm happy to represent Mr. O'Brien until he retains permanent counsel."

Mason raised an eyebrow. Look at his brother, acting all lawyerly. And for Liam "The Lion" O'Brien, no less. Of course, it was belief in the rule of law that had Jeep volunteering, but Mason appreciated it anyway.

A muscle in Agent Gutierrez' cheek jumped, but she nodded to the skinny agent who'd ridden in the back seat. "Take him back, Jones. We'll be in Room Three." Then she turned back to Mason and Priss. For a moment, Mason thought she might speak, but instead she shook her head and made a "follow me" signal with two fingers. He waved Priss ahead of him but stayed close on her heels as they followed the agent down another long hallway and into a corner conference room—if this was Room Three, it wasn't marked as such. This room, like the one back in holding, had the usual governmental feel and smelled of old wood, dust, and damp. An enormous wood and metal version of the FBI shield filled one wall, an assortment of cobwebs and dust motes clearly visible on its raised surfaces. Another wall was teched out with two flat screens, but there were no colorful paintings or photography to brighten up the rest of the room. The building's signature sunken windows made hanging anything along the other two walls impossible.

Room Three needed a makeover, stat. Mason grinned, imagining what his mother could do with two days and five hundred dollars.

"Glad you find this so amusing," Priss snapped, walking around to the other side of the long, veneered table that dominated the room.

Mason sighed, too tired to start an argument right now. He hadn't thought their relationship could get any more complicated, but he'd been wrong.

The ancient brass casters of the oversized pleather chairs creaked as they sat across the table from each other. He settled into his bucket seat, noting how the artificial, bluish glow of the fluorescent lighting overhead hummed as it illuminated a few tear tracks on Priss's face.

Great. Like he'd needed another gut punch.

He leaned back against the pleather. It was going to be a long evening.

****

Shit!

Mason shook himself awake. Damn his hospital training. He hadn't meant to fall asleep. He scanned the room for a clock. Had he been out long? The windows showed it was well and truly dark outside. He sneaked a peek at Priss. The look she shot back was pure venom. No doubt his little nap had moved the needle from "uncaring asshole" to "uncaring mega-asshole," from her point of view.

"Priss, I—"

Her eyes flashed. "I'd prefer it if we didn't talk."

Holy hell. Much more of this and they'll need to lock me up.

He tried box breathing, his usual go-to for stress relief, but it failed to slow his racing mind. He was halfway to a nuclear meltdown when Jeep, Liam, and the rest of the Feds entered the room.

The agent named Peters walked to the head of the table and plunked down a stack of file folders, then nodded in Mason's direction. Mason hadn't liked the guy at the airport, and he didn't like him now. The man carried an air of arrogance that rubbed Mason the wrong way. To be fair, he'd only spent about three minutes in the agent's company, so maybe he grew on a person. Mason doubted it, but time would tell.

Liam sat down next to Priss. He was no longer

handcuffed, but the dejected expression on his face was unchanged. Jones, the baby-faced agent, stood near the door. Mason managed a half-hearted grin. If this dude was the only line of defense against Liam O'Brien's escape, Mason's money was on his brawny brother-in-law.

Priss shot Mason a defiant look before rolling her chair closer to her brother, in an obvious attempt to present a united front. She patted the back of Liam's hand and whispered something in his ear.

Mason shook his head. Chances were, she'd said something along the lines of "Let's kill Mason and make a run for it."

Sweet heaven, he loved her. And had no more than a snowball's chance in hell of proving it after today.

Out of the corner of his eye, Mason caught the subtle nod Gutierrez gave Peters. The seasoned agent cleared his throat. Did it rankle the aging agent to have to take orders from a woman? Mason figured it did. Big time.

"I'd like to thank you all for coming." Peters smiled, as if he were the genial host at a garden party. *What a jerk.*

Still oozing bonhomie, Peters grabbed a couple of bottles of water from a wheezy credenza that looked older than Mason's grandfather and set them on the table. "Please, help yourselves. For the record, this conversation will be recorded."

Conversation. Like tea and cakes would soon follow. While Peters went on to list the names of those present around the table, Mason leaned toward Jeep, who'd taken a seat on his right.

"What do you know?"

"Not much. They booked him," Jeep whispered.

"The usual Mob-related charges, including tax evasion. Now, we'll see what they really have in mind."

"Here at the agency, we believe in transparency. I'm gonna set all our cards on the table." Peters' tone had a ring of memorization to it that sank any sincerity behind the words. He pulled more manila files out from a briefcase and set them on top of the stack on the table.

"Our primary goal is to understand the events of the past several months, as they relate to a Mr. Jonathan Bannion." He looked down the table at Liam. "In addition, we are very interested in the actions of your uncle, Sean O'Brien."

Hope stirred at the back of Mason's mind. Liam was the small fish in this pond. They had arrested him, but that might just be a show of power, a way of convincing him to talk. Maybe they could be trusted. Maybe they'd hand Liam a sweet deal.

Mason sent Priss an optimistic glance.

Once again, he got daggers in return.

****

Mason rolled over on the lumpy sofa for the eighth time in as many minutes. The safe house wasn't five-star, but it could have been worse. At least Liam wasn't behind bars. After eight hours' worth of interrogation, Mason needed all the points with Priss he could get. The revelation, earlier in the night, that the Feds had tracked The Lion through his cell phone, even though the device was turned off, hadn't mitigated her anger with him one little bit.

Sometimes they'd all been kept together, in Room Three. More often, they were apart, speaking to a pair of agents at a time. Every minute of it was hellish but, in Mason's opinion, the day's crazy events had yielded the best possible outcome for his brother-in-law: A new identity and new life in return for Liam's testimony against Bannion and Clan O'Brien.

So here he was—along with Priss, Liam, and a team of shoulder-holstered agents—snuggled into a two-bedroom ranch somewhere in rural Maryland. Of course, given the plethora of law enforcement and the alarmed doors and windows, it was uncomfortably like house arrest, although he and Priss could go home anytime, as Jeep had done. Mason had been in favor of that option, since the agency had eyes on their house and it should be safe enough, but Priss was determined to stick by her brother's side.

And Mason was determined to stick by Priss's side, so here they were.

Again, it could be worse. The sub sandwiches the agents brought in had been good, and the shower he'd taken after they ate had been hot. The only awkwardness occurred when Priss took the larger of the two bedrooms, and Liam followed suit with the other. Mason had stood in the hallway like a damn fool for a long minute before heading to the sofa in the miniscule den.

The couch was a good foot and a half shorter than he was, and the upholstery, as far as he could tell, was interwoven with straight pins, but other than that, he'd never been more comfortable. At least the gaggle of agents had retreated to the kitchen, two rooms away, where their voices had subsided to a dull roar punctuated, now and then, by cracks of laughter.

He didn't know what was worse, being trapped in a cabin with no heat, or sleeping—make that *not* sleeping—on this damn couch. He and Priss knew just how to warm each other up, which gave the cabin a leg up, pun intended.

His stomach growled. The subs had been small. There might be something in the kitchen, but that meant dealing with the agents again, so that was a nonstarter.

"Mason? Are you awake?" Priss's whisper in the darkness surprised him. She hadn't spoken an intentional word to him since their arrival at the FBI building a lifetime ago.

Opening his eyes, he spotted her silhouette in the doorway. Light from the hallway spilled around her and across the carpeted floor. Pushing himself up on his elbows, he blinked, trying to see her face. His Spidey senses started to tingle. "What's up?"

"Liam's not in his room."

"Okay." That was hardly a reason to sound an alarm.

She moved across the room and shoved at his legs, sitting down at the far end of the sofa. The warm, soft curve of her thigh pressed against the soles of his feet. "I don't like it."

Mason swung his legs to the floor and ran a hand through his mussed hair. "He's probably in the bathroom."

"He isn't. I checked."

He exhaled a curse. Honest to God, the last thing he felt like doing right now was playing hide-and-seek with his brother-in-law. "Then he must be talking to the agents in the kitchen."

Priss shook her head, sending tresses of her long hair flying. "He's not in there either."

The back of the couch scratched his neck as he leaned back and closed his eyes. "So what are you saying?"

"I'm saying I've searched every nook and cranny in

this house and Liam's gone."

His tired brain refused to be jump-started. "We're in a locked safe house with a team of armed agents sitting twenty feet away. What do you mean he's 'gone'?"

"I mean, he isn't here. He's disappeared."

Chapter Sixteen

The beehive of activity around her reminded Priss of something right out of *NCIS* but without the acting talent. Agents with guns drawn went from room to room, their faces so serious they became parodies of themselves. They checked in closets and behind furniture, under beds and in the shower, sending echoing shouts of "Clear!" throughout the house. The house was small and sparse. Within five minutes—six, counting their search of the garage—the team was back in the kitchen, reinforcing what Priss already knew to be true. Her brother was gone.

And that wasn't good.

"Unbelievable," Mason said, under his breath. He sat across the round kitchen table from her, wearing the same expression Dorothy had worn when she landed in Oz. A lifetime ago, Priss would be sitting next to him, holding his hand, giving and receiving comfort.

But they weren't in Kansas anymore.

She rubbed a finger along a deep scar in the tabletop while butterflies danced the jitterbug in her stomach. Something had happened to Liam. Something...*bad.*

Agent Gutierrez, her gray eyes as alert as a hawk's, snagged another chair and sat down. One of her colleagues hovered behind—the skinny young one named Jones. His round-eyed expression twinned with Mason's.

"I'm going to be honest with you, Dr. and Mrs. Hughes. I'm not sure what's going on. *Yet.*" Gutierrez spoke with the detached, almost robotic formality all Feds shared. Priss squashed an eyeroll. The agent couldn't help it. They probably put it in the water at Quantico.

Another agent, one Priss hadn't seen before, appeared in the doorway and Guttierez raised her eyebrows. He shook his head once and Gutierrez's nostrils flared as she pulled in a deep breath.

Hmm. Something else was up and it wasn't good either. "What aren't you telling us?" Priss asked.

Gutierrez threaded her ringless hands together on the table. "Agents Peters and Young also appear to be…well, we can't locate them, although we haven't completed our perimeter search."

Priss's butterflies began double-timing it.

"Wait. They're *missing*?" Mason lurched forward, propping his elbows on the table. "How in the hell does that happen? Can't you ping their cell phones or something?"

The tips of Gutierrez's ears turned red, but her stoic expression remained unchanged. "They left approximately forty-five minutes ago to go grab some hamburgers, and they haven't been in communication since. We are trying alternative ways of locating them."

"Damn it!" This time Priss did eye the ceiling. *Seriously?* Was this their first fricking Mob case? "I *told* you my uncle has long arms."

Mason raised a hand. "Hang on a minute. It's a long jump from going out to get a burger to being kidnapped by the Mob. Where's the restaurant? Maybe they're lost."

"Ha!" Priss shook her head. Bless Mason's sweet heart. He was so naïve.

"That seems…" Guitierrez cleared her throat. "That appears unlikely. The drive-thru's about five minutes away."

Mason shook his head. "All the same, it has to be a coincidence. I mean, I get why my brother-in-law would sneak out of here in the dead of night, but your agents have no reason to disappear."

Priss threw her hands up. "Of course, you would think that. You trust every move the Feds make. But what if they're bad apples? What if they're in bed with my uncle? Then they'd have every reason to take Lee."

"Ms. Hughes, both Agent Peters and Agent Young are experienced and trusted members of this team."

Guttierez emphasized each word, as if speaking to a child, and Priss swallowed a pithy retort. Not only would it mean a hefty donation to her mother-in-law's swear jar, it wouldn't get her anywhere with the Feds.

"Furthermore, we don't indulge in speculation. The fact is, the house doors," Guttierez flicked her thumb in the direction of the back door, "are locked at *all* times, unless the fire alarm is triggered. They can only be unlocked with our keycards." She lifted the lanyard she wore around her neck and met Priss's hard stare without batting an eyelash. "The only way your brother could leave this house is if he managed to get his hands on one. We can't speak for Peters or Young, but the rest of us have our cards."

Priss shook her head again. She didn't need to be a rocket scientist to hear the agent's subtext. "No. Absolutely not. You just offered Lee a new life. There's no way he'd jeopardize that by stealing a keycard, let alone kidnapping federal agents. I know it and you know it. Lee didn't…" She paused as heredity kicked in. *Never concede anything.* "*If* my brother is guilty of any crime—*if*—it's not a violent one. He's unarmed. The only thing that makes sense is that *your guys took him.*"

Gutierrez pursed her lips but remained silent.

Mason tunneled both hands through his hair, leaving it mussed. "Okay." He exhaled and glanced toward a ticking wall clock. "It's three-thirty. Liam was here an hour ago—we all saw him. Unless he had a plane waiting for him somewhere nearby, which seems way too James Bond-ish, he can't have gotten too far. As to your agents, they're probably in the drive-thru grabbing seconds, with their phones silenced."

"Oh, don't worry. We'll find Mr. O'Brien." Gutierrez's tone more than implied that, when they did, Liam's goose was cooked.

An angry scream rose in Priss's throat. Was she the only one worried about her brother's safety? The only one who realized just how pissed off both her uncle and that Bannion guy were? Her brother had been scared. Terrified. And no one else seemed to understand that.

Not even Mason.

A loud knock on the back door sent her heart hammering. The four other agents who'd accompanied them to the safe house tromped into the kitchen. Guttierez rose to meet them and, after a moment of whispered conversation, faced the table again.

"We'll arrange transportation for you both, back to the city, in about an hour from now. This manhunt will be orchestrated from DC. We have more resources there."

"*Manhunt.*" A wave of disappointment swept

through Priss, although she couldn't say why. The Feds were who they were. They wouldn't change their spots. Fine. She wouldn't either. She stood and took a step toward the agents. "That's a scary word. It sounds to me like you're planning to shoot first and ask questions later. I've seen that scenario play out before."

Guttierez frowned as she pulled her cell phone from her pants pocket. "Again, we aren't making any assumptions, Ms. Hughes. We don't use deadly force unless there's a perceived threat. Having said that, the moment he left the safety of this house, your brother became a fugitive and will be treated as such."

Priss thrust her hands forward. "That's my point! You know how my father died. Lee knows you'll come after him with guns blazing, so why would he leave willingly?"

Guttierez cradled her phone to her chest and shook her head. "Ms. Hughes, I'm sorry, but until we have evidence to the contrary, as far as we're concerned, your brother fled of his own free will. That being said, I can assure you that all protocol will be followed in this matter."

Once more, Priss bit back a scream. "You just don't get it! My brother's got two insanely powerful men on his tail. Why is it so difficult to believe that one of them got to him?"

The agent raised well-manicured eyebrows. "In an FBI safe house? With a team of agents inside?"

Priss glanced at the doubtful expressions of those around her, Mason included.

Fine. She was on her own. That was nothing new.

Guttierez exchanged a smirk with her fellow agents. "We'll keep your theory in mind, ma'am. Now, if you'll excuse us, we have work to do." With an about-face the military would be proud of, the agent headed through the swinging door to the living room, the rest of her team following along behind her like a bunch of well-tailored lemmings.

Priss clenched her fists. It would be a bonehead move to punch an FBI agent, but man, was she tempted.

As if sensing her thoughts, Mason walked over and waved a hand in front of her face. "They're on our side, remember?"

Something inside her snapped, like a twig in an ice storm, and she rounded on him so fast, she almost fell into his arms.

"No, they're not! They're on their own side. What I need to know is whose side you're on, because it sure as hell doesn't feel like you're on mine." She pulled in a deep breath and adjusted her volume. The agents didn't need to hear this. "These are the same folks that blew a thousand holes in a seventy-year-old man. They care about one thing and one thing only." Reaching out, she poked his breastbone. "Their. Own. Power. Why should I believe they have my brother's best interests at heart? Witness Protection costs a lot of the taxpayers' money, and Lee already told those agents quite a lot today." She pointed toward the living room. "Who's to say they didn't get all they needed out of him and took a cheaper way out?"

"Wow." Mason crossed his arms across his chest, his biceps straining the thin fabric of his long-sleeved T-shirt. "Believe me, I'm on your side—or at least I'm trying to be. But do you realize you've gone from 'my brother's missing' to 'crazy-ass conspiracy theory' in less than ten minutes?"

Priss stared at him for a couple of thundering heartbeats. "Do you call that helping?"

He had the decency to look chagrined. "Fair enough. But your father's case was completely different from your brother's."

"Was it? Lee suspects Uncle Sean had a hand in Dad's death. The only way that works is if he has contacts in the agency. Two FBI agents are 'missing,'" she said, with air quotes. "I know, as sure as I'm standing here, that my brother didn't kidnap them. I've had a bad feeling about Peters and Young from the start. I'm telling you. I think they're working for Uncle Sean."

Mason sighed. "Do you have anything besides a bad feeling? Any proof?" He backed up a step and raised his hands. "I'm not discounting how you feel, but we'll need more."

"I *know* my brother. He didn't leave this house of his own free will. He wouldn't. Not without telling me first."

****

Mason got it. Brotherly love could make you do crazy things. It was a long story, but he'd once taken the rap for Jeep when his oldest brother had dinged up one of the family cars. Priss wanted to believe her brother wouldn't scram without letting her know. And he agreed with her on one point, at least. Running away from a safe house was a huge mistake. Even his idiot brother-in-law should have figured out that much. But Liam had gotten on the wrong side of not one but two powerful men, and that had to mess with a man's head. The impulse to flee, while boneheaded, wasn't out of the question. On the other hand, if Liam had fled, how had he done it? Agent Guitierrez's argument cut both ways. They were in a locked-down safe house with a zillion FBI agents. Leaving wasn't as simple as opening the door and heading out into the night.

Puzzling it all out threatened to make his head explode, so he made his way through the living room and down the hallway toward the den. Packing up should take him all of three minutes.

"Mason," Priss called, as he passed her open doorway.

He slouched against her doorjamb. "Yep."

She finished making up the queen-sized bed that dominated the tiny room. "Do you still have those burner phones Jeep gave you?"

"Yeah, they're in the den."

"Good." Perching on the side of the bed, she pulled on the snow boots she'd worn from the cabin. Then, she shoved her T-shirt from earlier into a plastic grocery bag and stood up.

"You look like you're ready to skedaddle. Our transportation won't be here for at least another forty-five minutes," he pointed out.

She disappeared into the small bathroom for a few seconds and returned with a toothbrush and toothpaste in hand. They, too, went into the plastic bag. "I have to find Liam before the Feds do. I need one of those phones so I can call my own car."

His tired brain took a couple of seconds to compute the words, but once it had, he couldn't stop a bubble of panic from rising in his chest.

"Wait a minute. Let's talk about this."

She set one hand on a cocked hip. "I'm tired of talking. We talked all day yesterday and it's only made things worse. My brother is missing and I'm going to find him. It's as simple as that."

He took a step closer and caught a whiff of the clean scent of soap. Her complexion was pink, and curly wisps of damp hair clung to her forehead. She'd washed her face, but a dewy complexion didn't hide her determination.

Well, she'd have to go through him first. Regardless of where their relationship stood, there was no way he was allowing her to do this alone. "That doesn't sound simple at all. In fact, it sounds dangerous. And, at the risk of pointing out the obvious, you don't know where to begin looking."

Tossing the bag back onto the bed, she withdrew a small, pocket-sized diary from her sweatshirt pocket and waved it at him. "That's where you're wrong. I just found this in Lee's room, under his pillow. I think it'll lead me to him."

Wait…what? Mason shook his head, hoping to clear it. "Ten minutes ago, you tried to convince me he'd been kidnapped by federal agents. Now you're saying he told you where he was headed? I can't keep up."

"He didn't tell me *where* he was going or if he was on his own, but he told me how to track him."

He took another step in her direction and held out his hand. "Okay. Show me."

She clutched the diary to her chest, her eyes narrowing in suspicion. "I don't know if I can trust you."

Ouch. That cut right to the quick.

"Let me ask you something. How far would you go to help one of your brothers? Would you break the law in order to keep them safe?"

He rubbed a hand across his forehead. "Damn, woman. You aren't lobbing softballs here, are you?" Her question addressed the crux of the matter. The real issue between them.

"For most of my life, my dad's been a judge." Moving fully into the room, he began to pace. "The rule of law is something I've never questioned. Naïve of me, I guess, but that's how it was." He turned to make another pass and met her eyes. "Until now. Your entire family situation is nothing but shades of gray, and it's blown up my simplistic, black-and-white viewpoint."

Sadness darkened her eyes. "I know. There's a part of me that's sorry about that." She made a sweeping gesture with her hand. "And there's another part of me that realizes it's why there's no future for us." Her voice dropped to a whisper. "If they want you dead, you're dead. Even my father… Dad wasn't a saint. He had some bodies buried in his day." She tapped a finger against her chest. "That knowledge is my family legacy. I was lucky. I got out early. Lee… It's tougher for him—always has been. He knows right from wrong, though. That's what made this whole Gutenberg mess so frightening." Something close to a sob escaped her, but she kept on going. "My idolized older brother was slipping away from me, turning into something he'd fought against for so long." Sniffing, she fished a tissue out of her sweatshirt pocket and blew her nose before continuing. "Now that I've discovered he didn't cross that line, there isn't anything I won't do to guarantee he gets one more chance to break free of the family."

Mason stood there, unsure of what to say next. In all their time together, he'd never experienced such brutal, raw honesty from her before. And it was honest. Even she wasn't that good a liar.

Tiny pieces of paper fell like snow as she shredded

the tissue in her hands. Mason set a hand on her shoulder. She didn't resist when he pulled her close. Nothing sexual, just comfort.

"I'd be lying if I said I'm not moved by your loyalty, your love." He lowered his head until his chin rested on the top of her head. "I'm not convinced your brother deserves it, but I get it." He took a deep breath. "What if we compromise?"

"Um." She sniffled into his shoulder, then pulled back to look up at him, still staying within the embrace. "What do you have in mind?"

He straightened to his full height again but kept his arms looped around her waist, unwilling to break the contact. "We'll go meet Jeep, explain what's happened, and tell him we aren't ready to bring the Feds into the loop just yet, not until we have a better idea of what's what. With his contacts, he'll be able to figure out if the info in the diary does what you think it can do. Every step we take will be with the goal of trying to keep Liam safe, getting him connected to people we've vetted like crazy."

He watched as suspicion warred with hope in her eyes. "I promise, you'll control the narrative. Talk to Jeep first. Tell him as much or as little as you want. Give him—and me—a chance to surprise you."

"You mean it? You'll put the weight of the Hughes family behind a push to keep Lee safe?"

He raised a hand. "I pinky swear."

After a long moment, she linked her little finger with his and shook. The playful gesture was one they'd shared before, under more intimate circumstances and, just like that, his mood shifted from platonic to something a whole hell of a lot more primal.

Damn. This woman was every bit as dangerous as her uncle.

Oblivious to his predicament, Priss slipped out of his embrace and headed to the door. "Okay. C'mon, let's go."

Mason shook off a sense of foreboding that had nothing to do with his brother-in-law and followed her out of the room. The promises he'd just made took their relationship from slippery slope to avalanche.

Only time would tell if the Saint Bernard got to him in time.

Chapter Seventeen

Priss glanced around the hotel suite, noting the two bedrooms with a prickle of disappointment. Not that she'd expected otherwise. Nor did she expect to get much sleep anyway, while Liam was missing. All the same, deep in the delusional recesses of her heart floated the wish for one more night in her husband's arms. Not for wild sex, or even mild sex, though Lord knew they'd indulged in both in days past. No, she yearned for that sense of peace only he could give. A certainty that all was right with the world.

But it isn't all right. In fact, it's a train wreck. She couldn't explain it, but she was beyond certain that the Feds had her brother. Nothing else even began to make sense, given the two agents were also missing. The hurdle was convincing Mason and Jeep. She patted the zippered coat pocket of the oversized jacket she'd borrowed from the cabin. Liam's journal remained safe and sound. She hadn't lost it in the three minutes since she'd last checked.

The blue numbers on the kitchenette's small microwave announced it was now 8:00 a.m., a fact confirmed by both the bright sunlight streaming in through the gauzy curtains and the sounds of heavy traffic from the road below. Jeep would be here any minute and they could get this ball rolling.

Finally.

"I'll take this one, if that's okay," Mason called, from the bedroom on her right. It was the larger of the two rooms, but she didn't challenge him. With his height, he'd be far more comfortable in the king-sized bed, versus one of the two doubles visible in the other room.

During the ride back into the city, they'd debated the pros and cons of returning to their own house. Priss had won the argument, insisting that a hotel was a safer choice. She wouldn't be surprised to find that the Feds had, at a minimum, bugged their house. But more than that, she wasn't ready to face the home they'd made together—the home she'd fled all those weeks ago. It was a place of unity and forever, things she and Mason would never share again.

Since then, however, Mason's conversation had been minimal. She recognized the signs. He'd retreated inside himself, fallen into some serious introspection. In the past, he would share those thoughts when he was ready. Now, she might never know.

She entered the smaller of the bedrooms and tossed her bag on the nearest bed. It was a corner suite, and this room had floor-to-ceiling windows on two walls, with a leafy wallpaper on the others, which upped the airy, outdoorsy vibe. When she stepped into the adjoining marble and chrome bathroom, the lure of the fancy shower was strong, but she didn't want to miss a moment of the action once Jeep arrived. She had to convince a naval officer that the Feds couldn't be trusted. Not an easy task. Plus, why waste a good shower when she didn't have any clean clothes to change into?

Turning her back on the shower, she wandered again into the bedroom. Although the suite was temperate, she kept her puffy jacket on. The feel of the journal in its pocket acted like a talisman, giving her a sense that everything might, just maybe, work out okay. Glancing at the black-rimmed wall mirror was a mistake. Her face was drawn and pale, and the dark circles under her eyes could give a raccoon a run for its money. She pinched her cheeks and finger-combed her unruly hair. It didn't make a lick of difference, but it would have to do. At least it was only Jeep.

A loud growl from her stomach reminded her that it had been a while since she'd eaten anything. The complimentary package of microwave popcorn in the teeny kitchen beckoned. She picked up the package with a smile. Popcorn at eight in the morning was a page right out of Mason's dietary book. She didn't need to ask if he wanted any.

She'd just gotten the cellophane off when a loud knock on the door made her jump.

"Yo." Her brother-in-law's deep voice was as distinctive as his heavy knock. Ditching the popcorn with a sigh of relief, she unlatched the chain and rolled back the deadlock.

The door hadn't fully opened before she was pulled into one of her mother-in-law's giant hugs.

"Priscilla, dear. How awful this must be for you." Wearing a hand-knit, cream-colored poncho, with a matching beanie pulled over her sleek silver bob, Minna Hughes looked like she'd stepped out of an ad for a Swiss ski resort.

Damn it. She should have taken that shower after all.

"Mum." Jeep set a hand on his mother's back. "Step inside, please."

Minna loosened her grip and took an obedient step into the room before beginning the whole embrace all over again.

God help her, Priss couldn't pull away. There was something so…comforting about her mother-in-law. The older woman oozed maternal love and a reassuring sense that all would be well—the two things Priss had lacked most in life. Plus, *mmmm*. The woman always smelled like freshly baked cookies. Although, that could just be Priss's stomach talking.

"All the way in, Min." Patrick Hughes' voice was as deep as Jeep's, but rarely as somber. Tall and distinguished, with a full, gray head of hair and wire-rimmed spectacles, Patrick looked every inch the scholarly jurist he was. He took his wife by the shoulders and steered her into the sitting area, tossing Priss an encouraging wink as he passed by. He was dressed in what his sons called his "uniform"—buttoned-down shirt, navy sweater, and khakis.

"Wow. You brought the whole crew." Lounging in the doorway of his bedroom, Mason sounded anything but thrilled.

"Of course he did, dearest." With arms outstretched, Minna moved to her youngest son. "Where else would we be at a time like this?"

After the slightest of eye rolls, Mason kissed his mother's deftly made-up cheek and enveloped her in a hug. A lump formed in Priss's throat. That easy affection had once been hers.

"Are we safe?" Mason shot Jeep a concerned look over their mother's head.

Minna pulled back and swatted her youngest son's chest. "Perfectly. John took such a circuitous route, there's no way we were followed." She raised a hand to the side of her head. "I'm dizzy just thinking about it."

Priss fought the urge to laugh every time Minna referred to Jeep by his given name. While there was nothing wrong with his birth name, it suited his personality about as well as a mink coat worked on an iguana.

"I'm not worried," Priss added her two cents without being asked. "Everyone's after Liam now, not us." The words hinted at a confidence she didn't feel, but this was her fight, not her in-laws', and she wanted to keep their worry to a minimum.

As if reading her mind, Jeep glanced down the long hallway before crossing the threshold. He too had a hug for her—his usual, side-arm shoulder squeezer that said more than she'd ever heard him vocalize. The lump in her throat swelled. The night before last, she'd greeted her brother with a gun, and even when things had de-escalated, they hadn't embraced. It overwhelmed her at times, this ready exchange of affection in her husband's family. But oh, how she'd miss it when she moved on.

"Take a seat." Jeep nodded toward the small sitting area. "I'll fill you in."

Priss grabbed a bar stool from the counter and carried it over next to the couch. Mason did the same, while his parents relaxed onto the small loveseat. Jeep sank into the overstuffed armchair by the large window, his muscled bulk making the mid-sized chair appear dainty in comparison.

They hadn't been settled more than thirty seconds before Minna reached into her designer handbag and withdrew a plate covered by plastic wrap. "Biscuits and scones. No one thinks well on an empty stomach."

"What? No cream?" Mason asked, winking at Jeep.

"Ugh." Minna shook her head. "It is beyond me how

these Yankee heathens I raised can eat scones without clotted cream." She dug into her bag again and withdrew a jar and spoon. "Ta-da."

The fresh-baked aroma made Priss's mouth water, but hunger didn't dispel her sudden sense of the surreal. In the last few days, she and Mason had been submerged in more danger than most people experienced in a lifetime, and here was her mother-in-law hosting a tea party.

Minna reached over and patted Priss's knee. "You must be beside yourself, worrying about your brother, and here we're acting like it's all gone away."

Priss's cheeks warmed. Her mother-in-law had an uncanny knack for understanding the unspoken. "I admit to being a little impatient to get things going, although I do appreciate your thoughtfulness at bringing all this." She gestured toward food on the coffee table.

"Trust me. We'll all think better with a little something in our stomachs," Minna said, and passed her the plate.

Priss chose an oatmeal chocolate chip cookie the size of a salad plate and dug in. "Oh. My. God."

Jeep let out a humorous grunt. "Mum's cookies are better than sex."

"Huh," Mason said. "Not if you're doing it right."

Despite herself, Priss blushed again. She and Mason did it right and then some.

Minna rested her head on Patrick's shoulder, and he was quick to wrap an arm around her in return. "I agree with Mason, dear," she told Jeep. "You just haven't found the right partner yet."

Jeep's ears turned crimson. "Okay, enough. We are not here to talk about my love life," he ground out.

"What love life, darling?" Minna said, batting her long eyelashes. Mason and Patrick laughed.

Priss, her mouth full of cookie, hid a smile behind her hand. Nothing was sacred in the Hughes family, especially when it came to Jeep's dating—or lack thereof.

Jeep stood and grabbed the plate of goodies from Mason, then sat back down again. After selecting his own treat, he focused his laser-like gaze on her. "So, let's talk."

The cookie went down hard as her stress returned.

****

"We've got—" Mason clamped his mouth shut and shot Priss an apologetic look. He'd gone over this from every angle and here he was, messing it up before he even began. "I mean, *Priss* has some new information. But before she gets into it, I want you to understand that she…*we* have reason to believe the FBI can't be trusted. I've promised her that until we know exactly who we're dealing with, nothing we say here," he pointed around the small room, "goes any further. If you can't agree to that, you'll have to leave."

There. That should make it clear whose camp he was in. Earlier, Priss had doubted his trustworthiness. Well, he was one hundred percent Team Priss, and it was about time he made that clear.

Priss turned and looked at him. And looked. And then looked some more.

Mission accomplished.

"You might have teed that up a bit more," she said, fiddling with the strings to her sweatshirt hood.

Mason raised a shoulder. What was the use of sugarcoating things?

Priss swiveled to face his family. "Look, I don't mean to kick anyone out. I hope you know how much I care about each of you. But Mason's right. I don't know who to trust in law enforcement right now. And I realize that places you in a sticky situation."

"Not the way I see it," Mason's dad said. "Justice takes many forms, including Witness Protection, which has a long history of giving folks a second chance in return for valuable testimony. The FBI offered your brother that chance. If rogue agents are threatening to take that away from him, that's injustice, and none of us support that."

"Yes, but—"

"Dad's right. I'm not in the business of putting people in harm's way. Your brother deserves the right to due process," Jeep said. "First and foremost, that means finding him, safe and sound, and placing him into the hands of the right people."

Atta boy. One more to go. Mason caught his mother's gaze and raised an eyebrow.

"Oh, my dearest." She waved at him impatiently. "Need you even ask?"

Priss said nothing, but her eyes said everything.

Mason gave her a smile before continuing, "Great. I want to start, Dad, with a request. Do you know anyone who can reopen the investigation into Priss's father's death?"

"Oh, no," Priss said. "That's not necessary. I don't want you to put your reputation in jeopardy for Seamus O'Brien."

Mason's father shook his head. "If digging out the truth harms my reputation as a judge, then we're in a world of hurt. I've already started the wheels in motion."

"Thanks." Mason gave Priss a quick shoulder squeeze. "Then it's time to share what you've got."

Her hand shook as she slid the notebook out of her jacket. Clutching it to her chest, she took a deep breath. "Boston's a big city, but the world I grew up in was small. I wasn't allowed to socialize much outside of the private school I attended. My leisure time was confined to the house."

Mason shook his head. It wasn't any easier hearing this now than it had been the first time. Such a lonely existence, especially for a people-person like Priss.

His thoughts must have leaked into his expression. Priss lifted her chin into the defensive pose he knew so well. "I'm not saying this to make you feel sorry for me."

"But we do feel sorry for you, Priscilla, dear," his mother said, in her matter-of-fact way. "It's a natural reaction, after all, because we love you."

Mason's heart swelled. He and his brothers often joked about the one-letter difference between "mother" and "smother," but they wouldn't change her for the world. She was one in a kazillion.

"Thank you, Minna. That means more than I can say." Priss's smile didn't waver, even as she blinked away tears. After a moment, she cleared her throat, once, and then again. "Despite the differences in our ages, my brother did his best to make my cloistered life fun. One of the games he made up involved leaving cryptic little messages for me, revealing where some kind of 'treasure' was." Her eyes crinkled as she laughed. "It was just kids' stuff, of course. A piece of bubble gum, a candy cane, a yo-yo…whatever it was, the fun was in the finding."

Standing, she maneuvered around the square coffee

table to his brother's side. "I found this under Lee's pillow at the safe house." She tapped the open page before handing the notebook to Jeep. "I think this tells us how to track him."

Jeep pulled in a breath and began to read. "Hey, Sis. Your birthday gift keeps on giving. Pop the top and check it out." He shot Priss a questioning look. "You'll have to explain. What's the gift?"

She reached into her inside jacket pocket and pulled out a high-end pen, its onyx shell and gold accents a serious upgrade from any drugstore version. "This. Before he gave it to me, Lee put a tracking device in it—that's how he found us at the cabin." Unscrewing the nib, she exposed the ink cartridge. "Look at this." She removed a small piece of paper from around the cylinder and handed it to Jeep.

Jeep studied the paper, then shook his head. "Just a bunch of numbers. Do you know what they mean?"

Priss twisted the top of the pen's cap, separating a half-inch long section of the tip. "It's just like our old game, where one clue leads to another. Thank God I didn't throw this pen away." She tipped a small, rectangular piece into Jeep's outstretched hand. "This is the tracking device Liam attached to my pen. If you look closely, you'll see there's a series of numbers written on it—ten, in all. The first nine numbers on this tracker match the first nine numbers on that scrap of paper. Only the last digit is different. It's the next one, numerically." She gestured at the small piece of paper. "I think Liam is carrying a similar tracker and, what's more, I think the numbers on that paper are the ID or tracking number of that device."

Jeep studied the tracker for a long minute before

glancing at the paper again. Then, with a sound that was half grunt, half growl, he handed the tiny device back to Priss and reached for his backpack. In seconds, he was typing on his computer, his casual bearing gone, his face a mask of concentration.

Mason had seen this switch in his brother before and it never failed to impress. He imagined it wasn't unlike the mental compartmentalization that overtook him during a busy night in the ER. But it was his wife who got the lion's share of his admiration right now, no pun intended.

"That's amazing, Priss. Really good thinking." The words were inadequate. His naïve understanding of loyalty paled in comparison to her unshaken belief of the past few days. She'd schooled him, hard, but he'd deserved it. His brothers were right. He'd never fought for anything or anyone, not the way she'd fought for Liam. With no thoughts of herself. Only of her brother.

And of himself.

He should have gone after her the moment he'd gotten her note. Begged her to trust him. *Fought* for her. No wonder she had no faith in their future.

"Bingo!" Jeep interrupted. "The trackers are made by a company called Trakken. They're easy to get on the internet." He waved the small piece of paper Priss had pulled from the fountain pen. "I've got a buddy of mine tracing this one right now."

Mason whistled. "Is there anything you or your so-called buddies can't do, Admiral?"

"You'd better hope not," Jeep said, with a grin that just managed to stay on the good side of cocky. He got busy typing again, and in less than a minute, gave a fist-pump and turned the computer toward them. The screen showed a map with a beacon flashing in its center. It struck Mason as comically similar to what he'd seen hundreds of times on TV, but this was real and, maybe, even lifesaving.

"Is that him?" he asked.

"That's the *tracker,*" Jeep said, stressing the distinction. "But we'll assume Liam still has it on him. The signal's coming from a town just outside of Philly."

Priss nodded. "Okay. That's good news, I think." She returned to her stool and blew out a breath. "I mean, if they'd found the tracker, why would they take it all the way to Pennsylvania?" She slipped the journal back into her pocket, then slid off the stool once more. "When do we leave?"

Jeep gave her a hard stare. "Once we have a plan."

Good one, Mason telegraphed to his brother, as he, too, got to his feet. Priss was finished sitting back and relaxing, and so was he.

"I assume you've already sent some of your buddies to the location?" he asked.

"Yes, people I trust with my life." Jeep directed this comment to Priss.

"We'll be in good company, then." Mason hid a yawn behind his hand.

Jeep shoved the computer into his bag and slung the backpack over his shoulder. "No, *I* will be. You two," he waggled a finger between Priss and Mason and stood, "aren't going anywhere."

Mason opened his mouth, ready to argue, and out of the corner of his eye, he saw Priss do the same.

Neither of them got the chance.

"John, dear, don't be ridiculous. Would you wait in a hotel room if one of your brothers was in danger?"

Recognizing the determined look on his mother's face, Mason bit back a smile.

"Mason and Priscilla will go with you," she continued, in her signature, blasé-with-a-hint-of-steel manner. "I trust you to look out for one another and keep each other safe."

With the conversation clearly over, Mason's mother bit into a heavily creamed scone.

Chapter Eighteen

"Okay. This is how I see it going down," Mason said.

His voice, rusty with unuse, made Priss smile at her reflection in the truck's side window. It had to be some kind of record. According to the road signs, they were only about forty-five minutes from Philadelphia, which meant Mason had been quiet for well over two hours. Unusual for him, not so much for Jeep. Her brother-in-law could probably be quiet for days on end, if need be. The woman who married him would need the patience of a saint.

"This ought to be good." She didn't bother keeping the sigh out of her voice. "You've been thinking hard up there."

Mason wiggled around in the front passenger seat, and she faced him head on. If he thought he could tie her hands, keep her away from the action, he had a new think coming. But talking helped pass the time.

"I'm only saying this because I know you, Priss. You'll go off half-cocked and get yourself neck-deep in trouble if we don't have a game plan."

A few belly laughs bubbled up and out, releasing some of the tension that had built over the long drive. Mason never did macho convincingly, while she was a pro when it came to snark. "News flash. If I land in trouble, that's on me. Always has been. Always will be.

I'll either get myself out of it or I won't."

Mason's sexy mouth twisted into a frown. "That's just what I'm talking about. This is serious—"

She leaned forward, testing the limits of her seatbelt. "I swear. Sometimes you can be a total ass."

Jeep's broad shoulders shook, which Priss interpreted as agreement. At any rate, it spurred her on. "You think I don't know how serious this is?" She rolled her eyes. "Screw you. You like to go on and on about truthfulness. You want the truth? Here it is." Let him hear the worst of it. She was past giving a damn. "I was driven to and from school in a bulletproof car, by a man wearing a shoulder holster, who was accompanied by another man with an automatic. By the time I was ten, I could shoot with greater accuracy than most police officers and had earned top honors in three martial arts. Yeah, it was all done under the guise of 'sport,' " she said, raising her fingers in air quotes. "But it was also necessary, in case one of my father's rivals decided to kidnap the Skipper's only daughter. Now, there's a very real chance that my brother's been kidnapped and, guess what? I also grew up knowing that was a real possibility. Try living a lighthearted childhood with that hanging over your head. Serious? Don't you dare tell me how serious this is, because you have no idea."

She wilted against the pickup's leather seat and resumed her watch at the window. Let him think on that for a while.

"Okay." Mason spoke so low, she almost missed it.

"Okay?"

"Okay," he repeated, his eyes dark, unfathomable pools. "I get it now. You've always said you can take care of yourself, and you do. Every day. But even though

I was raised by a proud feminist, there was a lot of testosterone in our family, too. I can think back to about a thousand times when I came across like a high-handed ass hat during our marriage. Including a minute ago, right here in this truck. I apologize."

She folded her arms across her chest with a huff. *Damn it to hell.* Leave it to Mason to swallow the tragedy of her youth—not with revulsion, but with compassion. What would have happened if she'd revealed the truth from the outset? Would that kind of honesty have forged them together in an unbreakable bond? Or would they have parted ways from the get-go and never experienced the wonder of the past months?

She would never know.

"Look," he continued. "All I ask—all that I have the right to ask at this point—is that you're careful."

Priss squeezed her upper arms. "Don't worry. I promise I won't do anything stupid."

"That applies to all of us." Jeep's signature bark carried to the back seat. "My guys already have eyes on the location. They're acting in tandem with some…specialists I know, and *they're* the ones calling the shots. We're observers only. Got it?"

The leather seat squeaked as she squirmed. Catching Jeep's expectant look in the mirror, though, she nodded once. "Aye, aye, sir."

Her brother-in-law grinned. "That's the spirit."

Mason set a hand on her knee and her system flooded with more mixed signals. She wanted to attack; she wanted to flee. She wanted to climb into his lap and cry like a baby.

She settled on giving him a faint smile. "I get it. I do. And I appreciate everything you've done—and everything you and your friends are doing, Jeep. I just wish *I* could do more. I suck at inactivity."

Jeep's shoulders shook again, this time with audible laughter. "Damn! You figured this whole thing out. You're doing everything you can to get your brother through this in one piece. I'd say that's more than enough."

Mason nodded and pulled back, facing front again. "Jeep's right. We'd be nowhere without your insight and drive. You've taught me what it means to really fight for something."

Out of nowhere, Jeep offered his brother a fist bump, which Mason accepted.

Must be a brother thing.

She shrugged. "Thanks. It doesn't feel that way. I can't stop thinking about my brother, what he's going through." *Wondering whether or not he's alive.*

"Dad's working his end, too. He knows a lot of people in the DC food chain. He'll help weed out the bad apples," Mason said.

"I appreciate that, too. But Uncle Sean is cagey and just as well connected within his own circles. Even if Liam enters Witness Protection, I don't believe there's any guarantee he'll be safe. If the O'Briens have infiltrated the FBI, I guarantee they've got connections in the US Marshals, too."

Mason's shoulders squared and, even without a clear view of his face, Priss could feel his frown.

Lurching forward, she pushed her luck. "I still say he needs to disappear, without the Feds. Don't tell me that with all your contacts you guys can't make that happen!"

Her plea fell on deaf ears. Mason and Jeep, the most

physically unlike of all the Hugheses, wore identical expressions, their firm lips flattened together, strong jaws clenched. Immovable.

"It's not that simple," Mason said, after a beat. "We have to act within the scope of the law."

Priss threw up her hands. "It *is* that simple. You're just too goody-goody to consider it."

Mason aimed his frown her way. "No. I see people take the law into their own hands every day, and believe me, it isn't pretty. Jeep's gathered a good team. We know who we can trust."

"Shit, Mace," Jeep butted in. "I don't know why I tell you anything. You've never been able to keep your fucking pie hole shut."

"I didn't say anyth—" Mason began, but Priss clamped a hand around his forearm.

"Wait. What exactly is going on here?" Fear sent goosebumps racing up her arms. "You said we're meeting a few friends of yours, Jeep. Now we've got a whole team?"

Jeep waggled his head from side to side, stretching his neck and shoulders. "More or less."

"More or less? What the hell does that mean?"

Long seconds ticked off in her head before Mason turned to her again. "It means the specialists Jeep told you we're meeting are members of a special task force from the Boston FBI office. They're in charge of this whole thing."

Priss counted to five, ready to lose her shit. So this was how it felt to be ambushed. Again. "Do you have any idea how *Boston* law enforcement feels about the O'Brien family? Dear God! You've exchanged one death squad for another!"

"This is different," Mason said. "Jeep checked them out—up, down, and sideways. Hell, he probably knows what their PSAs are. They're all seasoned vets with outstanding records. Plus, their goal is clear—they're after your uncle, not your brother."

"That doesn't mean Liam won't get caught in the crossfire." She kicked the back of Mason's seat until her toes hurt. "Aargh! I can't believe I was stupid enough to trust you again."

She muttered a few choice words in English and Gaelic before throwing herself back against the seat and squeezing her eyes shut.

She couldn't even stomach looking at the back of her husband's head right now.

****

Jeep sneezed once, twice.

"Bless you." Mason said, without registering the words. He couldn't shake Priss's reaction to, well, *everything*. Every way he turned, he stepped right in it, knee-deep.

"I hoped you were sleeping," Jeep said, punching Mason's deltoid. It didn't hurt, but Mason rubbed the area anyway.

"Wallowing in self-pity instead, huh?" At Jeep's whispered question, Mason darted a glance at the back seat. Priss appeared to be sleeping, but he still shushed his brother.

"I was thinking about work," he lied, careful to keep his own voice down.

Jeep shook his head. "Man, get your head out of your ass."

"I don't know what you're talking about." Mason took another sneak peek at the back seat. Yeah, Priss was out cold. How often had he teased her about those puffy little snores?

Jeep shot him a look that was both skeptical and amused. "Bullshit." He rubbed a hand over his heart. "You said you've learned how to fight. Prove it."

"Easier said than done." Mason punched the armrest. "Do I fight the FBI? Take on Clan O'Brien with one hand tied behind my back?"

Jeep laughed. "Don't be an idiot. You know when I say 'fight,' I don't mean it literally. You've stuck with Priss throughout this past week, which, for my money, gets you more than halfway there. Now, finish the job."

"Again, easy for you to say. Every time I think we might be moving closer together, another bombshell goes off and sends us miles apart again. I mean, here we are, trying to save her brother's butt, and she still claims she can't trust me."

Jeep shrugged. "Adam's father-in-law killed his first wife, but he couldn't be more in love with Callie if he tried. Nothing's impossible if you want it bad enough."

Mason frowned. "You're one to talk about love." It was a cheap shot, one he regretted as grief shadowed his brother's face. There were those secrets again. He wanted to ask, but now wasn't the time.

"You're right." Jeep raised a shoulder. "But as I've said before, even a lone wolf like me can see you two are meant for each other."

Mason folded his arms over his chest but remained silent. There was no comeback for that. Only hope.

After the long hours on the highway, Jeep's GPS awakened and directed them to the outer belt, around the sprawling city of Philadelphia and toward the western suburbs.

"Anything else I need to know about what we're headed into?" As he spoke, Mason forced his muscles to relax. His sympathetic nervous system was so jacked, he could lift a freaking car off someone.

Jeep shook his head. "Nope. I have a couple of my guys keeping tabs on things, but I meant it when I said this isn't our op. We won't interfere—unless shit goes sideways. There's a spot or two near the house where we'll keep eyes on the situation without being in plain sight. I can tell you this much. In civilian terms, they're prepared to raid the house."

Another surge of adrenaline left Mason's entire body zinging. "Isn't that dangerous? I mean, if Liam's there, and still alive, shouldn't they try to negotiate first?"

"Sometimes, the element of surprise works best. This Boston team is good at extraction. And my team's got their six."

Something in his tone reminded Mason that what he *didn't* know about his brother's livelihood far outweighed what he did. For once, he pushed a little. "You don't work for JAG, do you?"

Jeep kept his eyes on the road, his usual stoic mask back in place. "No, I do. My law degree is legit. But occasionally, given my, um...*unique* skill set, I'm assigned other jobs for the Navy."

Mason studied his brother's profile. "Some kind of naval intelligence, I'm guessing." He shook his head. "I don't know why it took me so long to figure it out. Too busy with my own shi—shoreline shrimp, I guess." He gave Jeep a smile. "It makes sense. The thrill of the chase defines you."

"Yeah, well. It stays within the family, okay?"

"Yep." *And the jury's still out on whether that includes my wife or not.* Mason cleared his throat. "Speaking of, have you heard from Callie and Adam lately?" The couple was more than a diversion. They allowed Mason to step back, even for a minute, into some semblance of his old regular life. A life now divided into three distinct periods: Before Priss, During Priss, and whatever the hell this time now was.

Jeep's mouth twitched. "Barely. They sent a selfie from outside their hotel in Paris and a text saying they 'hearted' London, and the Chunnel was 'cool.' "

"They took a selfie at the hotel? They're in Paris. Why not the Eiffel Tower or the Louvre or... Oh, yeah. They're on their honeymoon."

Jeep made a humming sound. " 'Loved London' my ass. Probably didn't even leave their room."

Despite the implosion of his own love life, Mason was happy for his brother. Adam had endured a long season of sorrow before falling in love with Callie, and he deserved all the wedded bliss that came his way.

The GPS spoke again, and Jeep steered onto another off-ramp. Mason's nerves jangled as they exited the highway and joined the teeming traffic on a suburban main drag. Tall trees, their bare branches swelling with spring buds, lined the median like a platoon of scrawny soldiers.

Mason laughed at himself. He was waxing poetic, a sure sign he was short on sleep. And hungry.

In the back seat, Priss stretched, arms wide, arching herself off the seat like a cat. "Mmmm."

His mouth watered, but it had nothing to do with his hunger. At least, not *that* kind of hunger. She moved more sensually than any other woman he'd ever met, and his body pulsed in response.

Primitive. That's what it was, the way it had always been with them. And, if there was a way to shut it off, he hadn't discovered it yet.

They hit a pothole, and the jostling of the truck pulled his attention back to the road. Jeep pulled into a gas station, snagging a spot near the door to the convenience mart. After checking his phone, he typed a short message.

Priss slid off her seatbelt and scooted forward to lean between the large front seats. "What's going on? Why are we stopping?"

Jeep gave her his lopsided smile. "It's all good. My guys have eyes on the house, and they just spotted your brother, alive and well. He was escorted out to a car, but then the plans must have changed, because they took him back into the house. Lucky for us."

"Are Young and Peters with him?"

"They are."

If that brought her a sense of triumph, she didn't show it. Didn't show much of anything right now, in fact, except a brave face.

Mason's heart lurched. Now he was the one wishing there was more they could do. He reached for the door handle, needing to stretch his legs. "I'm going to get a cup of coffee. Anyone else want any?"

Jeep raised a finger, but Priss shook her head. "For heaven's sake, be quick about it."

Jeep placed a hand on her forearm. "Haste makes waste, Priss. We're still waiting for the team from Boston to arrive. They're about forty minutes out. Your brother's been fine up until now, so chances are they're holding him for someone else. We do this the right way and everyone stays safe, okay?"

She frowned before giving a jerky nod.

Mason's scalp tingled. "So even though you've basically been trained to be a lethal weapon, we're talking absolutely no heroics. Okay?" He mitigated his words with a smile.

She shrugged, but he caught the trace of an answering grin on her lips.

"*Okay?*" he repeated, still smiling.

"Okay," she said, and waved him away.

With her affirmative ringing in his ears, he exited the truck and headed toward the store. Idly, he wondered if they sold handcuffs. He had a sneaking suspicion that the only way to keep Priss out of trouble was to chain her to the truck.

Chapter Nineteen

Stakeouts looked fun on television. Hanging out, drinking coffee and eating greasy burgers, spying at people through binoculars. Who knew they were such misery?

Priss glanced at the dash clock for the thirty-eighth time and threw her hands up. "Oh, my God, how can forty minutes feel like three days?"

A muscle jumped in Mason's jaw. He was probably swallowing a couple hundred dollars' worth of swear words. *Good.* It was a two-way street.

He kept saying he was on her side, but he relied on law enforcement at every turn. That was the problem. The Hughes family couldn't stop trusting the system.

And she couldn't start.

"I warned you." Jeep hid a yawn before tapping around on his tablet for a minute. "The good news is these guys must be overconfident, because they're being sloppy. They haven't covered the windows, which is something even a rookie should know. We're able to get good intel. Right now, your brother appears to be confined to a room, but he's otherwise okay. So, we wait." Jeep met her eyes in the rearview mirror.

In response, Priss obliterated the wrapper on the protein bar she'd originally planned on having in a few hours. Eating it now would waste another minute or so.

Chewing, she raised the high-tech binoculars Jeep

had given her and panned up and down the sleepy street that stretched out below. The houses were older but not ancient. 1960s and '70s ranches, all well-cared for except for the house they watched. The grass had been mowed, but the shrubbery had grown wild. It might be her Hollywood-fueled imagination talking, but *meth house* kept reverberating in Priss's brain. Had it been seized by the FBI? If Peters and Young were behind this, that might explain how the house had been chosen.

"Uh-oh." Jeep swore under his breath.

Priss lowered the binoculars to her chest and met her brother-in-law's gaze in the mirror again. "What?"

He pointed to a speck, way down the road. "Unless I'm mistaken, we're about to have company."

Mason aimed his own pair of binoculars toward the windshield. "What makes you think—oh. That can't be good."

The half-eaten protein bar fell to the floor as Priss raised her lenses again. Several blocks away, a car approached. A black luxury sedan with darkened side windows. Not an unheard-of sight in a suburban neighborhood. "So?"

Mason and Jeep shook their heads in unison. "Look at the license plate," Mason said, over his shoulder.

She lowered her sight a fraction. "Massachusetts." *Shit and double shit.* She swung around in Mason's direction, dropping the lenses when his blue eyes appeared in blurry, 144x magnification. "Maybe it's the Boston FBI." The hopeful lilt in her voice wasn't fooling anyone. Both men looked as cheerful as a firing squad.

"In a Mercedes?" Jeep scoffed.

Priss timed a long exhale. She would not panic. "Uncle Sean prefers Jags—used to, anyway."

Jeep grunted and returned to his tablet while she and Mason raised their binoculars again. The black car kept on coming, and the butterflies in her stomach switched from the box step to a polka.

"Damn." A lump rose in her throat. "I can't see who else is in the car, but I'd swear that's Danny Walsh at the wheel. He was a teenager when I last saw him, but it's hard to mistake that mop of red hair. Besides, he looks just like his father." She shivered. Davey Walsh had been one of her father's enforcers, a hard, intimidating man who'd frightened her even as a child. He'd been no fan of Liam's, either, often mocking her brother's preference for the "softer" side of the business. Was the elder Walsh in the car, too? She squinted, trying to make out the other passengers.

"What do we do now? If that's Uncle Sean—or anyone from the clan—Lee's a dead man."

Her brother-in-law paused his typing and twisted in his seat, facing her, and she lowered the binoculars once more. Priss knew Jeep's hard shell protected a sweet, gooey center. She'd glimpsed it a time or two, but now wasn't one of those times. Right now, his intense expression was intimidating as hell.

"I'll tell you what we don't do. We don't go off half-cocked. We have a plan, a good plan, and we'll stick to it until we can't anymore." He raised a hand, cutting her off before she could speak. "I get it. Ambush or not, your father was killed by law enforcement bullets. We're here to prevent that, but not by putting ourselves or anyone else in danger."

Without warning, the anger that had fueled her over the past several hours ran dry, leaving her as limp as a deflated beachball. Good thing she'd left her seatbelt buckled or she'd slide to the floor. "Okay. I get it. Right now, we need to get Lee out of this, pronto, and I don't care who does the rescuing."

Jeep raised a hand to his earbud. "Copy that." He met Priss's eyes again. "Boston is stuck in traffic—a wreck on the highway—so they're mobilizing the local police."

He must have seen her panic, because he was quick to continue. "They've been told your brother's one of the good guys." He typed a sentence or two onto his tablet. "My team has set up a high-powered microphone near the house. That enables us to monitor the parley—the conversation—inside. We have clearance to go in, if necessary, but I hope it doesn't come to that."

"And by 'we,' he means—"

"Yes, I've got it," Priss snapped at Mason. "You and I keep sitting here, even if the sky falls."

Jeep started the truck, shifted, and pulled away from the curb.

"Wait. We're not leaving?" Priss clutched at Jeep's headrest. Despite the agonizing inactivity, she didn't want to abandon their post.

"Nope," Jeep said. "Going around the corner. Don't want to attract any attention by staying in one place too long."

"But we can't see the house as well from over here."

"That's okay. We've got audio now."

As if on cue, a burst of static erupted from his tablet, and Peters' gravelly voice became clear.

"…any minute now. Right now, we hold the cards, but that changes the second we hand over the Lion. Did you rough him up?"

"Enough to make him bleed, like you told me." That

229

was Young.

"Bastards!" Priss whispered.

"Good," Peters voice came through the speaker again. "They want him alive, but it's better for us if we hand him over with a few scratches. Make it look too easy and it'll cost us. We want them to think we worked hard for the money."

Young's answering laughter had Priss fisting her hands in her lap. "I'd like to walk in there and kick both of those assholes right in the—"

Jeep shushed her.

"We're good. I hogtied him, too. You should've seen him. When I mentioned his uncle, he tried to bribe me. I was like, 'with what?' " Young laughed again. "He's shitting bricks. Speak of the devil, guess who just pulled up?"

Priss leaned forward as a wild idea began to take root. "I need to go in there. The surprise of seeing me will throw Sean off, gain us some time. Besides, I have an inside track to the Gutenberg, and I guarantee you my uncle still wants to get his hands on it."

Mason shook his head. "Let's leave it to the professionals."

Their eyes met, and her heart stuttered as he read her soul.

She looked down at his long fingers, threaded together in his lap. His platinum wedding band glinted in the gray light. He still wore it. She still wore hers. They were still linked. Perhaps now, more than ever.

And he was still in danger because of it.

"This is an O'Brien problem, and I'm an O'Brien."

Mason's fingers clenched. "You're a Hughes, too."

"Where's that no-good nephew of mine?" Sean

O'Brien's booming voice, so familiar, so reminiscent of her father's, made Priss jump. "I'll make that boyo sorry he ever lived."

She clutched at Jeep's arm, with fingers that shook. "You know I'm right. I'm our best chance for buying time."

Jeep's lips flattened into a straight line as he reached back and grabbed a duffel off the seat beside her. She'd recognized it when she first got into the vehicle. It was his go-bag. "Un-uh. Not without a bodyguard."

Mason grabbed his brother's wrist. "Wait. No way. She's staying out of there."

Jeep shook his head. "She's right. She's got something unique to offer, which will give us the time we need until the cavalry arrives. Besides," he gave Priss half a grin, "it sounds like she's got mad skills."

Priss released a breath she hadn't even known she was holding.

"So…what? I just sit here twiddling my thumbs?"

Jeep frowned. "What is it with civilians? Sometimes you just gotta wait."

"Yeah, but—"

"No buts. If we play this the way I want to, don't worry. You'll have your moment." Jeep stared Priss right in the eye.

"Are you sure you want to do this?"

She nodded once.

"Okay, then. There're a few things we need to get straight first."

****

Mason watched the truck door close behind Priss. The bulky sweatshirt she wore hid the bulletproof vest well, but that didn't stop his nerves from jangling. She could be swathed from head to toe in Kevlar and he'd still be a nervous wreck.

He grabbed his brother's wrist, right before Jeep left the vehicle. "Can you promise me she'll stay safe?"

Jeep shook his head. "You're a doctor. You know as well as I do there's no guarantee when it comes to life or death. What I *can* promise is that I wouldn't risk my life for Liam O'Brien but I will for Priss."

Mason swore. "I'd like it best if you both come out of this without a scratch, please."

"Believe me, that's the plan."

"Okay." Mason nodded toward sidewalk, where Priss stood waiting. "Stick with her like white on rice."

"Will do." Jeep passed him the tablet. "My guys are the best, and they'll have ears and eyes on us. In fact, Nutter is setting up heat sensors now. You can watch *and* listen. The back of the house is completely overgrown, the windows covered by huge evergreen shrubs. The back door is substandard construction, to boot. It couldn't be better, really, if we have to make a surprise attack."

Mason raised his eyebrows. "I'll take your word on that. My last surprise attack was jumping out from behind the sofa, on Mum's fiftieth."

Jeep grinned. "You're okay, you know that, kid?"

"…goddamn sonofabitch. This is how you treat family?" Sean O'Brien's snarl came through the tablet's speaker as clearly as if they were standing inside the house.

Jeep opened his door. "Touching little reunion. Priss and I will make it complete. Remember, we'll call you if we need you."

Mason nodded, and murmured a quick prayer as two

of the people he cared most about walked into harm's way.

Losing sight of them when they rounded the corner sent the blood pounding in his ears, but right when he was ready to send the agreed-upon distress signal to Jeep's team, the tablet's speaker amplified steady knocking at the house door.

Inside the house, the men's voices telegraphed their confusion.

"Who the hell—?"

"For God's sake, answer it, you dumb shit," Sean O'Brien barked out.

Footsteps sounded and bolts flipped.

"Surprise!"

Despite his terror, Mason couldn't hold back a bubble of pride. His wife was one tough cookie.

"What the—" Several voices sounded at once.

"Priscilla?" Sean O'Brien sounded shocked to the core, just as Priss had predicted. So far, so good.

"What the hell are you doing here? You left us for greener pastures long ago." The sneer in the mob boss's voice didn't tone down the heavy dose of Boston in his words.

"Okay. You've thrown them for a loop," Mason said, to the empty truck. "Now finish things and get the hell out of there." His finger shook as he swiped to a display of thermal images.

Priss, Jeep, Peters, Yates. Mason pointed at each distinctive silhouette in turn. *I think that's Liam. Shorter guy might be Sean. These guys I don't recognize, but they're flanking the short guy so...bodyguards.*

"Shit, O'Brien. You brought your niece into this? That wasn't part of the plan."

Mason smiled. Peters wasn't happy with the change in the script.

"No shit, Sherlock. I had nothing to do with it. I'm guessing we have you to thank for this?" On screen, the smaller heat shadow reached out and slapped the back of the head on the image Mason had identified as Liam.

"I'm just as surprised as you are to see her here," Liam said.

"I'll bet you are," Mason whispered. Would Liam have done things differently if he'd known his sister would put herself in harm's way? No. Probably not. *Selfish little prick.*

"Is that any way to greet me after all this time?" Priss's footsteps echoed as she crossed the large room, Jeep at her heels. The heat sensor didn't pick up the automatic weapon in his brother's hands, but Mason knew it was there. Priss stopped near her uncle and set her hands on her hips.

"What's the matter? Wasn't setting Dad up enough for you?"

Easy girl. She was supposed to stall, not piss anyone off. His brother wasn't the only one in there with a gun.

"I don't know what you're talking about. Your father was my older brother. I adored him."

Huh. Mason gave Sean's acting skills about a C minus.

"Sure, you did." Priss's tone revealed she hadn't bought her uncle's act either. "You loved him all the way to a fatal ambush. And now you've paired Liam up with a seriously scary dude. I suppose that's all out of love, too?"

"Your brother's problems are of his own making. He's lucky—"

"Uh-oh." Mason tapped the screen, zooming out. The heat sensor picked up the figures of three men heading toward the house's front door. He couldn't tell from the screen, but he was willing to bet the hefty characters were armed to the teeth.

Mason activated the microphone of the earpiece he wore. "Tell me those are your guys." The acidic churning of dread in his stomach gave him the answer before he got a response from Nutter, Jeep's number two.

"Negative, Doc. They just arrived in another Massachusetts car. Looks like they may be backup for O'Brien."

Mason didn't waste a moment relishing his new call sign. He pressed the earbud again. "What the hell do we do now?"

"Stick with the plan. Eagle hasn't signaled any distress."

Eagle. Jeep's nickname, from the Jeep-Eagle car manufacturer, couldn't have fit him any better. Yes, in his heart, Mason would prefer to be in there with Priss, stuck closer to her than that bulletproof vest she was wearing. His head, however, recognized that Jeep was, by far, the better choice.

He leaned forward as loud knocks came through the speaker once again.

"It's worse than fucking Grand Central here," Yates said.

Mason kept his eyes glued to the tablet's screen as the agent's shadow moved toward the front door. Before he reached it, there was a tremendous bang and the sound of splintering wood. The three newcomers fanned out with what Mason could only assume were weapons drawn.

Shit.

Chapter Twenty

Priss stared at the business ends of three pistols and smothered a laugh.

If this day was a movie, she'd walk out of the theater. It was too much of...*everything* to be believed. Were they Feds? More of Uncle Sean's minions? Aliens from Mars visiting an old meth house?

Today, anything seemed possible.

Jeep, on her right, stood still, holding his automatic in a face-off with the newcomers. Liam, on her left, leaned an inch in her direction.

"Who are these jokers?" he whispered.

She gave him the merest of shrugs. Through narrowed eyes, she studied the three men behind the weapons. They didn't look like law enforcement. Oh, they were brawny enough, but their faces were rough, their gazes hard.

In short, they looked like they meant business. Bad business.

"Who the fuck are you?" The look Uncle Sean gave the three men was full of the machismo only a mob boss could muster.

Never let anyone know you're outgunned. Like much of her father's advice, this was easier said than done. If these men weren't cops and they didn't work for Uncle Sean, that left the Martian theory or...

"We work for Mr. Bannion. You..." the tallest of

the three aimed his gun right at Liam, "have made him very unhappy."

Flippity Flapjacks.

Liam flinched, but for once in his life, he didn't argue. And, really, what could he say? The men obviously knew who he was. The question was, were they here merely to scare him, or were they here to kill him?

The guns indicated the latter.

Time to get this party started. The more the merrier.

Taking a deep breath, she slid one foot forward. She wasn't packing so much as a stick of chewing gum, but she had Jeep Hughes protecting her six, which wasn't too shabby.

"Mr. Bannion wants the Gutenberg, right?"

The smallest thug, the guy on her right, met her eyes. "It's a little late for that, honey."

If there was anything she hated more than being called "honey" by a condescending male, even in this crazy situation, she couldn't think of it.

The tallest man trained his gun straight at her heart. Jeep met the move by aiming his weapon right at the man's forehead, as if they were playing some kind of lethal game of chess.

Okay. She hated that a hell of a lot more than being called "honey."

"What do you know about it?" the tall man asked.

"I'm—" She cleared the lump of fear from her throat. "I'm Priscilla Hughes. I can get the Bible for you."

She sensed rather than saw Lee's eyes bulge and prayed he didn't mess this up by opening his big fat mouth. If he did, she'd kill him herself.

The third man in the trio rolled his eyes before speaking for the first time. "Lou, we're here for the Lion. Let's just grab him and go."

Lou, the tall guy, shut him down with a raised hand. "Wait a minute. Doesn't hurt to listen." He nodded at Priss. "You were saying?"

"I-I can get the Bible. You know how badly Mr. Bannion wants it. It's extremely rare and worth a fortune."

Lou nodded again and his mouth split in a sinister smile, revealing large, surprisingly white teeth that made him look like the wolf who ate Grandma. "Yeah. That's what I hear. What makes you think you can get it?"

Another teeny, tiny step forward. "It's the *Hughes Family* Gutenberg." She raised her eyebrows with all the haughtiness she could muster and waited.

Lou didn't so much as blink.

"I'm a card-carrying member." She flipped a thumb toward Jeep. "So's he."

Nope. Still nothing. All brawn, no brains? Surely one of them would take their bait. "If a Hughes—if *I* ask for it, they'll release it in a heartbeat," she said, pushing her point.

A thoughtful gleam appeared in Lou's eyes. "Prove it."

"Yeah." Her uncle gave her a suspicious glance. "Prove it."

Sheer will alone kept her upright. The greedy bastards had fallen for it. Now to finish the job.

She raised her hands. "I'll need to pull out my phone."

Lou jerked his head once. "So, do it. Nice and slow."

With a shaking hand, she slipped the smart phone

Jeep had given her mere minutes before out of the front pocket of her sweatshirt. The room was dead silent as she made a show of bringing up the University's library website, just as Jeep had instructed.

"Put it on speaker," Lou ordered, with a little wave of his gun.

Priss gave Jeep a side-eye glance, but his stony demeanor hadn't changed. Her jangling nerves quieted a bit. He trusted his team. She'd have to trust them too.

"Just dial already!" Lou barked.

She dialed. The line rang once, twice, three times, and her heart sank a little more each time. Maybe Jeep's buddies hadn't had enough time to set things up. Maybe she should hang up before the call actually reached the antiquities librarian.

Her finger hovered over the disconnect button as it rang one more time.

"National University Antiquities Library. Abernathy Wilson, head librarian, speaking." Mason's voice, wrapped in a crisp British accent, echoed through the room.

Priss drew in a deep breath. "This is Mrs. Hughes— Mrs. Priscilla Hughes. I have…" she swallowed, "a gentleman who's interested in seeing the Gutenberg, but I'm afraid it's impossible for me to come to you right now."

"Not to worry, Mrs. Hughes. We can arrange to bring it to you. Where are you?"

"I'm in Philadelphia."

"Ah. Very good. I have an associate at the university there. I'll make the necessary arrangements, but it will take several—"

"That's good enough," Lou broke in. "Tell him

you'll figure out the timing and will call back."

Priss did as he directed with a cautious sense of hope. Had Lou bought it? She thought she saw genuine interest in his eyes. Her uncle, she noted, was nearly drooling. Liam, for his part, looked like he was struggling to breathe, but he'd recover.

If this bought them the time they hoped for, maybe, just maybe, she'd saved his sorry ass.

****

Mason muted the tablet and pressed on his ear bud. "Nutter, where in the hell are the Feds?"

"Still a good twenty minutes out. Over."

Mason's grin faded. He wanted Priss out of that house now. Wanted her far away from her brother, her uncle, and the three gunmen. Wanted her safe, so he could have a chance to repair their marriage and raise it from the ashes of deception.

He wanted Priss, O'Brien family and all. Hell, everything she'd fought for over the past several weeks proved she was one hundred percent Hughes. Besides, he wasn't a perfect catch himself.

But he was perfect for her. And he'd spend the rest of his life proving it, if—when—they got out of this mess.

He hit the volume button on the tablet again.

"I need to speak to the boss," Lou said.

Mason pushed his seat back as far as it would go and stretched out his legs. In a weird way, this wasn't too different from hanging out, watching a television show, albeit one with a strange-looking video feed. Except that two of the actors were his wife and brother.

And the guns and danger weren't fake.

"Hey, it's Lou." Lou must have made his own phone

call, because he proceeded to provide a short recitation of what Priss had offered.

"So, what do you think? Do we go for it?" There was a long pause. "Okay…Okay, will do."

"Was that Bannion?" Sean O'Brien asked. "I hope he knows I'm brokering this deal."

Someone snorted. Mason would lay money it was Priss.

"Don't worry, you'll get what you have coming." Lou pointed in Priss's direction. "Here's what we're going to do. You're going to call your museum friend again and tell him we're coming down to DC to pick up the Bible."

Jeep took a step forward.

"Don't worry, hotshot. You can come with her, make sure everything stays friendly. In the meantime, my friends will accompany the rest of you to a location of *our* choosing."

Mason reached for his ear again. "Damn it. Are you hearing this, Nutter?"

"Copy that. Don't worry, Doc. That's why we have Plan B. Over."

Plan B? What in the hell is Plan B? The only plan Mason was aware of kept everybody cool until the Feds arrived, Jeep covered Priss's escape, and the bad guys got arrested.

"I'm sure that's not necessary," Priss said.

C'mon, girl. Start tap dancing again.

"It's not up to you," Lou reminded her. "Whose black SUV is that in the driveway?"

Priss's footsteps echoed as she started across the room. Immediately, Lou's arm stretched out in her direction. Mason had no doubt that, at the end of that long arm, there was a gun, because Jeep wasted no time in stepping in front of her.

"Where do you think you're going?" Lou asked.

"Nature calls. There's a bathroom over here, right? Near the back door?" Priss's shadow circled around Jeep's and advanced again.

"Okay, but make it snappy." Lou said.

"It will take as long as it takes," was Priss's spunky response.

"Doc, Eagle just flashed the bat signal." Mason jumped as Nutter's voice sounded in his earpiece. "Boys, you know the drill. We'll go in and neutralize. Over."

Mason knew what "neutralize" meant. He'd seen the results in the ER. "Wait." He grabbed the door handle and slid out of the truck, ignoring the stiffness from too much sitting. "That bathroom's at the back of the house. Give me a chance to get Priss out of there first."

"Stay where you are, Doc. But what do you have in mind?" Nutter asked.

Mason put a hand on the truck's hood and scanned the empty street. Jeep's team must have eyes on him somehow. "Wouldn't a diversion be helpful? Something that creates a little chaos?"

"Copy that, Doc. We'll go in with flash bangs. Those are a pretty damn good diversion. Over."

Mason nodded. "I'm sure they are, but I might have a better idea…Over," he added.

"Copy that. Care to explain? Over."

"That black sedan in the driveway. My grandad has the same model. I'm betting that, like his, it has a very sensitive, very loud alarm. Goes off like a fire engine at the slightest jarring. Lights. Sirens… Over."

Mason held his breath a beat.

"Copy that, Doc." A smile was evident in Nutter's tone. "You might have missed your calling. That's a pretty good tactic. We'll set that mother off before we breach the house. They won't know what hit them. Over."

"Okay." Mason jetted across the street. "I'm heading up the alley."

"Negative, Doc. We've got it handled. Over."

"My wife, my decision, Nutter."

Nutter sighed into the walkie. "Copy that, Doc. The Eagle warned us you'd feel that way. We're on our way to meet you. Over."

****

Mason checked and rechecked his own Kevlar vest. Any tighter and it would cut off his oxygen supply.

"Let's do this." Nutter, a muscle-bound redhead with a Yosemite Sam mustache, and Buzz, a tall man with a flat-top haircut, exchanged quick fist-bumps before they headed through the overgrown back yard. Mason followed, sticking closer than their shadows. Within seconds, Buzz had picked the lock on the door. Using hand motions, he counted down.

Just as he reached zero, ear-shattering sirens filled the air. Buzz and Nutter disappeared inside the house before Mason knew what was happening. He spotted the closed bathroom door as he crossed the threshold. "Priss!"

There was no time to celebrate when she opened the door to the wildly pink room. Mason grabbed her hand and took off like a bat out of hell.

Priss tugged on his arm as they reached the alley. "Wait. Lee—"

Over his shoulder, Mason caught sight of his

brother-in-law, sprinting across the back yard.

"Follow me," Mason yelled, and picked up his pace once more. With every step, he expected to feel the bite of a bullet in his back—or worse, see Priss fall—but by some miracle, they made it to the truck unharmed.

"Nice work," Liam said.

"Yeah, well." Mason glanced back up the alley. "I haven't heard any shots fired, so that's a plus."

"Nope, your brother and his team have it handled. It was like watching some kind of bad-ass ballet. They had everyone disarmed and down on the ground before I knew what side they were on."

Mason would have sighed with relief, but his vest wouldn't allow it.

"No one pinned you down?" he couldn't help asking his brother-in-law.

"I'm not a threat, so…" Liam met Mason's eyes with a shrug.

"You ran." Mason didn't know whether to laugh or punch the guy.

Liam gave him another shrug. "I figured my attorney wouldn't shoot me. Plus, I didn't go far. I'm here, talking to you…" He glanced around, as if making his mind up about which way to flee.

Mason looked down at Priss, surprised to see their hands still linked. Being connected to her was everything. Without her, he was simply going through the motions.

What little air he had in his lungs drained out of him. Her face, those emerald eyes, they said it all. He knew what she was asking him to do. A week ago—hell, a day ago—he'd have refused. But it was different now. He was different now. He'd learned how to fight.

"Get in," he told his brother-in-law. "I'll take you to the nearest train station and give you all the cash I have. After that, you're on your own."

Chapter Twenty-One

Priss walked with her brother into the train station. People filled the two-story depot, although it wasn't even three o'clock yet.

Where are all these folks going? Looking up, she met her brother's gaze. *Where are you going?* She swallowed the question. It was better that she didn't know.

"Come with me," Lee said, setting his big hands on her shoulders.

Priss shook her head. "You know I can't."

Lee gave her his don't-bullshit-me look. "You could. But…"

"I won't leave him again. Not unless he asks me to," she said. "Either way, I'm done running."

Bending, he kissed the top of her head. "I guess I'm glad to hear that. I'm going to miss you, though." He pulled back a little and fiddled with a strand of her hair. "No matter how old you get, I always think of you in pigtails."

Priss laughed. "And I can't hear thunder without wondering where you are."

His eyes gleamed in the bright, fluorescent light. "It wasn't all bad, was it?"

She let her forehead rest against his chest. "No," she said, blinking back sudden tears. "It wasn't all bad."

"If only Uncle Sean hadn't—"

247

"No." Straightening, she shoved at him with both hands, forcing him back a step. "Our whole lives, there's always been someone to blame. First Mom, then Dad, then Uncle Sean. We make our own choices, Lee. We always have, and it's time to own that."

"Yeah." He nodded again. "You're right." His mouth twisted into a half-smile, but it didn't reach his eyes. "As usual."

"Ha!" She smiled back but suspected the glad expression didn't make it north of her nose either. "Finally, you admit it." Taking a step, she slipped her arms around his neck and hugged him until she was breathless. "You'd better get going. D-don't risk anything. I mean, don't try to make any contact. It's too dangerous."

"Okay. Tell Mason thanks. I can never repay him for what he's done."

She gave him one more squeeze. "That's the crazy thing about the Hugheses. They never expect anything in return."

"What a concept." Lee chuckled near her ear, then stopped and took a shaky breath. "I love you, sis."

"I love you, too." With that, she let him go. In seconds, the crowd had taken his place, pressing against her, threatening to sweep her away.

A warm hand cupped the back of her neck. "Are you okay?"

Mason.

"No. But I will be."

"You will," he said, and dropped his hand. "Jeep just called. It's time to face the music."

She pulled her hair back over her shoulders and started making her way to the exit. "How mad is he?"

Mason dodged a handholding couple, then fell into step at her side. "Hard to say. He gave me an earful about driving his truck without permission, but he didn't mention the rest of it, except to say that the take-down—his words—was a piece of cake. Your uncle's headed to jail and, according to the Boston guys, they have enough to keep him there for a long time."

A wave of relief swept through her, followed by sudden, bone-deep weariness and, of all things, hunger.

"Where are we going to meet him?"

"Somewhere in downtown Philly. Not too far from here, I think."

"Any chance of hitting a drive-thru on the way?"

His naughty schoolboy grin made her heart go pitty-pat. "I've already mapped out the nearest cheesesteak truck. We'll be there in five."

****

Mason leaned back, staring up at the water-stained ceiling tiles. There were thirty-four and a half of them, stretched across the small, windowless room in one of Philadelphia's federal buildings. It smelled of stale air, coffee, and sweat, but that didn't bother him. It was the endless barrage of questions from the Feds, who'd double-teamed with the local authorities, that had pushed him to his last nerve.

All he wanted was to grab his wife and go home. *If only life was that simple.* His chair creaked as he lifted the cup of coffee off the rectangular table in front of him and took a sip. His life had been that simple, and he'd taken it for granted. Somehow, things were sweeter when you fought for them.

And, boy, over the last week, he'd put up quite a fight. He'd fought to believe Priss again. He'd fought to understand her upbringing and her beliefs. Most of all, he'd fought against his own prejudice, his own conviction that things were either right or wrong, with nothing in between.

Now, he faced another battle, one he wasn't fooling himself about. Convincing Priss that, despite the astronomical differences in their life experiences, they could make their relationship work, wouldn't be simple. They had a lot to overcome. But he loved her, to the depths of his soul and back again, so failure wasn't an option.

Unless she felt differently.

A sudden commotion in the hallway sent him to his feet. Who would it be this time? The locals, or the Feds?

"Mason, dear. Thank goodness you and Priscilla are all right." His mother's flowery scent enveloped him seconds before she wrapped him in a bear hug.

His father squeezed his shoulder as he filed past them. "Let's sit down, Min."

Mason pulled out a chair for his mum before dropping back into his own chair. His father circled the table and took his seat. They both gave him a onceover, concern obvious in their eyes.

"She's two doors down. Exhausted, I think, but holding up magnificently," his mother said.

Mason nodded. "Thanks for checking on her. They've kept us apart, but I guess that's standard, given the situation. They don't want us influencing each other's story."

His father nodded. "I've spoken to the agents in charge. It shouldn't be long now before you're both let go."

"Thanks." Mason set his elbows on the table and

threaded his fingers together. "I need to talk to you both anyway."

His mother patted his forearm. "Of course, dearest. We're all ears."

Mason met his father's eyes with a smile. His mother's forte was talking, but whenever she announced she was listening, she meant it.

"Thanks," he said, again. "My marriage to Priss... To say 'it's complicated' is an understatement. No matter what she's done to distance herself from her family, she's still Seamus O'Brien's daughter—always will be. That could make things difficult, especially for you, Dad."

"Go on." Ever a jurist, his father never weighed in on something without hearing the complete argument.

"That being said, I believe that what we have—or, at least, what I hope we *still* have—is worth fighting for. She shouldn't be blamed for being born an O'Brien or for loving her brother. In other words, I won't give her up. If that makes a mess for you, I'm sorry. We'll try and keep a low profile. We can even move, if we have to."

His mother jerked back, as if struck by something, but remained silent.

His dad removed his glasses and began polishing them on his sweater. "Son, I have long been on the record as a believer in second chances. I also believe—and I think I've instilled similar thinking in you and your brothers—that we are defined by our actions instead of by our relatives. My feelings toward Priss haven't changed. I know her to be an intelligent, kind, and loving woman. What's more, I know she's the love of your life." His father replaced his glasses, then turned his hands over, palms up. "As for my career, I have nothing to hide. My record speaks for itself. I've never been connected, in any way, shape, or form, to any case having to do with the O'Briens, and I defy anyone to try and claim otherwise." Reaching over, he placed his hand on Mason's and squeezed.

Mason sandwiched his father's hand between his own. "I love you guys. More than I can say."

His mother ran a hand along his back. "Of course you do, darling." She leaned close. "We're awesome," she whispered.

Mason's tension evaporated as he threw back his head and laughed.

Chapter Twenty-Two

For Priss, the ride back to her home—*their* home—with her in-laws had been notable only because of its complete failure to resolve anything. Instead, by some unspoken agreement, they'd filled the time with a benign assortment of funny stories and good-natured teasing, as well as the surprise announcement that Adam and Callie were expecting.

In other words, it had been pleasant. So pleasant, Priss had nearly ripped her hair out. Back in the train station, the air between herself and Mason had shifted, but it hadn't cleared.

Now, she was stuck in the fog while a thousand questions swirled around in her head like a mental tornado, leaving doubt and fear in its wake. Where did they go from here? She loved him, plain and simple, but how did he feel about her? She was still a mobster's daughter. Her closest relatives had plotted to cheat his family out of a fortune and almost gotten him killed in the process. And she'd left him—for his own good, yes, but it was still a lot to forgive.

Maybe too much.

Those doubts threatened to suffocate her as she stood there in the middle of her own guest room. She'd sprinted into the sunny yellow-and-blue-themed room as soon as they'd arrived at the apartment, stating something about them both needing showers before shutting the door in her husband's face.

Ugh. She bent over and wrapped a towel around her wet hair. She was such a coward. It was past time she put an end to all this anxiety.

Crossing the room, she reached for the doorknob and jumped as it turned beneath her hand.

"Priss?" Mason took a step into the room, but stopped as she peeked around the open door.

"May I come in?"

She nodded, but stayed rooted to the spot, her pulse pounding hard in her ears.

"I think we need to talk."

With fumbling fingers, she rebelted the fluffy white bathrobe she kept for guests and perched on the edge of the king-sized bed. He followed suit, managing to sit not too close but not too far away either. His hair was damp, and his worn, navy-blue T-shirt was wet where it stretched across his breastbone. Gray athletic shorts left his long legs bare. She caught a whiff of the stringent antiseptic soap he used after a stint at the hospital.

"It's been a long night." A glance at the pair of windows along the far wall showed the gray light of dawn slipping between the slats in the miniblinds.

"One of the longest," he agreed. "But that's not why I'm here."

There was a determined glint in his eyes, but she couldn't decipher any more than that.

She swallowed. "No. But, before you start, I have something I need to say. I—I am who I am, Mason. My upbringing, my family…that's never going to change. I've spent the last twelve years of my life distancing myself from it, but the old saying is true: *Wherever you go, there you are.* Wherever I go, whatever my name, my family history remains the same. I'm always going to be a mob boss's daughter and that, plus the Hughes family, well, it's oil and water, isn't it?"

Mason's eyes crinkled at the edges as he smiled. "We've been oil and water from the moment we first laid eyes on each other." Reaching out, he took her hand, lacing his fingers through hers. "Oil and water help make a very good cake."

Her gaze locked on the simple physical connection. His warmth spread through her body, licking through her bloodstream, firing up her nerve endings, seeping into her bones.

Only Mason had this effect.

He traced her jawline with his free hand, looping a loose strand of hair behind her ear. By sheer force of will, she remained upright, wondering, waiting, wanting.

"I've thought about it a lot," he admitted. "Your relationship with Liam is just that, *your* relationship. It's not my place to judge it, place conditions on it, or interfere with it in any way, so long as he keeps his troubles to himself."

Tears welled in her eyes. "You mean it?"

He nodded, and his fingers kept exploring, under her hair, across her shoulder bone and back, under her chin. "I do. I love my brothers to hell and back. It's not fair for me to expect you to feel any less for your own brother." He brushed her lips with his thumb.

"But…" She blinked, trying to keep her focus. "Your family—"

The mattress creaked as he leaned forward, until his forehead touched hers. "I love the batter you and I make, Priss, even if it is immiscible."

She almost lunged at his mouth. Curiosity held her

back.

"Immis-what?"

That sexy mouth of his split into an even sexier grin. "Immiscible. It's more of a layering rather than a true mixture." His arms slipped around her, tugging her more fully against his torso. "We each retain our own, separate properties, even when we're together. And I want us together. Forever." His eyes telegraphed everything that remained unsaid between them.

Smiling, she let go of her doubts and trusted. Scary but exhilarating. There were no guarantees, but the risk was more than worth it. "Layering, huh? As in one on top of the other?"

His deep laugh vibrated under her wandering fingertips as he rocked against her.

"Exactly like that," he said, and brought his lips down on hers. His kiss was hard and thorough, and she answered it with a passion borne of the weeks of loneliness and uncertainty.

She was home at last.

****

"Umm." For Mason, the warmth and weight of his wife's naked body, nestled with his, was the epitome of comfort. Too bad he couldn't say the same of their guest room's bed.

"This mattress has to go. I've known concrete slabs that were more comfortable." He arched a shoulder, trying to avoid a wayward spring.

Priss nuzzled his neck. "Wanna know what I discovered while sleeping on Callie's couch?"

Picturing his sister-in-law's sorry-looking sofa, he gave her a doubtful grunt. "That rocks would be better?"

"Sometimes you're better off sleeping on the floor."

"Ah." Lunging, he tumbled her up and over the edge of the bed, onto the throw pillows and comforter they'd pushed onto the carpet while in the midst of their earlier passion. "You're right. This is much better," he said, draping her on top of him again.

She slapped his chest. "Ha-ha. I can't wait to sleep in our own bed tonight." Apology flickered in her eyes. "These past weeks… They've been hell in so many ways."

He gave her a squeeze. "The future will be better than our honeymoon. I promise."

Grinning, she sank her fingers in his hair. "That's big talk. As I remember, our honeymoon was just about perfect." She shimmied against him. "And very…athletic."

"That it was." He scanned her face, taking in the high cheekbones, the smiling eyes, the tumbling hair.

"Happy?" He cupped her cheek, felt as well as saw her smile.

"More than I ever dared to dream."

He raised his head for a lingering kiss. "I love you."

She kissed along his shoulder before snuggling against his chest. "I love you, too."

It was all that mattered. Against all odds, they'd found their way back to each other. Despite his words, Mason knew their future wouldn't always be easy. But, whatever happened, they'd face it together, with complete honesty and trust between them. He relaxed into the blankets beneath him, allowing his body to go heavy with relief as he soaked up the heat of the sexy woman on top of him.

He was halfway to dreamland when he heard Big Ben's chimes.

"No," he said.

Priss's lips curved against his skin. "She'll just keep calling."

"No." He shuddered. "I absolutely won't talk to my mother when I'm naked. That's wrong on so many levels."

"Well, if that's your attitude…" Priss sent a hand gliding over his stomach, stealing his breath. "I can think of something you *do* enjoy doing when you're naked."

"Mmm," he agreed, as she ventured lower. "That's one of the many things I love about you. You always have such terrific ideas."

****

"Someday soon, I'll tell you the whole, sordid story of my childhood," Priss pressed her frontside against Mason's backside, making him want to get naked again.

Instead, he checked the date on a container of pudding, decided to risk it, and ripped the foil lid off. Their energetic lovemaking had made him hungry. "You can trust me with anything."

"I know."

He fed her a spoonful of pudding, then kissed her, full on the mouth.

"You taste like strawberries."

She raised a brow and gestured toward the container. "We have a problem then, because that's vanilla pudding."

He shrugged. "Desperate times. How can I not have any food here?"

Stepping to his side, Priss set her hands on her hips. "Obviously, you were pining for me."

"You know it." He kissed her again, then straightened. "Um, about that. The coffee table in our living room may, or may not, be broken."

Her nose crinkled. "The glass-topped one? Why? What happened?"

He went for an innocent routine. "Beats me. It's possible that someone threw the wrought iron lamp at it while having a first class, um…temper tantrum."

Smiling, she slid her arms around his midsection. Without relinquishing either pudding or spoon, he embraced her as well.

"Let's make a promise."

He grinned down at her. "Anything." After scooping blindly, he popped another spoonful into his mouth.

"Let's try our very best to be kind to one another from now on. I've had enough hostility to last me a lifetime."

"Amen." He stole another fruit-flavored kiss. This one grew more involved, and he only just managed to avoid spilling pudding down her back.

Priss broke the kiss with a heavy sigh and rested her forehead against his chest.

He kissed the top of her head. "Thinking about your brother?"

She gave a forlorn chuckle. "Yeah. I can't help but wonder where he is. I hope he's okay." Leaning her head back, she met his eyes. "Thank you for letting him go. I know you did it for me."

Mason walked her backward and set his pudding and spoon down on the kitchen counter before looping his arms around her hips.

"I don't know what the next hours, let alone months or years, hold for him. We're honesty only, from here, right?"

She squeezed his waist. "Yep. Do your worst."

"Just because I helped him escape doesn't mean I think it was the smart decision. Despite everything, I still think most Feds are trustworthy."

Standing on tiptoe, she kissed his chin. "I did some thinking of my own last night. Believe it or not, I came around to that same point of view. I don't expect him to be around, but if I do hear from him, I'm going to encourage him to turn himself in."

Any spots of tension his body held onto melted at her words and he grinned down at her. "You know, you're a pretty remarkable woman, Priscilla O'Brien."

Priss returned the grin and stood on tiptoe, wrapping her arms around his neck. "It's Hughes, mister. No more of that O'Brien bad luck for me."

Mason leaned down for another promise-filled kiss. "You've got that right. We're married." He nibbled his way to her ear. "And that makes me the luckiest man in the world."

Epilogue

Priss licked her lips as she gazed at the table full of Halloween-themed goodies. There were Frankenstein frankfurters and Vampire *vol-au-vents* and a bat-shaped brie *en croute*, not to mention the array of purple, green, and orange cupcakes, cookies, and chocolates at the far end of the spread. The fact that it was only April fifth didn't appear to bother anyone. The whole family had gathered at the Hughes farm to welcome Adam and Callie home from their extended honeymoon.

"Who goes to Paris and doesn't visit the Louvre?" Mason asked Callie.

"Don't look at me." Callie pointed at her husband. "Ask the good professor.

"I know it's hard to believe, but after London, I was museumed out," Adam said. "Besides," he winked at his wife. "We found plenty of other things to do."

"I'll just bet you did," Jeep said, wiggling his eyebrows.

"They brought me back a French unicorn." Callie's sister, Gretchen, raised a stuffed toy from her lap. "See?" She shoved the toy under Jeep's nose. "It has a beret."

"Well, I for one am glad to have everyone home, safe and sound. I'm also happy to know the Gutenberg is right where it belongs." Minna shivered. "Such a palaver, all that extra security. I can't wait to have company round again. It was like having another pandemic."

"We'll need the company, to help us eat all this food," Priss said, accepting a steaming bowl of Spider Web soup.

"Sssh!" Mason said, in a stage whisper as he rubbed his hands together. "I have plans for the leftovers."

Priss held up a fluted crystal bowl of bright yellow mustard. "I'm guessing those plans involve some of this."

The laughter that erupted around the table made her day. She would never take this family's unwavering acceptance for granted. Never.

"When do you guys leave on your trip?" Gretchen asked, once the merriment had died down.

Priss leaned forward, in order to see around her husband. "Next Tuesday, after Mason's done at the hospital."

"Where did you finally land?" Patrick asked. "I heard you discussing both Florida and Puerto Rico. Good beaches in both spots."

"True," Mason said. "But, in the end, we decided to go with a more…rustic vibe."

Jeep paused, a loaded fork hovering in one hand. "Don't tell me you're going to the cabin?"

Priss glanced at Mason, savoring the hungry look in his eyes that had nothing to do with food. "I can't think of a better place," she said, with a smile.

A word about the author…

Eva Fox Mate has been writing ever since she could hold a pencil. An avid reader, crafter, and lover of history, when she isn't writing or volunteering at a house museum, she's wielding a crochet hook or glue gun and looking for something to DIY. A transplanted Ohioan, she now lives in the Mile High City of Denver, Colorado, with her husband of over 30 wonderful years. Empty nesters, they enjoy golfing, traveling, and spending time with their two adult children and their two zany and much-spoiled dogs. evafoxmate.com

Thank you for purchasing
this publication of The Wild Rose Press, Inc.

For questions or more information
contact us at
info@thewildrosepress.com.

The Wild Rose Press, Inc.
www.thewildrosepress.com